# Poppy Harmon and the Hung Jury

## LEE HOLLIS

**KENSINGTON**
PUBLISHING CORP.

www.kensingtonbooks.com

KENSINGTON BOOKS are published by

Kensington Publishing Corp.
119 West 40th Street
New York, NY 10018

All Kensington titles, imprints and distributed lines are available at special quantity discounts for bulk purchases for sales promotion, premiums, fund-raising, educational or institutional use. Special book excerpts or customized printings can also be created to fit specific needs. For details, write or phone the office of the Kensington Special Sales Manager: Kensington Publishing Corp., 119 West 40th Street, New York, NY, 10018. Attn. Special Sales Department. Phone: 1-800-221-2647.

The K logo is a trademark of Kensington Publishing Corp.

ISBN-13: 978-1-4967-1392-6
ISBN-10: 1-4967-1392-3
First Kensington Hardcover Edition: January 2020
First Kensington Mass Market Edition: March 2021

ISBN-13: 978-1-4967-1393-3 (ebook)
ISBN-10: 1-4967-1393-1 (ebook)

10 9 8 7 6 5 4 3 2 1

Printed in the United States of America

# Chapter 1

"**M**r. Cicci, are you a fan of Tony Molina?" the prosecutor asked as she crossed from her desk in the small courtroom and strolled casually over to the witness box. She was pint sized, barely cracking five feet, and she sported a giant mass of curly red hair on top of her head that threatened to swallow her up whole. She wore a smart gray designer suit and black dress shoes that looked more like what a man would wear. She was a tiny thing, but her abundance of confidence and ferocious, almost predatory attitude gave her an unexpected stature.

"Tony Molina was my hero," Carmine Cicci spoke into the microphone that had been set up in front of him. He was plump and bald, wearing a purple tie and pink dress shirt, with the sleeves rolled up to show off his tattoos of various New Agey phrases and dragons and other symbols that he had collected in his fifty-some-odd years.

"When did you first see him perform live?" the prosecutor asked.

"Nineteen eighty-one at Madison Square Garden. I'll never forget it. I went with my high school sweetheart Antonette. She got the tickets for my eighteenth birthday, and we took the train in from Massapequa Park to see him. When Tony sang, 'My Heart Beats in Manhattan,' I wept. I felt as if I was in the presence of greatness. Tony's God-given talent was just so inspiring and overwhelming."

"And for how many years after that night when you first saw Tony Molina in concert did you consider yourself an unabashed fan?" the prosecutor asked, leaning forward and placing her small hands on the witness box.

"My whole life. I saw all his movies and collected all his music. When I opened my first restaurant in the East Village, I invented a dish called steak Molina, named after him. Even now, seeing him sitting over there, my heart is racing and I'm . . . uh . . . well . . . I'm tongue-tied."

The prosecutor chuckled. "That's very sweet. But you are famous in your own right, are you not?"

"I'm just a chef lucky enough to have a few successful restaurants around the country, and who also gets to judge a cable TV food competition show for three months out of the year. Tony Molina is a legend. He'll be remembered for generations. . . ."

Poppy Harmon, who was juror number four, was perched in the front row of the jury box. She glanced over to where

Tony Molina was seated next to his defense team—three high-powered, impeccably dressed sharks. They all stared at the prosecutor, pretending to be unimpressed with her talents as an attorney. Poppy couldn't help but notice how handsome Tony Molina, now in his midsixties, still was. He didn't appear to be nervous that he was on trial. In fact, he seemed almost relaxed.

Tony noticed Poppy looking at him. He gave her a sexy smile and a suggestive wink. She quickly averted her eyes back to Chef Cicci, who was still testifying.

". . . Which is why it's so heartbreaking what happened," Chef Cicci said quietly, lowering his head and looking down at his feet in the witness box.

"Were you expecting Mr. Molina to come into your restaurant that night?" the prosecutor asked.

Chef Cicci nodded and slowly glanced back up. "Yes, his assistant had made a reservation earlier in the day. Needless to say, I was ecstatic. I wasn't even supposed to be at the restaurant that night. My parents were having a party celebrating their fiftieth wedding anniversary. But I cancelled because there was no way I was going to miss preparing a dish for *the* Mr. Tony Molina!"

"You sacrificed your parents' fiftieth wedding anniversary party to cook for Mr. Molina?" the prosecutor asked, glancing wide eyed at the jury, as if she was surprised to hear this news and hadn't worked it into her prepared questioning of the witness.

"Yes. Of course, my parents understood. They knew how much I loved Tony . . . I mean Mr. Molina."

Poppy glanced back over to Tony, who sat up straight, a stoic look on his face.

The prosecutor also looked over at Molina and shook her head, disgusted, before returning her attention back to Chef Cicci. "Take us through what happened after Mr. Molina arrived with his party."

"Well, I greeted them personally and offered them drinks on the house. He was there with his wife. . . ."

"Tofu."

"Yes."

Poppy thought Chef Cicci had suddenly shifted gears to talk about what everyone had ordered before remembering that Tony Molina was married to a woman named Tofu, a songstress best known for singing the theme song from a Timothy Dalton–era James Bond movie. Like Cher, Rihanna, and Beyoncé, Tofu had at one time been popular enough to go by just one name. Tofu was not in attendance for the trial. In fact, the only family member present was Tony's handsome twenty-something son from his first marriage, Dominick. He sat in the gallery, dutifully loyal with a look of dismay on his face, as if he could not believe his poor father had to go through all this drama.

Chef Cicci continued his testimony. "There was also his business manager, Mr. Kurtzman, and the stand-up comedian who always opens for him whose name I forget. . . ."

"Robby Stone," the prosecutor offered helpfully.

"Yes, right, Mr. Stone. Oh, and also Mr. Molina's two bodyguards, a man and a woman. I remember thinking how cool it was that Tony invited two of his employees to have dinner with him. It struck me as very nice and—"

The prosecutor was not happy with Chef Cicci complimenting the accused, so she promptly cut him off. "Then what happened?"

"I had some calamari sent over and told one of my waitresses, Mary Grace, to go over and take their order. Mr. Molina ordered the steak, not the steak Molina that I had named after him that is on all my menus at all my restaurants. He ordered the steak bordelaise, which is a New York steak with sautéed mushrooms, garlic, and a red wine demi-glace sauce."

"And how did he request his steak be prepared?"

Chef Cicci frowned. "Medium well."

"And was the steak medium well when it was served to Mr. Molina?"

Chef Cicci shrugged. "I thought it was. It was slightly pink when I last checked it and so I prepared the plate and gave it to Mary Grace to take it out to him."

The prosecutor folded her arms and shot Tony Molina a knowing look. "What happened next?"

"The next thing I knew Mr. Molina came storming into the kitchen. He was carrying the steak in his hand and started screaming at me that I had overcooked it. Then he threw it against the wall. I thought he was going to bean our busboy Raul in the head but luckily the steak missed him by a few inches."

"But you were not so lucky as Raul, were you, Chef?"

Chef Cicci glanced around at all the people in the courtroom, embarrassed. "No. I tried to apologize to Mr. Molina and I started to tell him that I would cook him a new steak, but he wasn't interested in listening to anything I had to say at that point. . . ."

"What did Mr. Molina do?"

"He . . . he picked up a frying pan that was on the stove top and he hit me on the head with it," Chef Cicci muttered.

Poppy looked around at her fellow jurors, all of whom,

by the luck of the draw during jury selection, were men. She was the lone woman on the entire jury. Most of them had appalled looks on their faces as they listened to Chef Cicci recount the assault at his restaurant on the night in question, aptly named Cicci's, one of the more popular Italian eateries in Palm Springs.

"Did he hit you really hard or, as the defense maintains, just tap you with it to show his displeasure?" the prosecutor asked with a smirk on her face because she was already acutely aware of his answer.

"He hit me kind of hard."

"*How* hard, Chef?"

"The blow knocked me out cold," he said softly.

"In fact, when you awoke hours later, you were in a hospital room, is that correct?"

Chef Cicci nodded and sighed. "Yes, ma'am."

"The doctors informed you that you had a concussion!"

"That's right."

"All because Mr. Molina was unhappy with his steak!"

Poppy saw Tony Molina shifting uncomfortably in his chair as he rested his elbow on the table and cupped his hand underneath his chin as he gazed with sad, regretful eyes at Chef Cicci, perched in the witness box.

Chef Cicci noticed and appeared to be devastated that he had just delivered such damning testimony against his favorite singer in the world.

Poppy also liked Tony Molina. She must have played one of his ballads, "Lovely Girl," a million times when it first came out in the late seventies. But now, the bloom was definitely off the rose because she staunchly believed Chef Cicci's version of events. And the fiery prosecutor had already informed them during her opening statement that she would call to the stand Raul the busboy and a few other kitchen staff who were in the kitchen at the time of the incident to back up his story.

"Nothing further, Your Honor," the prosecutor bellowed as she whirled around, threw one more disgusted look at the defendant, and crossed back to her table.

Judge Linscott, a dapper, refined, friendly man, leaned forward and in a sweet, unassuming voice said to the jury, "Ladies and gentlemen, it's ten minutes to five so I am going to wrap this up for the day. We will resume tomorrow at nine o'clock. Please do not discuss any of the particulars of this case with anyone, not even with each other, until after closing arguments when you begin deliberations. Is that clear?"

Poppy nodded, as did the eleven men sitting with her in the jury box.

"Have a lovely evening," the judge said before banging his gavel. "We're adjourned."

As she stood up to leave, Poppy couldn't resist peeking one last time over at Tony Molina, who was now on his feet, conferring with his three high-priced lawyers. Almost as if on cue, his head turned and he focused right in on her and offered a dazzling smile. No doubt a bid to charm the lone female on the jury. Fearing the judge might notice her gawking star-struck at the incredibly handsome defendant, she quickly turned away and ran right into the back of juror number seven.

"I'm so sorry," she whispered as she filed out of the courtroom, determined to follow the judge's instructions and not discuss the case with anyone, least of all her friend Iris Becker, who just happened to be *the* biggest

Tony Molina fan on the planet. Iris had made no secret that she was supremely jealous that it was Poppy and not her who had received the fateful jury duty summons that had landed her on the high-profile criminal trial of her favorite celebrity.

# Chapter 2

"My Tony could never do such a vile, vicious act!" Iris bellowed, having just arrived at the garage office of the Desert Flowers Detective Agency after playing eighteen holes of golf in her white polo shirt, yellow skirt, and matching yellow visor. "I believe that overrated cook is making the whole thing up just to get more publicity for his restaurants and TV show."

Poppy, who sat behind her desk, threw up her arms and said, "I'm sorry, Iris, like I already told you a *hundred* times, the judge has given us strict instructions not to discuss the case with *anyone*!"

Violet, who was at the coffee machine in the small kitchenette, brought Poppy a cup of coffee and handed it to her. "I saw on the news that there were about a half-dozen witnesses in the kitchen who saw Tony do it, right, Poppy?"

"I am not allowed to talk about it!" Poppy wailed.

Violet's twelve-year-old grandson, Wyatt, who worked part-time for the agency after school and was completely bored, totally uninterested in some case about an ancient crooner he had never even heard of, stared at his computer in a trance-like state playing some kind of video game.

"Well, I certainly hope you are planning to vote *not guilty*. I mean, let's be honest, no one with the voice of an angel like Tony Molina deserves to go to prison even if he *did* do it!" Iris huffed.

Poppy, mouth agape, and with a disbelieving look, simply stared at Iris. She could not imagine why, despite her pleas, Iris refused to drop the matter.

Always the peacemaker, Violet finally intervened. "Iris, I think we should respect Poppy's wishes and stop talking about the Tony Molina trial."

Iris finally got the hint and muttered, "Fine! I was not aware that it is now against the law to offer one's objective opinion!"

"I hardly think your opinion is objective, Iris," Violet laughed. "You own every album the man ever recorded."

"Nobody asked you to tell us what you think, Violet!" Iris snapped.

Whenever Iris barked loudly at her, dear Violet became, well, much like her namesake, a shrinking violet. She quickly retreated to her corner of the room, desperate to avoid any further confrontation.

Poppy sighed, stood up, and was about to demand the two kiss and make up when mercifully the door to the garage office attached to Iris's midcentury home flew open, and the ladies' fourth partner in their detective agency, Matt Cameron, hustled in with a big grin on his face. Matt was impossibly handsome, an aspiring actor who was toiling part-time as the "face" of the Desert Flowers Detective Agency after it became painfully apparent that not a lot of potential clients in the Coachella Valley were eager to hire three capable women north of sixty to solve their various cases. Hence, Matt created the persona of crack investigator "Matt Flowers," relegating the real brains behind the operation—Poppy, Iris, and Violet—to pose as his loyal assistants. The whole setup, in Poppy's mind, was right out of *Remington Steele*, a popular detective show starring Pierce Brosnan from the 1980s, long before he played James Bond, but surprisingly it worked. Matt's gorgeous face and appealing personality were actually drawing in business on a regular basis.

"Good afternoon, ladies, I'm pretty sure I just wrangled us a brand new client *and* he's got deep pockets!" Matt declared as he ambled over to the minifridge and opened it. "Is it too early for champagne?"

"Who is it? He didn't leave a message on the office voicemail," Poppy said, surprised since that was how most potential clients contacted the agency.

"He contacted me directly through my Facebook page," Matt said proudly before adding, "Did you know my Matt Flowers fan page has almost four thousand 'likes' already?"

Poppy refrained from rolling her eyes, choosing to stay positive and supportive. "That's wonderful, Matt. So who is this new client?"

"Rod Harper," he said.

The room fell silent except for Wyatt, who continued playing his video game, which seemed to have a lot of retro-futuristic sound effects.

Poppy was stunned. She had not seen Rod, her former

costar on the popular 1980s detective series *Jack Colt, PI,* in almost ten years.

"Rod reached out to *you*?" Poppy asked, incredulous.

"Yes, what a nice guy," Matt said. "He's on Instagram, too, so I started following him. He has all of these photos of himself running on the beach shirtless with his dog, and, man, he still looks good for an old-timer."

"He's only two years older than I am," Poppy said, seething.

Matt's eyes popped open as he realized his faux pas and tried to quickly recover. "I forget because you look at least ten years younger than your actual age."

"Nice save," Iris sneered.

Violet, who was done hiding in the corner, scurried back over, curious. "What kind of case is it?"

"Missing person," Matt said excitedly as he bent down to peer inside the minifridge. "Oh, hey, my lucky day. There is a bottle of bubbly in here."

He yanked it out and then began unwrapping the foil from around the cork.

"Who is missing?" Violet asked.

"His daughter, Lara," Matt said.

"Lara? I remember when she was a little girl. She was so shy. She used to hide behind her father's pant leg whenever they were in public. Oh my, she must be in her early twenties by now," Poppy said, smiling at the memory.

"She's a singer, or trying to be," Matt said. "Rod saw her a few weeks ago and after that she just seemed to vanish. He hasn't heard from her since."

"Did he go to the police?" Iris asked.

"No," Matt answered.

"Is that not what most people would do first?" Iris scoffed, shaking her head.

"I guess he has his reasons. I didn't push it because we could really use the hefty retainer fee that I quoted to him and that he's totally offering to cough up, like right now if we decide to take the case."

Poppy smiled to herself. This young man, who should be in Los Angeles auditioning for guest parts on TV shows but instead was in Palm Springs fronting a detective agency run by three women old enough to be his grandmother, was looking out for their livelihood, and she deeply appreciated it. But she did have questions.

"Rod lives in LA. Why does he want to hire a Palm Springs–based firm?" Poppy asked.

"I'm not sure, but he has a house out here and mentioned that he had read some local articles about our first case and me being the big hero and all. I told you that publicity would be invaluable. We can find out all the details tomorrow when you and I have breakfast with him," he said, pointing at Poppy.

"Matt, I have jury duty," Poppy said.

"I know, that's why we're doing it really early," he said with a wink.

"I see," Poppy said. "Does Rod know that I'm a part of Desert Flowers?"

"Of course he does," Matt said. "But don't worry, I let him believe that this was my agency and you were just a hired hand, like we agreed."

Matt was only doing what Poppy had ordered him to do. Keep the idea alive that he was the one in charge. But it bothered her on some deeper level mostly because Rod Harper had played Jack Colt, a crackerjack private eye, and she had toiled as his loyal secretary Daphne for three seasons. And now, decades later, Rod, who had always been somewhat of a male chauvinist pig, to coin an old phrase, was under the impression that Poppy herself was still consigned to that same familiar role in real life. In his mind, she was exactly the same, except with many more years under her belt.

Still, once Matt told her the five-figure retainer fee he was willing to pony up the following morning at breakfast once they officially accepted the case, Poppy was able to put her ego aside.

Having a wealthy new client was far more important. Let Rod Harper assume that Matt was the Flowers in the Desert Flowers Detective Agency.

# Chapter 3

Rod Harper placed a big, strong hand over Poppy's much smaller one that rested on the table and gently squeezed it. She looked up from the small pad of paper on which she was jotting down some notes, startled.

"Look at her," Rod seemed to say to no one in particular. "She's just as beautiful today as she was when we worked together back in the eighties."

Matt couldn't resist cracking a smile. "I caught some old episodes of *Jack Colt* on the Nostalgia Network recently, and I could not agree more."

Poppy was more embarrassed than flattered by the free-flowing compliments, and so she was relieved when the perky waitress appeared with their breakfast. They were dining at Spencer's, part of the Palm Springs Tennis Club that was nestled against the soaring San Jacinto Mountains. It boasted an elegant outdoor patio surrounded by large banyan trees. Poppy and Matt were seated with Rod at a corner table that was hidden enough so they would not be bothered by any old fans who might be excited by this *Jack Colt, PI* cast reunion.

When Poppy and Matt had first arrived at the restaurant to find Rod already at the table waiting for them, she was struck by how much of a star he still was. It wasn't just his ruggedly handsome good looks that had aged so well or his intoxicating masculinity; he still had that swagger and confidence that had made him so popular in the 1980s. As they quickly caught up on their lives, Poppy learned that Rod was still a working actor, appearing occasionally in some TV movies for cable, mostly Westerns and detective retreads that were reminiscent of his glory days playing Jack Colt, only more age appropriate. His last role was as a sixty-something CIA spy with heart problems and early signs of Alzheimer's who was forced to recruit his antigovernment son to help him carry out his last mission. Matt had seen it on Netflix and gave it a rave review, although Poppy suspected he hadn't really watched the whole thing and was just using that as an excuse to butter up their new client.

Rod kept holding Poppy's hand as the waitress set the breakfast plates down, and it was only when she reached for her fork to eat her eggs over easy that she managed to slip her hand out of his warm grip. She glanced up and found him staring at her, beaming. She looked to Matt for help in steering the conversation back to the case of his missing daughter.

Matt dove into his waffles and turned to Rod. "So what was it like starring in your own TV show back in the days when there were only three networks?"

Poppy sighed. This was not some reunion special for

TV Land. This was about getting their hands on Rod's retainer fee check.

"We had a lot more eyes on our show than you get today, that's for sure. What was it, Poppy, something like twenty-seven million viewers a week?"

"Something like that," Poppy said, forcing a smile.

"Wow," Matt said, shaking his head. "Sometimes I wish I could have been an actor back then instead of now just to know what it was like to have that wide of an audience watching my work."

Poppy kicked Matt under the table. He jumped in his chair, his eyes nearly popping out of his head. He looked at Poppy, and suddenly it dawned on him that he had just blown his cover as Matt Flowers, Private Eye.

Rod looked up from his spinach and wild mushroom frittata. "Did you say you're an actor?"

"I dabbled," Matt said, laughing, quickly covering. "In college. But I didn't take it too seriously and got bored very quickly, so instead I followed my true passion . . . criminal investigation."

"I see," Rod said, seeming to buy his story.

Poppy piped in, attempting to coax Matt into moving on to the topic at hand. "So Matt says you're worried about Lara?"

"Yes," Rod said solemnly, looking down at his plate. "Did you know she's twenty-two now?"

"I can hardly believe it," Poppy said, smiling, before shifting into a more serious mode. "And you say she's *missing*?"

Rod nodded.

"When did you last see her?" Poppy asked, picking up her pen to write down the facts as she heard them.

"A few weeks ago last Sunday," Rod said, setting down

his fork. "We had an argument. She showed up at my house in Beverly Hills wanting me to bankroll an album she was planning to record. I am already supporting her with rent and an allowance, and I had already paid for three other recording studio sessions that went nowhere, so I finally put my foot down and refused, and boy, she did not like that at all."

"She's not used to Daddy saying no?" Matt asked.

"That's an understatement. Ever since her mother took off to parts unknown when Lara was twelve and cut off ties with both of us, I have felt terribly guilty about it, and so I spoiled Lara. I gave her everything she wanted, thinking that might help with the healing and bring us closer together. But it hasn't exactly worked out that way. Now she just blames me for everything that's wrong in her life."

Poppy scribbled everything down as fast as she could.

Rod noticed her bent over writing furiously and grinned. "I'm having déjà vu watching you right now, Poppy."

Poppy glanced up from her notepad. "I'm sorry?"

"Seeing you take notes for Matt makes me think I'm in a scene with Daphne on an episode of *Jack Colt*."

Poppy was not amused nor nostalgic. She just wanted to get all the facts down and finish her breakfast and deposit his check. But knowing he was in a wistful mood, she nodded and smiled sweetly. "Daphne lives on apparently."

Rod couldn't take his eyes off her to the point where Poppy was starting to feel uncomfortable, so she decided now was the time to change the subject. "So how did the argument end?"

"She called me a bunch of names I don't care to repeat, and then I told her that I was going to cut her off financially if she couldn't show me some respect. After that, she stormed out of my house, and that was the last time I saw her."

"Did you go through with your threat and cut her off?" Matt asked before stuffing his face with a big hunk of waffle.

"Not really. Her rent is paid for the next three months and I didn't cancel her Platinum Visa card so it was pretty much an empty threat."

Poppy stopped writing. "Why didn't you call the police?"

Rod sighed. "Lara has gotten into some trouble before with her wild behavior. A joy ride on the Pacific Coast Highway that turned into an arrest for DUI. A case of kleptomania that resulted in a shoplifting charge at a boutique on Melrose Avenue. A false accusation of sexual assault against one of her professors at USC who was going to fail her for skipping the final exam. The police have long run out of patience for her antics and I'm afraid my very expensive lawyers are not going to be able to keep her out of jail the next time."

Matt leaned forward. "But she's missing and could be in real trouble. . . ."

"Yes, that's possible, but my gut is telling me she's just angry with me and acting out, and this is all just a ploy to get me worried enough so that when she does eventually turn up, I'll have my checkbook ready."

"Then why not just wait for her to reappear?" Matt asked.

"Because I could be wrong. I just want to make sure she's really all right," Rod said, shaking his head, frustrated. "So instead of involving the cops, I'm hiring you."

"Rod, there is one thing I don't understand. There are

plenty of private investigation firms in LA. Why us?" Poppy asked.

"Besides the fact it's a good excuse to see you again?" Rod asked with a wink. "I've been in contact with some of her old Beverly Hills friends, and although they all claim not to know where she is, they did tell me she had been spending a lot of time recently here in Palm Springs, so I wanted a detective familiar with the desert, who could be on the ground here."

"Any idea why she would be out here?" Matt asked.

"Not a clue," Rod answered.

"Well, don't worry, Rod, I'll find her," Matt said, brimming with all the confidence in the world.

"Thank you," Rod said, heartened as he pulled a checkbook out of his back pocket. "Oh, before I forget . . ."

As Rod wrote enough zeroes on the check to delight both Poppy and Matt, Poppy slowly began to worry that despite how cocksure Matt was of locating Lara, she was still a newbie in the PI game. She was going to have to pay a lot more than just lip service in order to get results. And she had no idea just how challenging and dangerous this run-of-the-mill missing person case was about to get.

# Chapter 4

Poppy listened with intense interest as the feisty prose-cutor with the mop of curly red hair walked around the table and approached the jury, making eye contact with each and every one of them as she delivered her closing argument. "I'm sure you probably listen to Tony Molina's music and have watched many of his movies. I know I have. And I have to admit, I love the sound of his soothing, melodic, and, yes, dare I say, sexy voice."

Poppy glanced over at Tony, who couldn't suppress a smile.

"In fact, I'm a *huge* fan! There. I said it. I adore him. My mother adores him. My grandmother adores him."

Tony's smile slowly faded. He didn't like to be dated.

"He is a national treasure, in my humble opinion."

Poppy knew a "but" was coming.

"But . . . that does not excuse him from having to pay

a debt to society when he breaks the law. And lady and gentlemen of the jury, the evidence is clear. Tony Molina broke the law. We have eyewitnesses who saw him assault Chef Carmine Cicci. We have Mr. Molina's fingerprints on the weapon he used to attack Chef Carmine, a frying pan. We have the medical records from the hospital confirming Chef Carmine's serious injury. And we have the testimony of the victim himself, a world-renowned celebrity chef, with absolutely no reason in the world to lie. You heard him yourself. He loved Tony. Just like I do."

The prosecutor pointed to a few jurors in the second row. "And you probably do. And you. And you . . ."

Poppy stole another glance over at Tony, who was now scowling, not happy where this was going.

"Unfortunately, this case has nothing to do with whether we love someone or not. This case is about a vicious, unprovoked attack by a privileged crooner and movie star who believed his fame was sufficient enough to save him from having to face justice. Well, ladies and gentlemen, it's time to send the message that no one, and I mean no one, not even Tony Molina, is above the law. And so, as you go back to the deliberation room with this overwhelming amount of evidence, I believe that you all know in your hearts that, despite any personal feelings you may have for the defendant, there is no other choice here but to find Mr. Molina guilty of aggravated assault."

She stopped, her hands gripping the wooden railing of the jury box, and stared at the entire jury, her intense eyes daring them to disagree with her. Then she offered them a brief but pleasant smile. "Thank you." She dramatically turned to Judge Linscott, who was listening, stone faced. "And thank *you*, Your Honor."

The prosecutor marched back to her table and sat down.

The juror sitting next to Poppy, a pudgy man with a bulbous nose and wisps of white hair on the sides of his otherwise bald head, wrote copious notes on a pad of paper with a pen. It suddenly dawned on Poppy that she hadn't taken any notes during the trial and suddenly she began to feel guilty about it.

"Mr. Calloway?" Judge Linscott nodded to one of the sharks surrounding Tony Molina. The oldest one of the three, a strikingly handsome man with gray hair, a lanky build, and an expensive Brooks Brothers suit, slowly stood up.

"Thank you, Your Honor. We have no closing argument."

There was silence in the courtroom.

Poppy noticed the prosecutor's jaw drop open.

Judge Linscott raised an eyebrow. "Excuse me? You already waived calling any witnesses for the defense, and now you're not going to make a closing argument before the jury deliberates?"

Molina's first-chair lawyer, Mr. Calloway, calmly opened his arms and shrugged. "Why waste the jury's time when the prosecutor has already failed, spectacularly, I might add, to present a compelling case."

Poppy, along with her fellow jurors, couldn't believe what was happening. In Poppy's mind, Chef Carmine was a believable victim, the kitchen staff were credible witnesses, and there was strong physical evidence. It was unfathomable that Tony Molina would not want his team of expensive lawyers to at least try to refute the charges. When it had been time to cross-examine the witnesses who had observed Tony Molina bashing Chef Carmine in the head with the frying pan, the lawyers had declined, except for a busboy, whom they revealed was an illegal alien and thereby should not be taken seriously, which Poppy found abhorrently offensive.

Judge Linscott leaned forward, almost trying to help them. "Are you *sure*, Mr. Calloway?"

"Your Honor, it's plainly clear what happened here," he said calmly and confidently. "The members of the jury appear to be smart people. I'm not going to insult their intelligence by walking them through it. They know what *really* happened."

Poppy was dying to hear what he had to say since she was already convinced in her mind that Tony Molina was guilty.

"Go ahead and insult my intelligence. I really want to hear what you think happened," Judge Linscott strongly suggested.

"If you insist, Your Honor. Chef Carmine's TV ratings have plummeted in recent months and he badly needed some publicity to goose his public profile. My client just happened to be in the wrong place at the wrong time. He walked into a trap. A setup. Chef Carmine staged the whole thing to make it look like my client hit him with that frying pan. The kitchen staff all worked for him. He probably put a little extra in their paychecks if they backed up his story. As for the fingerprints, Mr. Molina was dining at the restaurant. They could have easily transferred his fingerprints from a wine glass to the handle of the frying pan. There are ways to do that. We've all seen it done on TV. There were no security cameras in the kitchen, so we have no photographic evidence, just the testimony of some devoted employees and one illegal immigrant who was probably blackmailed with deportation if he didn't go along with this abject fantasy. These charges are a joke, Your Honor, and we refuse to play this game anymore. The good people of the jury have their own lives to get back to. . . ." He paused dramatically and then turned to the prosecutor. "This woman has wasted enough of their time."

Judge Linscott wasn't wholly convinced and decided to give the defense team one last chance. "Are you absolutely sure about this, Mr. Calloway?"

"One hundred percent, Your Honor," Mr. Calloway said with a wolfish smile. "We believe the jury has far more than just reasonable doubt."

Poppy was repulsed by the lawyer's cocky and sleazy demeanor. She didn't like his tone or his attitude or his dismissiveness of the female prosecutor by addressing her as "*this woman*." She wanted to pop him one right in the kisser.

Judge Linscott shrugged. "Okay, then. We shall proceed to jury instructions."

The judge droned on for about twenty minutes, and as much as Poppy tried to pay attention, it got boring very quickly. She was still stunned by the fact that Mr. Molina would risk not making a case after the prosecutor's argument appeared to be pretty much open and shut. Was this some kind of psychological ploy? Were they trying to convince the jury that the case was a sham by pretending to be unconcerned and uninterested in refuting any of the testimony and evidence? It made absolutely no sense.

Poppy noticed the pudgy man next to her still writing furiously until his pen finally ran out of ink. He shook it and tried again to no avail. He looked up at Poppy in a panic. She gently patted his hand. "I'm sure they have more pens in the deliberation room."

That did not calm him down. He wanted to write everything he was hearing down on paper. Mercifully the judge was just wrapping up his instructions to the jury and asked the bailiff to escort them out of the courtroom. They were led down a hall and filed into a stuffy conference room with a coffeemaker and large round table. Pens and paper were set out in the center. The pudgy man was the first to grab a pen before sitting down. Poppy looked around at the eleven men surrounding her of various ages and types. She guessed the oldest was around sixty-seven and the youngest about twenty-five.

"I feel like Dolly Levi at the Harmonia Gardens. One woman surrounded by all the handsome dancing waiters."

Only one man, a fiftyish man in a bright blue tracksuit, probably gay, got the joke and chuckled. The others just stared at her, dumbfounded.

They sat in silence for a few moments. No one wanted to speak. It was starting to get a little awkward so Poppy decided to take the lead. "I suppose our first order of business should be selecting a jury foreman."

The gay one in the tracksuit nodded in agreement. "I nominate you."

Poppy quickly moved to squelch that idea. "No, I really don't want—"

The pudgy one, practically stroking his new pen, then piped in, "I second it."

Before Poppy could stop them they were voting.

It was eleven to zero, with Poppy abstaining.

She was going to be the jury foreman for this trial whether she liked it or not.

# Chapter 5

"Perhaps we should take an initial vote to see where we all stand," Poppy suggested before picking up a piece of paper and tearing it into twelve pieces and handing one to each of the jurors. Everyone reached for a pen to scribble down their verdict. Once Poppy retrieved all eleven folded pieces of paper and wrote down her own opinion, she began reading the various verdicts.

"Guilty," she said, setting down the piece of paper on the table. She picked up another piece and read it aloud. "Guilty." She set the paper down on top of the other guilty verdict. She unfolded a third verdict. "Not guilty." She started a new pile. When she was done, it was six "guilty" and six "not guilty."

"Split right down the middle," said one of the jurors who hadn't spoken before. He was small and spindly with thick glasses and a perpetual puzzled look on his face, like he was constantly confused. "What do we do now?"

"I say we break for lunch," another juror with a pronounced paunch suggested. "I'm starving."

"It's not even noon yet, so why don't we spend an hour going over the evidence before we take a break?" Poppy advised with a smile.

The big-bellied juror sighed loudly, annoyed, and threw up his thick, chubby hands. "Whatever!"

Poppy picked up a sealed manila envelope and tore it open. She took out a stack of papers and set them down in the middle of the table for everyone to look at. The juror in the blue tracksuit was the first to reach for some of the papers. "I'm not sure why we have to go over the evidence again. It's crystal clear to me that Tony Molina is guilty."

The big-bellied juror nodded in agreement. "I mean, come on, there were eyewitnesses who saw him crack the poor chef's head with the frying pan! Who here voted not guilty?"

A young juror, no more than thirty years old, with curly blond hair, a handsome face, and wearing a shirt and tie that seemed too big for his lean frame, shot a hand in the air. "I think the defense has a very good point about those kitchen workers! They're employed by the chef. They're loyal to him. They could be lying, which gives me reasonable doubt!"

An older professorial type in a tweed jacket rolled his eyes, irked. "Oh, please, are you seriously going to buy their argument that the worker was an illegal immigrant who was so scared of being deported that he was willing to lie for his boss? That's preposterous, not to mention downright racist!"

An African American man with a round face and friendly demeanor leaned forward. "How come there were no security cameras in the kitchen?"

The juror in the blue tracksuit shrugged. "Who knows? If there were, it would make our job a whole lot easier."

The young blond man in the oversized shirt, who was sitting next to Poppy, reached over and suggestively placed his hand over hers. "This could be a remake of that old movie with Henry Fonda except we would have to call it *Eleven Angry Men and One Very Sexy Woman*."

Poppy quickly extricated her hand out from under his. The kid made her skin crawl. He was obviously trying to flatter her, perhaps in some vain attempt to get her to change her vote from guilty to not guilty. It was condescending and sexist, and she was not going to fall for it. "Let's stay focused on the evidence."

"What's that perfume you're wearing? It smells really nice," the blond kid commented, flashing a megawatt smile.

"Vera Wang," Poppy answered, picking up a piece of paper with some testimony and reading it over.

"It's borderline hypnotic," the blond man said. "By the way, I'm Alden. Alden Kenny. If we're going to be spending some time together, we might as well get to know each other."

"Poppy Harmon," Poppy said brusquely. "Why don't we go around the room and introduce ourselves?"

Everyone took turns. Big belly was Bart. Blue tracksuit was Chuck. There were two Johns and a Luther. A Max. One Jerry. A Phil, a Jesus, and a Rodrigo.

Alden didn't seem at all interested in the other male jurors. He was laser focused on Poppy, and it made her supremely uncomfortable. He was blatantly pouring on the charm, not stopping at her perfume, but also complimenting her outfit, her shoes, her hairstyle. At one point, she had to scold him for distracting the other jurors from the task at hand. He shut up for a little while as Poppy and the other jurors discussed the overwhelming amount of evidence against the defendant. Max, who admitted he was an unabashed fan of Tony Molina and had earlier voted not guilty was finally swayed over to the other side. He was joined by Rodrigo, who initially had been reticent to convict, and eventually another holdout, one of the Johns, also changed his vote.

"Okay, instead of doing another anonymous vote, let's just have a show of hands. Guilty?" Poppy said, raising her hand.

She was joined by Chuck, Bart, Luther, Max, Phil, the two Johns, Rodrigo, and Jesus.

Poppy nodded. "Not guilty?"

Alden leaned back, smiling seductively at Poppy and raised his hand.

He was joined by Jerry.

Chuck folded his arms, annoyed. "Come on, people. We could be out of here before lunchtime. It's so obvious he's guilty. Why are you holding out?"

Jerry, who was soft spoken, whispered, "My wife will kill me if I vote to toss her favorite singer, Tony Molina, in jail."

"Your wife did not take a sworn oath to be an impartial juror," Poppy fired back, glaring at Jerry. "But *you* did."

Jerry was easy to convince after that. He didn't want trouble and, after some coaxing, admitted that deep down he believed Tony was guilty of the assault. Another quick show of hands and Jerry was a "guilty" vote.

That left Alden Kenny.

And he made it very clear to everyone in the room that he was not going to budge.

Poppy called the bailiff and requested that the jury be released from deliberations until after lunch. She hoped that by then, with some time to consider the mountain of evidence, Alden Kenny might ultimately join the majority in voting to convict.

She was dead wrong.

Once the jury reconvened at the conference table an hour and a half later, Poppy turned to Alden. "Have you reconsidered your vote, Alden?"

Alden shook his head. "Sorry, I'm still a 'not guilty,' and I'm afraid it's going to stay that way."

Bart looked as if he was going to lunge across the table at Alden and strangle him. "You've got to be kidding me! It's so obvious he did it! Why can't you see that?"

"I have reasonable doubt," Alden answered calmly, with an irritating smirk on his face.

"And there is absolutely nothing we can do to convince you otherwise?" Poppy asked as a looming sense of hopelessness began to settle over the deliberation room.

Alden pursed his lips. "Nope."

He was acting so smug and superior and smarmy.

Poppy found him repulsive.

"So going over the overabundance of evidence one more time will not change your mind?" Poppy asked, sighing.

"As much as I would love to spend more time with you, Poppy, I'm afraid it would be pointless if your goal is to switch my vote. However, once this is over, I would be happy to spend as much time together as your heart desires."

God, he was such a little creep.

"No thank you," Poppy said curtly. "I'm good."

"Can I ask why you're being so stubborn?" Phil barked. He was around Poppy's age and scowled a lot and seemed deeply miffed all the time.

Alden smiled. "I grew up in Abilene, Texas. My whole family were huge fans of Tony Molina. He was so suave and cool and had such a soothing voice that would melt butter. He was so different from what we were used to, and he had such an impact on me, and I just wouldn't feel right ruining his life because of a small scuffle over a steak."

"So the fact that Chef Carmine was hospitalized with a very serious concussion doesn't affect you at all?" Poppy asked with a raised eyebrow.

"Not particularly," Alden said. "He looked fine to me in the courtroom. Let's be honest. It's not like he suffered any brain damage."

"So it's okay to assault someone as long as they manage to recover? Is that your opinion?" Rodrigo asked, shaking his head, disgusted.

Alden folded his arms and sat back in his chair. "We're talking about *the* Tony Molina."

Poppy knew there was no convincing him.

The jury was hopelessly deadlocked.

# Chapter 6

"Who is the jury foreman?" Judge Linscott asked, a weary look on his face.

Poppy reluctantly raised her hand, as if the deadlocked jury would somehow be perceived as being her fault.

Judge Linscott unexpectedly brightened. "Ah, Ms. Harmon, it's a pleasure to see you in my courtroom, so actively embracing your civic duty."

Poppy was utterly confused. The judge was acting as if they had met before. But she was fairly confident their paths had never crossed. And during jury selection, he had shown no signs of recognizing her.

"Thank you, Your Honor," Poppy said.

"I thought you looked familiar when the jury was first assembled, but I couldn't quite place you," Judge Linscott said, beaming. "But last night, my wife was watching the Nostalgia Network. . . ."

Poppy silently groaned. She hadn't expected this moment and was not looking forward to it. Her past always seemed to be a distraction.

"And what should come on but an old episode of *Jack Colt, PI*," Judge Linscott said excitedly, leaning forward, hands clasped together.

Max, who was sitting directly behind Poppy, shouted, "Of course! That's where I've seen you before! You played Daphne, Jack's loyal secretary!"

Poppy wanted to shrink and disappear, but she knew that was impossible in the moment so she just nodded and forced a smile.

The judge, who was oblivious to just how uncomfortable he was making her feel, continued to carry on. "You were quite good in the show. In the episode my wife saw, you went to deposit your paycheck at your local bank and walked right into a holdup, and you were taken hostage by the robbers, and Jack had to race against time to rescue you before they escaped with you across the Mexican border! Do you remember that one?"

"I'm afraid not, Your Honor. We did over seventy episodes so I don't really remember a lot of the story lines. . . ." Poppy said, shifting in her seat, silently praying this would be over soon.

"It must have been around nineteen eighty-six or eighty-seven. You looked so young," the judge said before quickly catching himself and attempting to recover. "And, may I add, you have aged beautifully."

"Thank you, Your Honor," Poppy sighed.

"Now," the judge said, clearing his throat. "Let's get back to the business at hand."

Alden, who was sitting next to Poppy, leaned in and

whispered in her ear, "I didn't realize I was on the jury with a celebrity!"

She had no desire to answer him and so she didn't.

The judge returned to his professional, stoic demeanor. "It has been brought to my attention that the jury is dead-locked. Is that correct, Ms. Harmon?"

"Yes, Your Honor."

"And if I send you back to deliberate some more, you believe it would be a waste of time and impossible to reach a unanimous verdict?"

"I believe so, yes, Your Honor," Poppy said with a frown.

"And what was the final vote?" Judge Linscott in-quired, glancing over at Poppy.

"Eleven to one to convict," Poppy said, glaring at Alden, sitting next to her.

Alden began playing footsie with Poppy, bumping his shoe into hers like a little kid who was smitten with the girl sitting next to him in church. Poppy was having none of that. She raised her foot and drove the sharp heel of her Steve Madden block heel sandal down on top of Alden's scuffed dress shoe. He had to suppress a yelp at the pain shooting through his toe.

The judge took time shuffling through some paper-work before looking up and nodding to the jury. "Very well, then, since the jury is hung and no verdict can be reached, I have no choice but to declare a mistrial on the assault charge against Mr. Molina."

Tony Molina slammed his fist down on the desk tri-umphantly and broke into a wide smile before excitedly shaking hands with his three lawyers. His son, Dominick, jumped up from his seat in the gallery and raced over to hug his father. Father and son then high-fived each other.

"It will be up to the district attorney's office whether or not the charges will be refiled for another trial," the judge said, eyes fixed on the redheaded prosecutor.

Frustrated, she stood up to address the judge. "They certainly will, Your Honor."

"That's up to you," Judge Linscott said with a shrug. He then turned to the jury box. "Lady and gentlemen of the jury, I thank you on behalf of the Riverside County district court for your service. I hereby excuse you. You are free to go."

Poppy and the eleven men of the jury all stood up and began filing out. Alden Kenny was in front of her, and as they passed Tony Molina, who was now hugging the older attorney, she saw the singer give a slight nod to Alden as he walked by him. She could not be 100 percent sure, but she thought she saw Alden nod back as if the two men knew each other. Molina could not have known Alden Kenny was the lone holdout, the one juror who had resolutely refused to find him guilty despite the clear evidence in front of him.

Was Alden a plant?

Did they have some kind of secret pact?

Perhaps she should go to the judge and tell him what she had just witnessed. But again, she wasn't confident enough to make any kind of fact-based accusation. It was just a nod, a half smile; it might have meant nothing. And the trial was over. It was time to get back to her life and start focusing on the search for Rod Harper's AWOL daughter. She decided in that moment to just let it go, blissfully unaware that forgetting about it would be far easier said than done.

# Chapter 7

Poppy was halfway to her car when she noticed Tony Molina and his son, Dominick, along with the small entourage of slick lawyers outside, slapping each other on the back, laughing uproariously, truly enjoying their victorious moment. The sight made her slightly nauseous. She knew in her gut that Molina had indeed physically assaulted Chef Carmine Cicci, and watching him now, cracking jokes, well, it just didn't sit well with her. She had half a mind to march right up and give him a piece of her mind and remind him just how close he came to serving jail time, and that perhaps in the future he should think twice before going off half cocked and indulging in a childish temper tantrum by whacking a poor man in the head with a cast-iron frying pan. Just because he was famous and had a lot of money didn't give him a license to break the law. But she refrained from causing any kind of scene. The only thing she would probably do going forward was to ban Iris from playing any of his CDs at the Desert Flowers Detective Agency office. At least when she was present.

Poppy turned back around and pressed the button on her remote to unlock her car. She was startled to see Chef Carmine Cicci suddenly appear in front of her.

"Oh . . ." Poppy gasped.

"I'm sorry, I didn't mean to sneak up on you like that," Chef Carmine said with an apologetic smile.

"That's quite all right," Poppy said, a hand on her chest as her heartbeat thumped twice as fast as usual.

"I was already in my car about to leave when I saw you come out of the building, and so I dashed over here to catch you. . . ."

"What can I do for you, Mr. Cicci?"

"I just wanted to thank you."

"That's very sweet of you. I wish the outcome had been different."

"Me too. I want you to know I was telling the truth on the stand. I was a huge fan of Tony Molina. I was so honored to have him dine in my restaurant. I can't tell you what a blow it was to have him come at me like that."

"Both figuratively and literally," Poppy added.

Chef Carmine chuckled. "Yes, I suppose so. Anyway, I could tell from your body language and how you spoke to the judge that you truly wanted to find him guilty."

"Well, I commend you on how well you can read people. That's exactly what I wanted to do. But as you heard, unfortunately, we had one juror who refused to seriously consider the facts of the case, so I apologize that we couldn't collectively come to a just verdict."

Chef Carmine nodded. "For what it's worth, the prosecutor has assured me that she will be retrying the case."

"That's certainly encouraging," Poppy said, noticing for the first time that despite all the swirling attention given to Tony Molina and his good looks, Chef Carmine himself was actually a very good-looking man with a certain swagger to him that Poppy found overtly appealing. And he had a warm, irresistible smile, which he shared with her now. Actually she found it a bit overpowering. "Good luck with everything. I'll be watching for you on the Food Network," she managed to get out.

He bowed to her and took her hand. "Thank you. And I look forward to seeing you play your next role."

"Good heavens, I haven't acted in anything in over twenty years," Poppy said, laughing. "Those days are long over, I'm afraid."

"Never say never. You're still an exquisitely gorgeous woman and I would watch you read from the phone book," he said with a wink.

Poppy found herself giggling like a schoolgirl. "Oh, stop. . . ."

"I mean it," he said, still holding her hand.

She found his almost brazen attempts to butter her up intoxicating, unlike the far less charming Alden Kenny, who had tried playing footsie with her in the jury box. There was no mystery why the masculine, bald Chef Carmine had a lot fans. It wasn't just for his cooking skills.

"The next time you come into Cicci's, your dinner will be on me," he said before finally letting go of her hand.

"I just may take you up on that," Poppy said, feeling flushed and flustered. "I love a good steak."

"Let me guess. Medium rare?"

"Good guess."

"I promise not to mess it up."

"And I promise not to grab a frying pan if you do," Poppy joked.

They shared a laugh.

"Then it's a date," Chef Carmine said. "Good-bye, Ms. Harmon."

"Please, call me Poppy."

"With pleasure. Good-bye, Poppy."

And then he was gone.

Poppy didn't exactly take his overtures too seriously. After all, he was much younger and probably just grateful that she had been on his side during the trial. She hadn't thought much about men since her husband, Chester, had died over a year ago, and wasn't too anxious to jump back into the dating pool anytime soon, especially now, as she was trying to get her fledgling detective agency with Iris, Violet, and Matt off the ground.

There was Sam Emerson, the former cop and consultant on *Jack Colt* she had recently reconnected with, but he lived two hours away in Big Bear, and so they were both keeping it casual. That's about all she was willing to handle at the moment.

But Chef Carmine certainly was a charmer.

And he wouldn't be the last man in the coming days to cause Poppy Harmon's heart to flutter.

# Chapter 8

When Poppy pulled up in front of Iris's house, she met Violet in the driveway, who was picking up a bag of groceries from the open trunk of her car.

"Is Iris having you do her grocery shopping now?" Poppy asked.

"Oh, no, I picked up some snacks for the office. Wyatt has been working so hard. We just had a breakthrough in the Lara Harper case and it's all because of him!" Violet exclaimed, beaming like the proud grandmother she was.

Poppy clasped her hands together hopefully. "Did you find her?"

"Not exactly," Violet said as she scooted up the driveway toward the garage, clutching her plastic bag of junk food. "I'd better get these ice cream sandwiches in the freezer before they melt."

Poppy chased after her and got ahead of her in time to open the side door of the garage for Violet, who hurried past her. Once inside, she found her team of investigators hard at work. Wyatt was at his desktop computer, furiously punching keys as Matt hovered over him. Violet began unpacking her food in the kitchenette toward the back of the garage office, and Iris, well, Iris was on the couch, reading *Vanity Fair*. But she was reading her article so intently it almost appeared as if she were in the middle of some important research.

"What have you got?" Poppy asked, crossing over to Wyatt.

Iris suddenly noticed Poppy's presence and dropped her magazine down on the coffee table in front of the couch. "You're back! Is the trial over? Did you actually send that American treasure Tony Molina to prison?"

"No, Iris, he got off. At least for now. It was a hung jury," Poppy sighed. "But it looks like the prosecutor is going to try the case again."

"That poor man," Iris lamented, shaking her head. "Being targeted by an overzealous prosecutor only interested in advancing her career by going after a celebrity who has been falsely accused!"

"If that is what you think happened, Iris, then you've been fed a heaping serving of fake news," Poppy declared. "I have been listening to all the facts for days, and the man is definitely guilty! He just got lucky!"

Violet raced past them and over to Wyatt and handed him a wrapped ice cream sandwich. "There you go, sweetheart. Grandma's so pleased with your progress. You should get some kind of award."

Matt looked up at Violet. "Don't I get one?"

Violet patted him on the arm. "Of course, dear. But Wyatt's been working so hard and you . . ." She stopped short at the sight of Matt's crestfallen face. "Hold on. I've got one coming right up."

Violet flew back to the kitchenette.

Poppy turned to Iris. "I don't want to talk about Tony Molina anymore. I'll be happy if I never have to hear his name again. I want to know about what Wyatt's uncovered."

Iris threw her arms up in surrender as Matt dashed over to Poppy excitedly. "It could be big. Rod told us that after his fight with Lara he threatened to cut her off financially but he didn't follow through, so Wyatt has been tracking her credit card, which is still very much active."

Poppy lit up. "She's been using it?"

Violet returned with an ice cream sandwich for Matt and then hugged Wyatt from behind. "I wish Wyatt got his brains from me, but sadly that's not the case!"

"Nana, stop. . . ." Wyatt groaned, squirming and scrunching up his shoulders.

"Someone's been using it," Matt said. "Either Lara is alive and well and using the card or it's been stolen and someone is posing as her."

"But if we can see the charges, then we will know exactly where the card has been used," Poppy said, thrilled. "And if it is her, we can use those charges to trace her whereabouts."

"I love this! We're a real team! Whatever we're doing here is working like a dream!" Matt gushed.

The women ignored Matt's overenthusiasm as Poppy turned to Wyatt. "So where has the card been used?"

Wyatt scanned down the charges listed on his computer screen. "Right here. All over the Coachella Valley. At a Mexican restaurant in Cathedral City, a Macy's, a music store in Palm Desert, Starbucks in Rancho Mirage, a Regal movie theater in Palm Springs . . ."

"If it's her using the card," Matt said with a smile, "then that means she's right here in our own backyard."

# Chapter 9

The potbellied man with a ZZ Top gray beard that touched all the way down to his protruding navel and nearly covered the Grateful Dead logo on his T-shirt squinted as he held up Matt's phone and stared at the photo of Lara Harper on the screen. "Yeah, I remember her. She was in here with some guy, and they were browsing the guitars over there."

One of the charges on Lara's card had been processed at this small independent music shop in Palm Desert, east of downtown Palm Springs.

Matt, in his full-on Sam Spade mode, cleared his throat and asked, "The amount you charged her was $14.99. Do you recall what she bought?"

The gray-bearded man with the half-asleep eyes, which Poppy attributed to his probable generous use of the now fully legal marijuana in the state of California, nodded. "A guitar pick. That's why I remember them. They must have tried out every guitar on the wall over there. I thought I was going to make a big sale, but after almost an hour, the only thing they ended up buying was a lousy guitar pick!"

Poppy noticed a security camera set up above the register. "Is there any chance we can see the footage from that camera recorded on the day they were here?"

"Afraid not," Gray Beard said, shaking his head. "That thing's been on the fritz for about a year. I keep making a mental note to get it fixed, but then for some reason I forget. . . ."

Poppy grimaced. She was fairly certain the long-term effects of excessive drug use was the cause of his short-term memory issue.

"What about the young man she was with? Can you describe him?" Poppy asked.

Gray Beard shrugged. "Good-looking guy. To be honest, I didn't pay much attention to him because I was more interested in her. She was hot. She had this real tight—" He caught himself as he spotted Poppy's disdainful look. "She was pretty, ma'am."

"I see," Poppy said wearily. "Well, thank you for your time."

As they turned to go, Matt said, "Well, at least we can report to Rod that nothing bad has happened to her. It looks like she's just been hanging out in the desert with a new boyfriend."

"Perhaps. But I sure would like to know more about this young man she's keeping company with," Poppy said as her phone buzzed. She fished it out of her purse and glanced at the screen. "Iris and Violet are on their way to a yoga studio."

"Are you serious? I can't imagine Iris bending over for anything except maybe a glass of Chardonnay."

"It has to be connected to the case. She just texted me the address. I'm going to meet them there," Poppy said as they reached the door. Before Matt had a chance to open it for her, the door flew open and a tall, lanky, grizzled rocker in his late fifties or early sixties and wearing a leather vest with no shirt underneath ambled in with a glazed look in his eyes. He appeared to be more of a stoner than even the potbellied, gray-bearded owner of the music shop.

Suddenly his dull eyes, which had been at half mast, managed to pop all the way open at the sight of Poppy. "No way . . ."

"Good afternoon," Poppy said, trying to get past him.

He stepped in front of her, effectively blocking her exit. "I know you!"

Matt instinctively moved forward, protectively putting an arm in between them.

"You're Daphne!" the rocker exclaimed excitedly.

"Yes, you have a good memory," Poppy said, mustering as much politeness as she possibly could.

"I watched you every week! I can't tell you how sexy I thought you were! Especially in that one episode where you go undercover as an exotic dancer at the nightclub where your boss's niece was being held prisoner by that crazed nightclub owner! Man, I had that one playing on my VCR every night! I can't tell you how many times I watched you while—"

There was no way Poppy wanted to hear any more so she quickly cut him off. "Well, I'm thrilled you have such fond memories of watching that show."

First the judge remembered her and now Cheech of

Cheech and Chong. It was like TV of the 1980s was enjoying some kind of renaissance.

"Can I get a selfie with you?" the rocker asked, searching his pockets for his phone.

"We're really kind of in a hurry," Matt interjected.

Poppy gently pushed Matt's arm down that was separating her from her ardent fan. "It's all right, Matt," she said before smiling at the man. "I'd be happy to."

Unable to find his phone, the leather-vested rocker recruited Gray Beard to take the photo with his own phone with the promise of texting it to him later. It took three tries before he was happy with the picture since in the first two he had his eyes closed.

After a flurry of thank-yous, Poppy and Matt finally managed to escape the music shop and were on their way to the car, which was parked in a lot around the corner.

"That is so cool," Matt muttered wistfully.

"What?" Poppy asked.

"To get recognized like that."

"Well, these days it is exceedingly rare. I'm not exactly Beyoncé."

"I know, but it must be immensely gratifying having played a role that is so fondly remembered," Matt sighed, almost envious.

"I suppose so," Poppy said. "At the time, it was just a job. I didn't realize the impact of the show until much later, after it had been cancelled. I desperately wanted a more challenging role, on stage or in the movies. Nobody back then took TV too seriously. When I played Daphne, it was mostly just for the paycheck. I had no idea it would end up being the part people would remember me for."

"It's such a gift. I would give anything to play a role that gets some kind of a reaction. To know I moved people. That would be the most awesome thing in the world. . . ." Matt said, his voice trailing off, lost in thought.

They walked the rest of the way to the car in silence. Poppy let Matt daydream about the possibilities ahead of him, and suddenly she felt guilty. She feared she might be responsible for Matt putting his acting career on the back burner while helping her run the Desert Flowers Detective Agency in Palm Springs, a long two-hour drive from the producers and agents and casting directors in Los Angeles.

"Matt, I don't want you to . . ."

He looked at her expectantly.

She tried to find the right words.

"I don't want you to sacrifice valuable time out here in the desert if you need to be in LA focusing on your career. . . ."

He smiled and put a reassuring hand on her arm. "I don't see it that way at all. I'm here to play a role. I'm Matt Flowers, Private Eye, and I am one hundred percent committed."

She could tell his heart was in the right place.

His words were sincere.

But she could not shake the feeling that she was somehow holding him back by keeping him away from the center of Hollywood and the opportunities that could come his way. But for now she needed him, and she was grateful he was on board to keep her fledgling agency afloat.

# Chapter 10

When Poppy arrived at the Peaceful Yoga Studio in a mini mall just south of downtown Palm Springs, it was anything but peaceful. There was a loud commotion in the main studio, and when she heard ear-splitting screaming, she rushed in to find a crowd of people in loose-fitting clothing having deserted their yoga mats and now surrounding someone lying flat on the floor. Poppy pushed her way through and gasped at the sight of Iris stretched out, sweating, as Violet squeezed her hand. A handsome man in his midtwenties, with his long brown hair pulled back into a ponytail and a trim beard that made him look a little like Jesus, knelt down beside Iris. He cradled her head in his hand and spoke to her softly.

"Please, let me call you an ambulance," he said soothingly.

"No! I am not going to the hospital! I have a social hour at the club tonight that I am not going to miss! I will be just fine!"

"What happened?" Poppy exclaimed.

At the sight of Poppy, Violet sprang to her feet and grabbed her arm. "We came here to see Falcon, but he refused to talk to us until after class was finished, and he told us we couldn't stay unless we paid the donation and participated."

"Who is Falcon?" Poppy asked.

Violet pointed to the Jesus look-alike. "That's Falcon. He's the owner."

"Is Falcon a first name or a last name?" Poppy wondered.

Violet shrugged. "I don't know. I think he may just go by Falcon."

Poppy didn't like him already.

"We barely got started and were in the Downward Dog position when Iris's back went out," Violet recounted breathlessly. "Now she's in horrible pain."

Iris, flat on her back, looked up at Poppy, blinking. "It's about time you got here! Help me up so I can get out of here!"

"I'm not sure moving you is a good idea, Iris. Maybe you should just let us call the paramedics so they can take you to a doctor and have you checked out!"

"That's nonsense! I don't have time for that! Come on, take my hand!"

Poppy reached down and grabbed Iris's hand. Iris pulled on it and sat up. She screeched at the top of her lungs before quickly lying back down again.

"Iris, this is crazy. I'm calling an ambulance," Poppy insisted.

"You will do no such thing! I forbid it! There is no way

I am going to be wheeled out of here on a stretcher! I can do this! I just need to go home, get my heating pad out, and pop a couple of Advils."

Poppy stared down at her skeptically, but there was no talking to her. Iris turned to Falcon and barked, "On the count of three, I want you to put your arm around me and lift at the same time as Poppy to get me on my feet."

"You're not going to sue me or anything, are you?" Falcon asked, more than a bit concerned.

"Of course not! I don't want your money! I just want to go home!" Iris screamed. "Poppy, let's try again. . . ."

Poppy grabbed both of Iris's hands this time as Iris yelled, "One . . . two . . . three . . . !"

Poppy pulled with all her might. Falcon's sinewy arm served as a brace and they managed to haul Iris to her feet. She cried and cursed all the way up, but once she was steady and her back was straight, she calmed down, feeling some relief.

Iris turned to Poppy. "What a crock! I always knew twisting and stretching your body could not possibly be good for you! Do you know what the name of this class is? 'Healing Yoga'! *Healing?* Can you believe that? I nearly killed myself!"

Violet stepped forward and whispered, "You were not doing the pose correctly, Iris. You didn't watch the teacher as he demonstrated."

"Nobody asked you, Violet!" Iris spit out.

Poppy quietly pulled Violet to the side. "What were you doing here anyway? Why did you need to talk to this Falcon person?"

Violet leaned in, keeping an eye on Falcon, who was now apologizing profusely to Iris, still not convinced she would not sue him for negligence. "Wyatt went to Lara

Harper's Facebook page and did a little digging and found out from some past posts that she and Falcon had been dating at one point. So Iris and I came down here to get the scoop, but, unfortunately, Iris's back went out before we got the chance."

Poppy walked back over to the handsome, lean, tactile yoga instructor. "Mr. Falcon . . ."

"Falcon, just Falcon," he said, slightly annoyed.

"Falcon. Would you mind helping us escort our friend Iris to the car, and then I promise you we will let you get back to teaching your class."

Falcon sighed, and gently put Iris's arm around his neck as Poppy draped Iris's other arm around her shoulder. He turned to a young man in his early twenties, gorgeous, perfect build, in a tank top that showed off his curved muscles. "Ted, would you take over for me while I see these ladies off?"

The young man beamed. "I'd be glad to." And then Ted bounded to the front of the room and got everybody back to where they had left off before Iris's calamity in her Downward Dog position.

Poppy and Falcon delicately led Iris, who shuffled along, wincing in pain as they exited the studio and out past reception. Violet followed along behind them. Once they were outside and managed to get Iris settled in the reclined passenger's seat of Violet's car, Poppy was finally able to corner Falcon alone.

"If you have just a moment, I'd like to talk to you about—"

Falcon interrupted her. "I have a class waiting inside."

"Ted seems quite capable of filling in for you for just a few more minutes," Poppy pressed. "Please, it's very important."

Falcon sighed. "What's all this about?"

"Lara Harper."

His face darkened. "What about her?"

"Are you two dating?"

"Not anymore. For your information, I'm dating Ted."

Poppy raised an eyebrow.

"I don't see genders; I only see souls."

"I see," Poppy said, although frankly she did not understand at all. "But you were involved with Lara at some point?"

Falcon scratched his beard and scoffed. "Yes, I should have known better. We met while I was teaching a conscious breathing seminar in LA. She was in attendance, and after class, she approached me. She came on rather strong and told me she found me attractive and would like to explore my teachings more in depth, and, well, you can only imagine what she meant by that."

"And you went along?"

"She's a very pretty girl."

"How long did you two *explore*?" Poppy asked, trying valiantly to disguise the distaste in her mouth with a bland smile.

"Not long. Maybe a month."

"Why did it end?"

"I try to follow a deep and enlightening spiritual path and it is very important that I avoid any dark and negative energy," he said.

"And Lara had dark energy?"

"Loads of it. She's a very disturbed spirit."

"And so you broke it off?"

Falcon grimaced.

Iris, who had just rolled down the window and was

eavesdropping on the conversation, shouted, "Looks to me like she was the one who dumped you!"

Falcon shot Iris an irritated look but refrained from commenting out of fear she might still file a lawsuit against him.

Poppy stared at Falcon. "Is that true?"

"Yes," Falcon admitted bitterly. "For another guy."

"Do you know who she's with now?" Poppy asked.

"Not a clue. And I don't care. She did me a favor. I'm thrilled she's someone else's problem now. You have no idea what that crazy girl put me through. Now if you'll excuse me, I have paying customers inside," he said before turning to Iris. "Feel better."

Iris leaned out the window of Violet's car. "Oh, I most certainly will if I never have to come back here again!"

Falcon ignored the parting shot and stalked back inside his yoga studio.

Violet waved to Poppy outside the driver's-side window as she peeled away. "We'll meet you back at the office!"

Poppy headed to her car, frustrated the team had just hit another dead end and were no closer to finding Rod Harper's daughter.

# Chapter 11

Poppy perused the menu at Cicci's Italian Restaurant, debating on whether or not she should indulge by ordering the eggplant parmigiana or the chicken piccata. When Chef Cicci discovered she was in the restaurant dining with Rod Harper, he personally brought out his specialty appetizer, his mouthwatering calamari fritti, for them to share. Like the true gentleman he appeared to be, Chef Cicci presumed the two were on a date and politely refrained from shamelessly flirting with Poppy again.

For that, Poppy was grateful. However, she was rather uncomfortable with the assumption that she and Rod were on a date. When Rod called her and suggested they have dinner so they could discuss the case, Poppy's inclination was to invite Matt to join them. After all, in Rod's mind, Matt was the boss and would be the natural choice to provide an update. But Rod quickly refused, preferring to meet Poppy alone, making up some excuse as to feeling more comfortable with her rather than the brash, excitable, hotshot young private eye. Poppy reluctantly agreed, but when she arrived at the restaurant and met Rod at the hostess station, he kissed her lightly on the lips, and kept a hand on the small of her back as the hostess led them to their romantic candlelit corner table. It was feeling more like a date with each passing moment.

Rod was his usual charming self, complimenting her appearance and ordering them an expensive bottle of Petite Sirah from the Napa Valley. When Chef Cicci came out of the kitchen to personally greet them, Rod placed a hand over Poppy's, almost possessively, as if he was marking his territory and warning the charismatic chef that his dining companion was spoken for. This made Poppy slightly nervous. It wasn't that she was trying to deny the fact that she and Rod had a history dating back to the 1980s, but in her mind, that's exactly what it was— history. Long in the past. She wasn't sure why he was being so forward all of a sudden. In fact, she didn't want to know, so she decided to just plow ahead with why they were here in the first place.

"I don't want you to worry, Rod. Although we haven't found Lara yet, we're making progress," Poppy said as convincingly as she possibly could.

Rod filled her wine glass, then his, and set the bottle back down on the table. "I have full confidence Matt will get the job done."

That stung a bit. She had the urge to tell him right then and there that she was the one in charge at the Desert Flowers Detective Agency. It would be nice to impress him, but she remained silent.

The waitress appeared to take their order and Poppy finally made her decision. She went with the chicken piccata. Rod ordered the steak Molina, named after Tony. Poppy had assumed Chef Cicci would change the name of his signature steak after the trial, but he probably hadn't had time to fix the menus.

"Lara apparently has a new boyfriend," Poppy said. "Do you have any idea who it might be?"

"No," Rod said, almost disinterested. "But I'm sure he's another world-class loser. Lara has an unyielding talent for digging up lowlifes and adopting them."

"A father rarely approves of his daughter's choices in men," Poppy said, laughing.

"There was one I actually liked. They met when she was an undergrad at UCLA. He was studying anthropology, had a good head on his shoulders, and treated her well. The minute she realized I was fond of him, she dropped him faster than a hot brick. Let's just say Lara has left a long trail littered with broken hearts."

"Well, I remember back in the day you were quite the ladies' man cavorting with actresses and models, and if I recall correctly, even a Spanish royal."

"They were more interested in the idea of dating Jack Colt than Rod Harper, an electrician's son from Missouri, believe me," he said with a wan smile.

"That's hardly true. Rod Harper was sweet and kind and one of the nicest stars you could find in Hollywood. Remember, I said so in a *People* magazine profile," Poppy said.

"I thought the studio's PR department wrote that," Rod said, chuckling.

"No, I came up with that all by myself. I had your back."

Rod took Poppy's hand again and raised it to his mouth.

He softly kissed her fingers. Startled, Poppy quickly withdrew her hand, smacked the half-full bottle of red wine, and it spilled all over the table.

"I'm so sorry," Poppy cried.

The waitress and a pair of busboys appeared out of nowhere; removed the bottle, plates, glasses, and silverware; yanked off the wine-stained white tablecloth; spirited it away; and quickly replaced it with a clean one, before re-setting the table with all the precision of a NASCAR pit crew.

Once they finished and scooted off and she and Rod were alone again, Poppy flushed with embarrassment. "See, I'm just as clumsy as Daphne was on *Jack Colt. . . .*"

"I find it endearing. I apologize if I was out of line," Rod said tentatively, eyes fixed on Poppy, anxiously awaiting her response.

"No, Rod, you weren't. . . ."

Rod sighed, relieved.

"But . . ." she added.

"There's always a 'but.' "

"I think we should keep things on a professional level . . . at least until we find Lara and close the case. . . . Then maybe . . ."

She couldn't believe what she was saying. She was leaving the door open. That was the last thing she had intended to do. But in this moment, with Rod, the man she had been so hung up on all those years ago, she couldn't completely dismiss him out of hand and close off the possibility that perhaps one day in the future . . .

"I love you, Poppy," Rod said.

Poppy's mouth dropped open. "I beg your pardon?"

"I always have. Ever since we did that screen test at your audition to play Daphne to see if we had any chemistry. I never told you this, but the producers wanted to go with one of the Landers sisters, but I fought like hell for you. I said I wouldn't do the show without you. There was something about you. . . . I couldn't stop thinking about you. . . ."

"Then *why* . . . ?"

"I was young and stupid. Making thirty-five grand a week. I couldn't fathom settling down with one girl at the time. Plus, you intimidated me. You had class. Most of the girls I was hooking up with back then were sorely lacking in that department."

Poppy sipped her wine, not sure what to say.

"When the show got cancelled, and I fancied myself a movie actor after getting that one heist movie that bombed big-time, I was in a rut professionally, and I wanted to call you, but I was feeling like a washed-up has-been and my self-esteem was in the toilet and I just didn't want you to see me like that. . . . I wanted you to remember me when I was on top of the world. . . . So I didn't. . . . And then I got cast in that Larry McMurtry miniseries about the Old West and met Regina, who was doing hair on the set, and we got married, and eventually had Lara, and then it was too late. . . ."

"It was probably for the best. I had already met Chester by that time and was preparing to move to Palm Springs—"

"I thought about calling you after he died, but it just didn't seem right, showing up after all these years when you had just lost your husband, so I kept my distance . . . until now. . . ."

"Rod . . ."

"I know, I'm making a fool out of myself. I should just stop right now while I'm way behind."

Poppy wanted to reassure him that she was flattered and, on some level, tempted to pick up where they had left off in the mid-1980s when neither could resist the chemistry they had on set and took it to Rod's Star Waggons trailer late one Friday night. Rod had invited her to stop by his dressing room for a glass of champagne to celebrate wrapping the second season of the show. She had happy memories of their night together. But he never called her after that one encounter. Later, she sank into a depression during the hiatus when she realized it had just been a onetime thing, and she was just one of Rod's many conquests. When they returned for the third and final season of *Jack Colt*, they both pretended it had never happened and remained professional and cordial until the series was finally cancelled the following spring and they went their separate ways.

Poppy opened her mouth to speak when she spotted Tony Molina breezing into the restaurant flanked by two rather imposing figures, a man and a woman. The rattled hostess looked around as if she were on *Punk'd*, that MTV show that played practical jokes on unsuspecting marks. She couldn't believe Tony Molina had the gall to show up at Cicci's so soon after the trial. Tony turned on the charm, calling the hostess by her name, Nell, and requesting his usual table in the back.

One of the busboys dashed into the kitchen to alert Chef Cicci, who came bounding out of the kitchen to see for himself, as if he couldn't believe what he had just been told. But sure enough, there was Tony glad-handing the staff and a few patrons he knew from around town. When Tony spotted Chef Cicci, he slapped his hands on the chef's ears and pulled him close before kissing him on both cheeks. "I hope we can let bygones be bygones! I've missed this place! I've been dreaming of chowing down on a steak Molina all day!"

There was a palpable tension throughout the whole dining room. Everyone's eyes were locked on Chef Cicci, waiting to see if he was going to kick Tony Molina out of the restaurant, but the famous chef had already gone through enough drama for one year and was not about to cause a scene. He simply bowed and said with a tight smile, "Coming right up, Mr. Molina." And then he quietly retreated back into the kitchen.

Tony Molina, still flanked by the handsome couple, who were both sporting sunglasses in the already dim restaurant, and casual polo shirts and long pants, was passing by Poppy and Rod's table when he stopped suddenly.

"I know you," Tony said with a warm smile to Poppy as he completely ignored Rod.

"Hello, Mr. Molina," Poppy said coldly, taking another sip of her wine.

"Please, call me Tony. I remember you from my trial, but we've never been properly introduced."

"Poppy Harmon," she said before gesturing toward Rod. "And this is—"

Tony didn't seem eager to meet Rod, so he cut her off and turned to the couple next to him. "This is my security detail. Griffin and Tammy Goodwin. They're married and both ex-military. I find that so cool. I hired them because they remind me of Angelina Jolie and Brad Pitt in that movie where they played married spies. . . . What was it called?"

"*Mr. & Mrs. Smith*," Griffin mumbled.

"I loved that movie!" Tony exclaimed, before focusing

on Poppy again. "Anyway, you stood out to me probably because you were the only woman on the jury. . . ."

"I voted guilty," Poppy said abruptly.

This caught Tony off guard, but only for a split second. He quickly collected himself and was flashing that mega-watt smile again as he feigned getting a stake through the heart. "Ouch, that hurt."

Poppy never cracked a smile.

"I certainly don't want to interrupt your dinner with . . ." Tony said, finally deigning to glance at her dinner date. His face immediately darkened at the sight of Rod.

"Hello, Tony," Rod said with a knowing smile.

Tony was obviously shaken and, ignoring Rod's insincere greeting, returned his attention to Poppy. "Enjoy your evening."

He quickly moved on, followed by Angelina and Brad, or the real-life versions of them apparently.

Poppy leaned in, curious. "What was all that about? Do you know him?"

Rod nodded. "Not well, but let's just say he's *not* a fan."

"What went down between you two?"

"Back in the day, I dated his wife."

"Which one?"

"His current wife. The former pop star."

"Tofu?"

"Yes. It was right around the time she had that big hit with the theme song from that James Bond movie. I don't remember the title. They all sound alike. We only lasted a few months, and it was years before she even met Tony, let alone married him, but he decided he hated me for sleeping with his wife."

"Even though he didn't even know her at the time?" Poppy asked incredulously.

"The guy's a psychopath."

Poppy sat back in her chair and glanced over at Tony Molina's regular table, where he was ordering a stiff martini from the waitress while his bodyguards sat quietly on either side of him looking over their menus.

"I sure wish you and the rest of the jury had convicted that son of a bitch. We'd all be a lot safer if Tony Molina was behind bars," Rod said.

Watching Tony's casual and almost boastful return to the scene of the crime, Poppy was convinced that in this case Rod was 100 percent right.

# Chapter 12

The guard inspected the contents of her purse thoroughly and once satisfied handed it back to Poppy and waved her through the metal detector. Poppy took a deep breath and followed the instructions. She had been through this routine many times before. Another uniformed guard, this one female, led her and a handful of other visitors down a long hallway that was painted turquoise. Poppy had never liked the color turquoise. They finally reached the receiving room and were instructed to sit down at the various tables that filled the space and wait. Five minutes later, the door opened and a parade of women, all in tan prison-issued jumpsuits, marched in and were reunited with their loved ones. There were a lot of tears and hugs. Poppy craned her neck to see if she could find her daughter. She started to worry that she might not be among this group, but at the tail end of the line, she finally spotted her.

Her daughter, Heather, looked tired, her face drawn, her complexion pale. Poppy's heart broke every time she came to visit her at the penitentiary. She hated to see her only child incarcerated. Although her sentence was nearly finished due to an overcrowded system and her exemplary behavior, the ordeal had been overwhelming for Heather. Every visit, once a week for the last ten months, Poppy had noticed a deadening of Heather's spirit, a slow erosion of her will not to succumb to her challenging circumstances. Poppy had hoped Heather would take advantage of the therapists the prison provided in order to work through what had happened that led to her plea deal and two-year sentence. And although Heather reassured her mother that she would get the help she needed in order to stay positive, Poppy knew she had ignored her advice and was just keeping to herself in her cell and counting down the days until her eventual release. Poppy's only hope was when that day came, Heather would then finally be able to emotionally deal with what had led to her arrest and her experiences behind bars so it wouldn't haunt her for the rest of her life.

During her first two or three visits in the weeks following Heather's sentencing, Poppy had tried to get her to open up about what she had gone through and not bury her feelings, but Heather was not interested in dredging up those painful memories and refused to discuss them with her mother or anyone else, so Poppy finally had no choice but to let it go.

Heather's glazed eyes scanned the room and saw Poppy excitedly waving at her. She gave her mother a half smile and shuffled over to her. Poppy threw her arms around her slight frame and squeezed her tightly.

"I've missed you so much, darling," Poppy cried.

Heather rested her head on her mother's shoulder for a few seconds before pulling away and sitting down at the table. "I've missed you too."

"You look wonderful," Poppy lied.

Heather cracked another half smile and pushed her flat, matted, stringy brown hair behind her ears. "No I don't, Mother, and you know it."

"Well, at least you haven't lost any more weight. I've been worried you haven't been eating properly."

Heather shrugged. "It's hard when I wouldn't even feed the mystery meat they serve around here to a starving stray dog I found in an alley. But at least the Jell-O is tasty, if not a little bland."

"Well, when you get out soon, I'm going to cook you a delicious homemade meal every night for a month!"

Heather scoffed. "Mother, you can barely boil water."

"Okay, we'll go out. My treat. We'll start with prime rib and Yorkshire pudding at Lord Fletcher's. You love that place. Chester and I used to take you there all the time when you were a little girl. And we'll have Mexican food at all your favorite haunts. La Tablita, El Mirasol . . ."

Heather folded her arms and stared at the floor. "Have you spoken with Harvey?"

Harvey Kaplan was Heather's attorney.

"Yes, I did. He says your parole hearing is on the fast track, but he's just not sure if it will be scheduled in a matter of weeks or months. Unfortunately, they have a very full docket. But he told me to tell you to just hang in there. He's confident that when it does happen you will no doubt sail right through with flying colors and finally get out of here."

"I feel like I've been in this awful place forever," Heather moaned.

"It's only been ten months, darling, but I understand why you're so discouraged. You just need to stay strong. This will all be over soon."

Heather kept her eyes fixed on the floor. "How is Matt?"

Poppy had expected the question.

Heather asked it every time she came to see her.

Poppy leaned forward and patted her daughter's hand. "He's fine. Working hard to help me keep this whole new private investigation business afloat."

"He hasn't been here to see me in almost a month," Heather whispered, looking up at her mother with sad eyes.

"Has it been that long? Well, I'm sure he's just lost track of time. Between working cases for me and driving back and forth between Palm Springs and LA for acting auditions, he doesn't have much spare time."

Heather bowed her head and began wringing her hands together. "Does he still talk about me?"

"Of course, darling. All the time."

It wasn't a lie. Matt had dated Heather for a while before her arrest, and part of the reason he had so completely devoted himself to playing Matt Flowers, the de facto head of the Desert Flowers Agency, was to help Poppy make enough money to support her daughter once she was released.

Poppy had asked Matt numerous times if he still planned on seeing Heather once she was out of prison. She hardly expected him to wait for her, but Matt assured her he was in this for the long haul. He was fully aware of all the circumstances behind Heather's situation. She wasn't some cold-blooded murderer. It had been an accident. Involuntary manslaughter. That was the legal definition. And the judge knew it, which was why he was lenient when it came to her sentencing. Matt had never wavered in his support of Heather, and although it had become more difficult for him these last few months to stay loyal and remain committed to his relationship with Heather, Poppy knew deep down when Matt made a promise, he was a man of his word. He was going to be there for her when she got out. However, with the obvious emotional turmoil Heather had been going through while in prison, and the challenges ahead upon her release, Poppy was deeply concerned about whether their relationship could survive when Heather was finally a free woman.

"Do me a favor," Heather said. "When you see him, give him my love and tell him I can't wait to see him."

"Of course, darling," Poppy replied, desperately trying to stay stoic and not dissolve in a flood of tears. "He will be so happy to hear that."

She could not break down in front of her daughter. She prayed Matt would still be there for Heather because her poor daughter had suffered enough, and she dreaded the idea of seeing her get hurt again.

# Chapter 13

The drive back from the California Institute for Women in Chino was just under an hour and a half. Poppy left the facility around noon and expected to be back to her Desert Flowers garage office before two in the afternoon to rejoin her colleagues in the search for Lara Harper. She was just turning off the 10 Freeway onto Highway 111, which would bring her north of downtown Palm Springs, when her phone, which was in a holder attached to the dashboard, lit up with a 760 area code number she didn't recognize. Poppy pressed a call answer button on her steering wheel and had to roll up the driver's-side window so the whipping desert winds didn't drown out the sound of the caller's voice.

"Hello, this is Poppy."

"Is this really Poppy? Poppy Harmon?"

It was a man.

His voice sounded vaguely familiar but she couldn't quite place it.

"Yes, who is this?"

"Alden Kenny."

The name didn't ring a bell at first.

She remained silent repeating it over a few times in her head.

*Alden Kenny.*

*Who is Alden Kenny?*

The voice on the other end of the call finally answered the question for her.

"I was a juror with you on the Tony Molina trial."

Of course. The young, arrogant holdout who was solely responsible for the unfortunate mistrial. She wanted to wring the little bugger's neck at the time and had very little interest in ever speaking to him again, especially now with her mind preoccupied with worried thoughts about her daughter.

"How did you get this number?" Poppy asked coldly.

"I was sitting next to you when we were filling out the jury forms and I just happened to glance over and I saw you writing down your phone number."

"That was two weeks ago. How on earth did you remember it?"

"I kind of have a photographic memory."

Poppy wasn't sure if she should believe him, but she had no reason at the moment to doubt him, either, so she decided not to challenge him.

"What do you want, Alden?"

"I really need to see you."

"What for?"

"I don't want to discuss it over the phone. It's better if we talk in person."

"I'm sorry, but I'm very busy, and I'm not about to drop everything just because you say you want to talk to me, and you refuse to tell me what it's about."

There was a long pause and Poppy thought he had hung up. But then he spoke and there was a sudden urgency in his voice. "It's about the Tony Molina trial."

"What about it?"

"*Please* . . ." he said, sounding fidgety and nervous.

He was pleading with her. He sounded desperate. And that's when her curiosity was finally piqued. She took a deep breath and made a decision.

"Where are you?"

"At home. I live in Cathedral City."

"I'm about twenty minutes away. What's your address?"

He rattled off a number and street address and she promised she would drive there straight away. After ending the call, she repeated the address to Siri, who mapped out the fastest route. In less than twenty minutes, she was pulling up in front of a modest nondescript house in a run-down area south of the 111. As she got out of her car, she looked around at the neighboring houses and empty lots, the whole area still years away from gentrification. The house next door was abandoned with busted windows and wildly overgrown palm trees out front.

She walked up to the door of Alden's house and rang the bell. She heard nothing inside. She pressed the doorbell one more time. Again, no sound. She assumed it was broken and so she rapped on the door with her knuckles. Still no answer. She waited a few moments and then banged on the door with her fist.

Poppy was starting to get annoyed. Alden Kenny had sounded so desperate to see her and now he wasn't even answering the door. She did an about-face and started marching back to her car when suddenly she stopped. Perhaps he was in the backyard and hadn't heard her knocking. She turned around and saw a dilapidated metal gate that led around the house to the back. She debated with herself but decided to at least take a peek since she had driven all the way out to Cathedral City.

Poppy walked back, unlatched the gate, and headed to the backyard, which was much larger than she had anticipated. There were several palm trees, an outdoor bar, and some patio furniture with colors faded from the intense desert sunlight. There was even an impressive large kidney-shaped swimming pool, given the small-scale size of the house.

And then, suddenly her eyes fell upon something floating in the pool.

It was a body.

Poppy screamed.

She could tell it was a man.

He was floating facedown, but from what she could remember about his height and frame and blond hair when they had served on the same jury, she was certain it was Alden Kenny.

# Chapter 14

"I wish I could say I'm surprised to see you here, but nothing about you surprises me anymore, Ms. Harmon," Detective Lamar Jordan said wearily as he arrived on the scene. He was a tall, handsome African American man, very self-assured and charismatic. Poppy had crossed paths with him last year while investigating another case. She had heard recently that he had joined the Riverside County Central Homicide Unit and was now serving as a primary detective.

"It's nice to see you again, Detective Jordan," Poppy said, mustering as much sincerity as was possible given their rather strained, contentious relationship in the past. Detective Jordan had not taken Poppy seriously as a detective when they had first met, and so Poppy had worked very hard to blow up his first impression of her, which she had done rather successfully.

Detective Jordan gave Poppy a curt nod before brushing past her and walking to the edge of the swimming pool where Alden Kenny's body had yet to be pulled out of the water by the forensics team, which was milling about, taking careful stock of the possible crime scene. Kenny was shirtless but still wearing pants, so the idea of him drowning while taking a swim was ruled out almost immediately. Jordan crouched down and lowered his sunglasses to the bridge of his nose in order to examine the corpse.

Poppy couldn't resist wandering up behind him so she could observe him as well. After calling 911 and waiting for the police to arrive, she had taken the opportunity to do her own preliminary inspection and had discovered some interesting details she wanted to share with Detective Jordan. But she knew better than to hit him with her thoughts all at once. Police detectives liked to do their own investigating before hearing from the peanut gallery.

After silently studying the floating corpse, Detective Jordan stood back up and turned to Poppy, surprised to find her standing so close to him. She smiled apologetically and took a step back.

"I see you're continuing your little habit of stumbling across dead bodies," he said with a withering look.

"I wouldn't call it a habit. I'd say it's more a case of bad luck," Poppy said.

Detective Jordan folded his arms. "So what were you doing here?"

He stared at Poppy with a stern look, but she was never one to be thrown off her game by an alpha male wannabe. She found it absolutely adorable that Detective Jordan actually believed he could intimidate her.

"Mr. Kenny called me and asked me to come here," she said matter-of-factly.

"Why?"

"He mentioned he wanted to talk to me about the Tony Molina trial, which we served on as jurors together, but he never got the chance to tell me any more than that," Poppy said, glancing over at Kenny's floating corpse in the pool. "Although I will add that when he called me he sounded awfully upset, like something was bothering him, or he was scared about something."

"Any idea what it could have been?"

"No, I'm afraid not," Poppy said, shaking her head.

She crossed back over to the pool and stared down at Kenny. "Did you notice the bruising on his body?"

This question seemed to startle Detective Jordan, who hemmed and hawed a bit before muttering, "Yes, I did."

"Well, do you suppose that's a clear sign of some kind of struggle?"

"Possibly . . ."

"It appears to me that someone, or perhaps more than one person, might have held him under the water until he drowned."

"It's probably best we don't speculate until we have a report from forensics and the coroner about how he died."

"Well, you wouldn't be here if you didn't think there was foul play involved, am I right, Detective?" Poppy asked pointedly.

He gave her a thin smile and didn't bother answering the question because she already knew the answer.

Instead, he walked over to Poppy, hovering over her since he was just about a foot taller than she was, in another attempt to send the message that he was the big, strong detective in charge of this investigation and that she was simply a cooperative witness and not the able-minded sleuth she had proven herself to be during their last encounter.

"So you two became friends while serving on the jury for the Tony Molina case?"

"I would hardly call us friends, Detective. In fact, I was rather annoyed with him by the end of the trial."

"Why is that?"

"He was the lone holdout. Everyone else on the jury wanted to convict, but Alden refused to consider the very strong evidence in front of him and insisted on voting to acquit Mr. Molina, which is why the trial ended with a hung jury."

"That happens a lot, I guess," Detective Jordan said with a shrug.

"Yes, it does. But in this case, I found Alden's actions highly suspicious. After the judge dismissed the jury, I personally witnessed a look exchanged between Alden and the defendant, Mr. Molina."

"What kind of look?"

"It happened very fast, but I got the distinct impression that they somehow knew each other. It appeared to me as if they might be up to something. . . ."

"You think Alden Kenny was a plant?"

"I have no proof of that, but the thought did cross my mind," Poppy said.

Detective Jordan jotted down a few notes on his small pad of paper with a pen and then stuffed it in his pants pocket when he was finished. The forensics team was now pulling Alden Kenny's half-naked body out of the pool after having finished thoroughly photographing the whole scene.

"Thank you, Mrs. Harmon, you've been a big help," Detective Jordan said with a nod.

"Do you have my number in case you have any further questions?" Poppy asked.

"Yes, I still have it in my contacts from the last time we met," he said before turning and heading away from the pool.

Poppy took a step forward and called after him, "Will you please keep in touch about the case so I know what's going on?"

Detective Jordan stopped in his tracks, took a moment, then turned around and looked back at Poppy. "Probably not. This is police business. And you're not a police detective. You're a private detective. There is a big difference. Have a nice day, Mrs. Harmon."

He walked away. Poppy bristled at his rudeness. But he was right. And she honestly didn't expect him to keep in constant contact about his progress. Still, it had been worth a shot. But if she really wanted to be kept in the loop about what she was convinced was the murder of Alden Kenny, she was going to have to investigate the facts herself.

# Chapter 15

Poppy was impressed with Lara Harper's vocal talent as she watched her perform in a YouTube video on Wyatt's desktop computer at the Desert Flowers garage office. Poppy, along with Iris, Violet, and Matt, was huddled around Wyatt, who stared at the pretty singer with a wide-eyed crush.

"She's very good," Poppy remarked.

Iris crinkled her nose. "I could do better. I wish YouTube was around when I was singing torch songs in nightclubs all over Germany back in the day."

"What I would give to see that," Matt cracked.

"I had men falling at my feet," Iris boasted. "I received so many roses I could have opened my own flower shop."

On the computer screen, Lara finished her rousing rendition of Kelly Clarkson's "Miss Independent," with one off note at the end, to thunderous applause from the audience.

"This was from last year when she was a contestant on the new *American Idol*," Wyatt gushed, as he stared at her on the screen with his puppy dog eyes while she was being interviewed by the host Ryan Seacrest and then paraded before the judges. Two of whom were kind, but one critiqued the "pitchy" parts of her performance, especially that unfortunate garbled note at the end.

"I agree with the last judge, the sexy one in the cowboy hat," Iris said, nodding. "Her last high note sounded like a cat whose tail was stepped on."

"It cost her too," Wyatt said sadly. "She didn't make it into the top ten. She was voted out after this episode."

"She certainly has talent," Violet said.

"And she's so beautiful," Wyatt cooed.

"Is there a reason we're watching this besides indulging Wyatt, who is obviously Lara Harper's number one fan?" Poppy asked.

Wyatt spun around in his chair and sighed, annoyed. "Um, yes! It's not as if I just hang out here to waste time. I have my life. I thought you might be interested in what's at the end of the video, if you would give me just a few more seconds of your precious time?"

Poppy knew she had to do a little cleanup. "Of course, Wyatt. I know we are very lucky to have you here working for us. I am sincerely sorry."

Wyatt seemed to accept her apology. He whipped back around to face the computer just as a shot of Lara running backstage to greet her vocal coach appeared on screen. They hugged and the coach kissed her on top of her forehead. "I'm so proud of you, baby."

Lara pouted. "Do you think my chances of making the top ten are shot since I missed that last note?"

The coach shook his head vigorously. "Of course not! The audience loves you! Trust me, you'll make it. I'm always right!"

"Until he wasn't," Iris commented.

The video ended and Wyatt clicked out of YouTube and brought up a file on screen. "I did some research on this guy. His name is Stitch McKenzie. He was a singer on Broadway years ago, but now he's a vocal coach in LA. Lara's been with him for a couple of years and, according to his Web site, still is. He has a whole page on her because she's the most famous of his students."

Poppy leaned forward to read the file. "So he might have an idea where she is and how we can find her."

"I tried calling the number on his Web site, but I got his voicemail. I left a message but he hasn't returned my call, which I find very rude," Violet said, grimacing.

"Perhaps this calls for a road trip to LA," Poppy said.

"Oh, can we have lunch at the Ivy?" Violet asked, clasping her hands together. "I've always wanted to dine there among the movie stars."

"If we have time," Poppy promised. "I'll drive."

"Do we all have to go?" Matt asked.

His question surprised Poppy. "No, of course not, Matt. You don't have to join us if you don't want to."

"It's just that I drove there a few days ago for an audition and I'm not exactly looking forward to another four hours there and back in the car, and that's if you don't hit traffic," Matt said. "I thought I'd take the tram up the mountain and do a little hiking today."

Iris put her hands on her hips, aghast. "If you want

everybody to think that the name Flowers on the door is you, and that you're actually the one running things around here, you should be more committed—"

Poppy interrupted her. "Iris, the three of us can handle questioning the vocal coach. Let Matt take a break."

"Thank you, Poppy," he said quietly before heading out the door.

Poppy watched him go, concerned. There was something off about Matt. He seemed unusually preoccupied. She turned to Iris and Violet. "I'll be right back."

Poppy followed Matt outside, where she caught him just as he was climbing into his car, which was parked in front of Iris's house. "Matt, wait. . . ."

He stopped and got back out of the car as Poppy approached. "Yes?"

"Is everything all right with you? You're usually so upbeat and positive and, well, I don't know, today you seem strangely distant."

He placed a reassuring hand on her arm. "Nothing to worry about. I just have a lot on my mind lately."

This worried Poppy. Matt never appeared to have much on his mind at all. Most of the time he was enthusiastic and carefree. "Do you mind if I ask what?"

He hesitated, but then he smiled and shrugged. "Knowing you, you'll probably figure it out anyway eventually. I've been going up the mountain and hiking the trails a lot more lately because it clears my head and allows me to think about things."

Poppy suddenly knew. "Heather?"

Matt nodded. "See, I knew you'd figure it out. To be honest, Poppy, I'm a little scared."

"About what?"

"Whether she's changed. Don't get me wrong. I've

been to visit her, once a month at least, and I'm totally committed to continuing our relationship once she's paroled, and it's not like I've met someone else or even want to meet someone else, that's not the issue—"

"Matt, as her mother, I can tell you, she *has* changed. Anyone who spends time in prison is never going to be the same."

"We hadn't been together all that long before she . . . left . . . and I worry about how it's going to work once she gets out."

"No one will blame you if you decide . . ."

"She's been through so much, Poppy," Matt whispered.

Poppy hugged him, patting him gently on the back. "You have to be true to your own feelings, Matt, and if you no longer love her, then you have to end it. The worst thing you could do would be to drag it out and give her false hope."

Matt squeezed her tighter, almost as if he didn't want to let go, but finally Poppy pulled away and looked into his eyes, which showed just how tortured he was by having to make this decision.

"I appreciate how kind you've been to me, Poppy. I really do. . . . I don't have a particularly close relationship with my own mother and . . ." Matt's voice trailed off.

"That's enough of that," Poppy scolded. "I don't like being reminded I'm old enough to be your *mother*! Now go take a hike!"

Matt laughed at her double meaning, feeling better. He jumped back into his car and sped away.

Poppy's lip quivered as she watched the car round the corner and disappear. She wasn't sure she would be able to hold it together for the long drive to LA with Iris and

Violet. Because inside, her heart was breaking for Heather. She knew she had to advise Matt to follow his feelings, but it had been tough. Heather was her daughter and she didn't want to see her hurt, especially after what she was already going through. Poppy's instinct was to protect her baby girl at all costs, but she knew that was an impossible mission. And there was nothing worse for a mother than to know there was only so much she could do.

# Chapter 16

Stitch McKenzie opened the door to his multilevel Beachwood Canyon home, which was nestled into a ravine just southeast of the world-famous Hollywood sign in Los Angeles. He greeted Poppy, Iris, and Violet with a warm, friendly smile. He was tall with a dancer's body and had to be upward of sixty years old although he looked at least ten years younger. He had kept himself in remarkable shape and showed off his sculpted physique by wearing a skintight purple T-shirt and skinny jeans. Poppy had worried that he might be difficult to meet after Violet's failed attempts to contact him by phone, but once Poppy wrote him an e-mail and identified herself as Poppy Harmon, the *same* Poppy Harmon who had costarred with Rod Harper on *Jack Colt, PI,* the former Broadway hoofer and current vocal coach could not have been friendlier or more anxious to meet one of his favorite 1980s TV actresses.

"Poppy Harmon, as I live and breathe," Stitch squealed as he enveloped her in a hug. "And still such a classic beauty! My God, girl, what's your secret?"

"You're too kind," Poppy demurred.

Iris cracked, "A face full of Vaseline every night before bed certainly helps."

As excited as Stitch was to meet Poppy, he nearly fainted when he turned to introduce himself to Iris. "No! It can't be! Is that really *you*?"

"Do you *know* Iris?" Violet asked, probably feeling like she was an inconsequential third person in the foyer.

"*Know* her? I stalked Iris Becker all over Europe when she was playing the clubs back in the day!" Stitch cooed, on the verge of bowing in front of royalty.

"See, I told you I was popular as a singer! I did not need a network television show to be famous!" Iris boasted proudly.

"I was in a touring company of *Cats* and while we were doing the show in Munich, much of the cast ended up in a club late one night. It was there when I first heard this beautiful siren sing! I was totally hooked! After the tour ended, I spent another couple of months just bumming around Europe and I caught Iris's act again in Vienna and then Paris. We even went out drinking together one night after one of her shows!"

Iris studied his face carefully. "I do not remember you."

"Why would you? I was just one of a whole entourage of people who worshipped you! I am so fanboying out right now."

"If anyone cares, I'm Violet Hogan, another person in the room. Apparently forty years as a high school principal isn't as glamorous as being a TV star or European torch singer."

Stitch nodded, thoroughly uninterested, but managed a quick "Hello" in Violet's direction before returning his attention to Iris. "I promise I won't ask you to sing '99 Red Balloons.' I remember you opened the show with that song."

Iris thoroughly enjoyed basking in the glory of her yesteryears, and obviously wanted to hear more, but Poppy felt it was time to finally get to the point. "When I sent you that initial e-mail, Stitch, I mentioned I wanted to talk to you about Lara Harper."

The mention of Lara's name quickly soured Stitch's mood and he grumbled, "Yes. If you had not been the star of *Jack Colt* with those perfect legs, I would have absolutely refused. I'd rather forget all about Lara Harper."

"So your professional relationship ended badly?" Poppy asked.

"You could say that. Is it true the studio insured your legs for a million dollars back in nineteen eighty-six? I think I read that in *People* magazine."

"That's not true," Poppy said. "I believe some Fox executive started that rumor as a publicity stunt. I just had a good old Screen Actors Guild health insurance policy."

Stitch turned back to Iris. "Did you really date Wolfgang Petersen?"

"Who?" Violet asked.

"He was a German film director! He did that movie about the U-boat!" Stitch bellowed.

"*Das Boot*," Iris added before shaking her head. "I did

not date him. But I did barhop with Werner Fassbinder in the late nineteen seventies, but there was nothing romantic between us because he was gay and smelled."

"Wow, *so* much history," Stitch cooed. "Where are my manners? Can I get you ladies something to drink? If I remember correctly, Iris loves a Seven and Seven."

"It is ten-thirty in the morning, too early for a cocktail. Maybe if we are still here at noon," Iris said.

"I will take a cup of coffee, if you have some," Violet said.

Stitch looked at Violet, having completely forgotten she was even there. "Oh, sure. What do you take in your coffee, Daisy?"

"It's Violet," she huffed. "But I suppose I should at least be grateful you remembered my name was a flower. Cream and sugar, please."

"Nothing for me, thank you," Poppy sighed, checking her watch, frustrated she was having trouble keeping Stitch on topic. But once he returned with Violet's coffee and led the three women to his living room, which was accented with framed Playbills of all the shows he had appeared in back in New York, and after Iris had graciously sung the first refrain from "99 Red Balloons," Stitch finally managed to focus on the subject at hand.

"Lara fired me right after she got booted off *Idol*, as if that was in any way *my* fault!" Stitch sniffed.

"So she blamed you for getting eliminated?" Violet asked.

Stitch looked at Violet strangely, like he had forgotten again about her presence. "I'm sorry, did you say something, Daisy?"

Poppy leaned forward and helpfully asked, "What reason did she give you for parting ways?"

Stitch turned back to Poppy, once more ignoring Violet.

"She didn't give me any reason. She just sent me a very cold text that said, '*We're done.*' Not even 'Have a nice life.' Just '*We're done.*' Can you believe that? What a bitchy little ingrate! After all the hard work I put into her lousy career!"

"She does not sound like a very nice person," Iris remarked.

"The funny thing was, when we first met she was a lovely girl. I thought of her as my own daughter. We were very close. She was a hard worker and seemed very focused on making it as a performer. But after a couple of years, she slowly started to change."

"How so?" Poppy asked.

Stitch shrugged and leaned back, clasping his hands around his raised right knee. "I started to see a more ruthless side of her. She started trashing singers who she considered rivals on social media. Once she even talked a few of her friends into attending a club gig of a fellow *Idol* contestant. A girl named Tiffany. The poor dear was just doing her thing and Lara and her gang started heckling her to throw her off her game. Lara was also constantly bad-mouthing her own father. She called him 'a has-been' and 'out of touch' whenever he tried to counsel her. I was so angry that she dumped me as her vocal coach before I had the chance to even meet him. I harbored such a huge crush on him back when he played *Jack Colt*. Has he aged as beautifully as you, Poppy?"

"He's a very attractive man," Poppy answered. "Do you have any idea where we could find Lara? Rod's very worried about her."

Stitch excitedly wrapped his legs around each other

into the lotus position and whispered, "Did you two ever . . . you know . . . ?"

"No, never," Poppy said emphatically.

Violet started coughing. Poppy assumed she had swallowed the wrong way after hearing such a big and unambiguous lie coming out of Poppy's mouth.

"Are you all right, Daisy?" Stitch asked blankly.

"Yes," Violet managed to get out as her coughing fit subsided and she was able to finally clear her throat. "Daisy's just fine."

"I have no idea where Lara is nor do I care," Stitch said. "Last I heard she had a new guy in her life after she got rid of that loopy yoga instructor. He actually taught me how to sit like this. I liked him, but he wasn't exciting enough for her, I guess."

"So you don't know the name of her new boyfriend?" Poppy asked.

"Nope," Stitch said. "But I will tell you, I feel sorry for him. She's a messy handful and needs attention twenty-four/seven. Believe me, I was her caretaker for two long, painful years and I still haven't recovered from the whole ordeal yet."

From all she had learned so far about Rod's tempestuous daughter, Lara, Poppy was not exactly looking forward to ultimately finding her because the young woman sounded like she could be the star in a reboot of the black-and-white classic evil daughter movie *The Bad Seed*.

# Chapter 17

"I suspect that your initial assessment may be correct, and that Lara simply does not want to be found," Poppy said while sitting in the lush foliage of Rod Harper's backyard in his palatial Benedict Canyon home. After meeting with Stitch McKenzie in the Hollywood Hills, Iris and Violet had dropped Poppy off at Rod's house so she could give him a personal update before continuing on to the Ivy on Robertson Boulevard for Violet's long-awaited lunch among the stars.

"Does this mean Matt is dropping the case?" Rod inquired, a worried look on his face.

"Not at all. As long as you want us to keep searching, the Desert Flowers Detective Agency will be happy to stay in your employ."

"That's good. I know Lara can be challenging and difficult, but I do worry about her and want to know that she is okay. I'm her father, after all."

"Then we will stay on her trail until she turns up."

"Excellent. Now that we have business taken care of, can I convince you to stay in LA and have dinner with me tonight?"

Poppy smiled, slightly uncomfortable. "I'm afraid I can't. I came here with Iris and Violet, and once they're done having lunch at the Ivy, we're going to drive straight back to Palm Springs."

"Traffic will be a mess at this time of day," Rod said emphatically. "I have plenty of room for you all to stay here for the night."

Poppy shook her head. "I appreciate the offer, Rod, but I really have to say no. I'm sure Iris and Violet will want to get home."

"And what about you?"

The question startled Poppy. Mostly because deep down she already knew the answer. She quite liked the idea of having dinner with her former costar. She still found him engaging and charming and remarkably hand-some. But she had also promised when she opened the doors of the Desert Flowers Detective Agency that she would always maintain her professionalism, and socializ-ing with a client was, in her mind, strictly forbidden. She could already feel herself becoming compromised. She was still reeling from the fact that he had professed his love for her at Cicci's in Palm Springs. But she had de-cided to chalk that up to too much wine during dinner.

"Thank you, Rod. Perhaps another time."

"Well, no one can say I didn't try," he said with a wink.

God, he was so handsome.

Even more so with age. The gray in his hair had given him such gravitas and a confident, experienced, distinguished air. When he was in his late thirties doing *Jack Colt*, he certainly had an intoxicating swagger about him. He was tough and rugged with a Burt Reynolds–like macho mustache. He was swimming in masculinity and she sometimes confused the brute force aggression of his character with Rod's actual personality. Now that *Jack Colt* and his seventy-two episodes and three two-hour TV movies were relegated to Amazon Prime, she had a much clearer picture of the real man behind the character, and he was far more pleasing than she had remembered.

"Can I get you another cup of coffee?" Rod asked, reaching for her mug, which she had just set down on the glass coffee table between them.

"No, I'd better get going," Poppy said, standing up. "I'm sure Iris and Violet must be having dessert by now. They've been there almost two hours and will probably be ready to leave soon."

"I read about the drowning of that juror you served with on the Tony Molina trial," Rod said, as if searching for some subject that would keep her from fleeing his home.

"The police suspect the autopsy will reveal he was the victim of foul play," Poppy said gravely. "I know I do."

"Is it true *you* were the one who found him?"

Poppy sighed. "Yes, unfortunately. It was just like back when I played danger prone Daphne on *Jack Colt* and stumbled across corpses in at least five episodes over the course of three seasons.

Rod nodded and chuckled as he remembered. "The writers seemed to have run out of ideas awfully fast."

Poppy quickly filled him in on the mysterious phone

call she had received from Alden Kenny, his insistence on her coming over to his house, and how she had found him floating dead in his swimming pool barely twenty minutes later.

"Do you have any idea who might have had a motive to murder him?" Rod asked.

"No, but I'm quite certain that whatever the reason he was killed, it had something to do with Tony Molina. I believe that they knew each other before the trial, and that Kenny might have been a jury plant to ensure Molina was not convicted of that assault on Chef Carmine Cicci."

Rod sat back in his chair. "Wow. That makes perfect sense."

"Of course I have no proof, and it's not like anyone has hired me to look into it, so it's really none of my business. . . ."

"You found the body. Naturally you're curious," Rod said. "It's a shame you can't stay another day."

"Why is that?"

"Tofu is in town."

Poppy perked up. "She *is*?"

"Yes, her favorite artist, this guy who lives in Venice and paints a lot of Southern California landscapes that rich people wildly overpay for, is having an art show tomorrow at a gallery in Beverly Hills."

"And you're sure she is going to be there?"

"She's never missed one. I know because I have three of his works hanging in my upstairs hallway."

Poppy practically drooled at the prospect of talking with Tony Molina's wife. As much as that little voice inside was screaming at her not to worm her way into an official police investigation that she had nothing to do with, she just couldn't help herself.

"Excuse me," she said, then walked down the brick steps of the patio toward the expansive pool and waterfall for a bit of privacy. She scooped her phone from her bag and called Violet.

When Violet answered, she was breathless and delighted. "Poppy, I am so glad you called! Guess who is at the very next table!" Poppy opened her mouth to hazard a guess but didn't have the chance before Violet screamed, "Cate Blanchett!"

"How nice. Listen, I've decided—"

"She was so nice and allowed us to take a selfie with her! It's so lovely here. You should smell the fresh flowers everywhere! Iris was not impressed with her lobster ravioli, but she's normally so hard to please. My lime chicken breast was delicious, and this pecan square with praline gelato and hot fudge sauce I'm having for dessert is absolutely to *die* for!"

"Violet . . ."

She could hear Violet not paying attention and talking to someone. "I hate to interrupt your lunch again, but I have my dear friend Poppy on the phone, and she would be so appreciative if you said hello. . . ."

Poppy rolled her eyes and shouted, "Violet, no! I really don't need to speak with Cate Blanchett!"

"Hello, Poppy, this is Cate Blanchett."

"Ms. Blanchett, I'm a big fan of your work, and it is so nice of you to take the time to say hello," Poppy said, dying of embarrassment.

"Thank you," Cate Blanchett said. "What was your favorite film I did?"

Poppy went blank.

She couldn't think of one.

Finally, Violet blurted out in the background, "I loved *The Talented Mr. Ripley*! Oh, and of course the two movies where you played Queen Elizabeth!"

After some perfunctory small talk, Cate Blanchett finally handed the phone back to Violet, who squealed, "How exciting was *that*?"

"Violet, when you're done at the Ivy, I want you and Iris to drive home. I'm going to stay in LA one more day. I have some business to attend to tomorrow."

She heard Violet relating what she had just said to Iris, who promptly snatched the phone away from her and bellowed, "What *business* are you talking about?"

Poppy knew there was no hiding the truth from her two best friends, so she just came out with it and told them about her going with Rod to the art show so she could meet Tony Molina's wife, Tofu.

"Why are you focused on a murder case that the police are investigating that really has nothing to do with you instead of working on the case we're getting *paid* to investigate?" Iris demanded to know.

"I will be with our client, so technically I'm working on both at the same time. It's called multitasking."

"That's a load of crap and you know it, Poppy," Iris admonished. "How are you going to get back to the desert?"

"I'll rent a car."

Rod, who had stepped outside and overheard her, smiled. "There is no need. I was planning on heading out to my house in Palm Springs after the show tomorrow. I can drive you."

Poppy decided against sharing that part with Iris.

"Have you booked a hotel for tonight?" Iris asked pointedly.

"No, I haven't had a chance to book a hotel because I just now decided to stay," Poppy said quietly.

"There is no need. You can stay here," Rod eagerly offered.

"Did I just hear him say you can stay at *his* place?" Iris asked pointedly.

Poppy tried reassuring Iris. "Yes, but of course I know that's completely inappropriate and I will respectfully decline his generous offer."

"I have six bedrooms. Five of them are unoccupied. A hotel is a waste of money," Rod said, getting more excited by the minute about this impromptu slumber party.

Poppy threw him a stern look. She overheard Iris filling Violet in on her plans, and Violet gasped, "She's spending the night with our client?"

"It appears so, if you can believe it!" Iris shouted.

"I can hear you both right now. I am *not* spending the night with Rod! Now I have to go! I will see you back at the office late tomorrow afternoon."

She hung up and dropped her phone back in her bag.

Rod joined her by the pool. "I'm serious. You can stay here. And despite the fact I've been very clear about my feelings, I promise to be the perfect gentleman. And just so you know, the doors in all my guest rooms lock from the inside as an extra security measure."

Her gut told her that the last thing she should do was spend the night at Rod Harper's house. But she also didn't want to spend a lot of money on a hotel room. So she reluctantly accepted. She indulged in only one glass of wine at dinner so she could keep a clear head, and when they returned from the restaurant, she retired immediately to her room, making sure to lock it from the inside. Rod was true to his word and never showed up knocking on the door in the middle of the night.

The following morning, by the time she showered and dressed for the art show, Rod had a full breakfast waiting for her in the kitchen.

"You look absolutely ravishing," Rod said as she sat down at the table and he served her a vegetable omelette and a glass of orange juice.

"I'm wearing the same outfit as I did yesterday. I didn't expect I would need a change of clothes."

"I can take you shopping before the show if you like," Rod offered.

"No, I'll stay in this. And then after the show, we head straight to the desert."

"Whatever makes you happy," Rod said.

He had been such a player back in the day.

And she couldn't quite figure out if he still was.

Or, if by some chance, Rod Harper was actually sincere and *was* truly in love with her, as he had so passionately professed. The thought scared her. Because there was a time decades ago when she would have welcomed this unbridled attention from him. But so much time had passed. So many years were now in the rearview mirror. And after her husband had died so unexpectedly with so many upsetting secrets about him that came bubbling to the surface after he was gone, Poppy just wasn't sure if she could ever trust another man again.

Especially this man.

# Chapter 18

When Tofu spotted Poppy and Rod arrive at the Crystal Wick Gallery on Robertson Boulevard, named after its wealthy benefactor, a big movie studio executive, she was like a magnet drawn to Rod. Tofu made a beeline right for him, slipping her arm through his and ignoring the fact that he had just walked in the door with another woman.

"Shame on you, Rod. You didn't tell me you were coming today," Tofu cooed.

Poppy marveled at just how stunning Tofu still was. She hadn't had a hit song in decades and had kept a relatively low public profile since marrying Tony Molina ten years ago. Poppy studied her face, which appeared to have had very little work done on it. Many women in show business sadly succumbed to the pressure of a few nicks and tucks to keep the face tight and tidy, but Tofu was such a natural beauty with perfect dark skin and hardly a trace of wrinkles. Her youthful glow was quite astonishing.

"I only heard about Devon's show at the last minute. I've been entertaining a friend who is in town so I thought I would bring her along," Rod said, gesturing toward Poppy. "This is Poppy Harmon. She is from Palm Springs as well."

Tofu basically ignored her and kept her eyes trained on Rod. "There is an ocean painting over there I've already paid too much for. Devon has outdone himself this time. His entire collection is selling fast."

"What's Devon's last name?" Poppy asked.

"It's just Devon. He doesn't really have a last name," Tofu said, annoyed that she had to explain that to this interloper who was on the arm of the man she was currently lusting after.

"I saw Tony the last time I was in the desert," Rod said.

Tofu frowned. "He told me. I apologize if he was rude to you."

"It's totally fine. I understand," Rod said, chuckling. "I didn't expect to run into him at Cicci's, of all places."

"Tony wasn't about to let a little trial get in the way of him enjoying his namesake steak dinner," Tofu said, shaking her head. "He can be very determined and pig-headed and Chef Carmine wouldn't dare ban him from the restaurant. Tony's a living legend. It would destroy his business. By the way, Tony mentioned you were there on a date."

"I was there with Poppy," Rod said, gesturing toward Poppy again.

"And who are you again?" Tofu asked, not the least bit interested.

"An old friend of Rod's," Poppy said, careful to avoid

characterizing their relationship as anything other than just friends.

"You look awfully familiar," Tofu noted, staring at her.

"Poppy was my costar back in the nineteen eighties when I did *Jack Colt*. She played my faithful secretary, Daphne," Rod said, smiling.

"Maybe that's it," Tofu said, crinkling her nose and cocking her head. "You just look very different now."

"Well, it was over thirty years ago," Poppy said.

"Yes, I suppose . . . the ravages of time and all that," Tofu said with a knowing smile.

Poppy resisted the urge to kick her in her shins because she didn't want to scare her away before they could discuss the trial some more.

Rod tightened his grip on Poppy's hand and kept his eyes fixed on Tofu. "In a remarkable coincidence, Poppy here was on the jury in Tony's trial."

"*Really?* I heard the final vote was eleven to one guilty," Tofu said.

"Yes, Tony got lucky," Rod remarked.

"I would have been there to show my support for Tony, but, unfortunately, I had to stay away because frankly the stress of the trial, the constant calls from reporters, it all led to me having an anxiety attack. I had to check into the Rancho Valencia Spa to recuperate until the whole nasty business was finally over," Tofu said.

"I can certainly understand how you must have suffered," Rod said, intentionally placating her.

"Thank you, Rod, but there is nothing like a desert-fig facial to make your problems go away. I came back feeling refreshed, like a new woman, and I was elated that my husband was still a free man."

"All's well that ends well," Rod said, smiling.

Tofu spun around to face Poppy. "Tell me, Pansy . . ."

"Poppy," she said through gritted teeth. Now she knew how Violet must have felt at Stitch McKenzie's house.

Tofu folded her arms and glared at Poppy. "Were you on the side of guilty, or were you that one heroic juror who saw through all the noise and false accusations and voted for what was *right*?"

"I voted guilty," Poppy said with a fake smile without a moment's hesitation. "The one holdout unfortunately is no longer with us. He drowned in his swimming pool."

"I read about that. There was an article in the *Desert Sun*. How horrible. I knew he was a juror on the trial, but I had no idea he was the only one who believed my husband's side of the story. That makes it even more tragic."

"Yes, and there is a good chance his death will be ruled a homicide," Poppy added.

Tofu gasped. "Oh my! That's awful! Who on earth would want to harm a simple small-town boy from Abilene?"

Poppy shot a suspicious glance at Rod, who seemed to be oblivious to Tofu's last remark. "Abilene?"

"Yes. Abilene, Texas. I read in the *Sun* that he was from there originally, but had moved out to the Coachella Valley for some kind of a job," Tofu said.

Poppy knew for a fact that this was not true. She had pored over that same newspaper article online, so she knew that the reporter had only mentioned that Alden Kenny was from Texas. He had *never* mentioned the town of Abilene. How did Tofu know that specific detail? Before she had the chance to ask, they were accosted by a rail-thin man dressed all in black with spiky blond hair and thick dark glasses. This had to be the artist Devon.

"I see we have some prospective art buyers," Devon said with a sly smile. "I hope you see something that strikes your fancy, Mr. Harper."

"You know I'm a big fan of your talent, Devon," Rod said.

"Then help yourself to some wine and cheese and be sure to check out my more expensive pieces toward the back of the gallery," he said.

He wasn't joking.

He practically had dollar signs in his eyes before he floated away as a woman in an expensive designer jacket entered and caught his attention.

Poppy tried to redirect the conversation back to Alden Kenny. "It's funny, I don't remember the newspaper article mentioning—"

Tofu was bored with the conversation and cut her off. "Devon's going to need some hand-holding. Whenever he is around really rich people he gets nervous and tries making jokes, which are usually inappropriate and insulting. I don't want his social ineptitude to affect any potential sales." She sidled up to Rod's right side and with her luscious ruby red lips planted a soft kiss on Rod's cheek. "If you have any free time later, Rod, be sure to call me."

And then she flitted off, having completely forgotten that Poppy was standing next to him.

"She's lovely," Poppy sneered.

"I know she can be rather catty sometimes."

"And petty and jealous and rude . . ."

"You're right on all counts. She used to be nicer back when we dated . . . before she met Tony. . . ."

"She's also hiding something."

Rod raised an eyebrow. "Seriously?"

"Yes, she knows more about Alden Kenny, the dead juror, than she's letting on."

"Can you explain it to me in the car? I want to get out of here before I'm pressured into buying a painting by that tragic Andy Warhol wannabe!"

Rod grabbed Poppy by the arm and quickly steered her out the door.

# Chapter 19

When Rod slowly leaned in to kiss Poppy, her instinct was to resist, to pull back, put her hands up to separate them. But this time, she didn't. She kept her arms to her sides, and as his lips grazed hers, lightly at first, tentatively, still not completely sure if she would accept his advance, her whole body shivered. The warm memory of their one night of intimacy together, which happened over thirty years ago, washed over her, and she allowed him to put his arms around her and draw her close, enveloping her. He still wore the same inviting Calvin Klein cologne. He always smelled so good.

How did she let it get to this point? Their conversation on the car ride home from the art show had been innocent enough. Poppy had eagerly filled Rod in on why she thought Tofu had been lying about not knowing the mur-

dered juror Alden Kenny, the obvious detail of him having been born and raised in Abilene. How could she possibly know that information unless she knew more about
him than she was letting on? Poppy had also made a point
of calling her "boss" Matt on his cell phone for an update
in order to maintain the illusion that he was the one in
charge of finding Rod's daughter, Lara, but he didn't pick
up and the call went directly to his voicemail.

When they had arrived at Rod's home, he'd invited her
inside while he packed a bag for Palm Springs, still in-
sisting he would drive her back to the desert and there
was no need for her to book a rental car.

He had served her an iced tea and had her sit outside
by the pool to watch the sunset while he showered and
changed for the two-hour drive. When he had reappeared,
looking very sexy in a pair of khaki shorts, deck shoes,
and a casual orange Michael Kors button-up short-sleeved
shirt that was open enough to show off his manly tufts of
chest hair, Poppy had nearly gasped.

She had stood up, still clutching her glass of iced tea,
and had opened her mouth to comment on how handsome
he looked when he had suddenly seized the opportunity
and tried to kiss her. And now here they were. Smooching
in his backyard and Poppy knew she was officially done
rebuffing him.

He stroked her hair as his mouth closed over hers and
his probing tongue danced with hers until she began to
feel light-headed. As if they were ballroom dancing, he
glided her across the patio, leading her to a lounger by the
pool, and with his hand firmly on her back lowered her
down until she was lying flat and he was on top of her.
She felt safe and desired, and she welcomed him by
slinging an arm around his neck and pressing him down

against her. She ran her fingers through the hair on his chest as he devoured her.

Suddenly they heard a loud knocking coming from the front door inside the house. Rod ignored it and continued kissing her and so Poppy decided she would ignore it, too. That is, until she heard a familiar voice calling out from around the side of the house.

"Mr. Harper, are you here?"

It was Matt.

Matt Flowers.

What on earth was *he* doing here?

Poppy immediately broke free from the lip-lock with Rod, her eyes popping open in a panic. "Rod, quick! Get off me!"

Rod quickly sprang to his feet and Poppy barely had time to roll off the lounger and fix her mess of hair enough to at least appear presentable and hopefully hide what they had been up to when Matt bounded around the corner, stopping short when he spotted the two of them.

"Oh, there you are! I'm so glad I caught you!" he said with a smile.

"Matt, what are you doing here?" Poppy asked, thoroughly confused.

"I have some potentially useful information about Lara that Rod should hear," Matt said, staring at Poppy, who had reached into her bag for a compact in order to make sure her lipstick wasn't smeared. "Iris and Violet told me you were still in LA and I could probably find you here."

"Well, what is it?" Rod asked, annoyed his long-awaited tryst with Poppy had been so rudely interrupted as he casually buttoned up his orange shirt, which had been inadvertently ripped open to his navel by Poppy.

"I saw a blurb on a trade paper Web site when I was researching Lara about a big-time talent agent by the name of Carl Menkin who had recently signed her."

Poppy turned to Rod. "Do you know him?"

"I've heard of him. He's known for grooming young singers, boy bands, kids just starting out," Rod said.

"Get this. I called him and conned my way into a meeting," Matt said excitedly. "I had Wyatt take a video of me singing on his phone and he added shots of an audience cheering, making it look like they were watching me perform at a club. Then he edited in some professionals talking about how impressed they were about this up-and-coming talent, as if they were talking about me, and he bought it! That kid is an absolute genius!"

"I'm impressed," Rod said, nodding.

"He's only in town today. He flies to New York tomorrow night, so he told me I could have ten minutes at five o'clock. I raced here in record time. We need to be there in forty-five minutes so we'd better go. I told him I'd be bringing my mother, who is currently managing my career," Matt said, gesturing to Poppy.

"*Mother?*" Poppy cried.

"It was the first thing that came to mind," Matt said sheepishly.

"That I'm old enough to be your mother?" Poppy huffed.

"Well, I couldn't very well tell him you were my boss," Matt said.

Poppy's heart sank.

She glared at Matt, waiting for him to realize his mistake.

But he wasn't getting it just yet.

Rod stepped forward. "*Boss?* But I thought . . ."

It finally dawned on Matt, and his face turned beet red. "I mean . . ."

Rod turned to Poppy. "What's he talking about?"

She considered spinning another lie, trying to convince him that the slipup was just a private joke between her and Matt, that sometimes he teased her and called her "boss" to make her feel more important, or as a term of endearment since as his secretary she was essentially "in charge" of his schedule. But at this point, after falling into Rod's arms and picking up where they had left off thirty years ago, deception just didn't seem to be an option anymore.

Matt tried to cover and quickly interjected, "What I meant was—"

Poppy stopped him. "No, Matt. Rod deserves to know the truth."

Rod looked from Poppy to Matt, his face tense. "What truth?"

"The 'Flowers' in Desert Flowers Detective Agency does not stand for Matt Flowers. Matt's real name is Matt Cameron. The 'Flowers' is really the three of us . . . Iris, Violet, and . . ."

"Poppy," Rod said quietly. "Three kinds of flowers."

"Yes," Poppy said.

"I don't understand what's going on," Rod said.

Matt decided to keep his mouth shut and let Poppy do the talking. He had screwed things up enough as it was.

"When I started the business, no one wanted to hire one, let alone three, women in their sixties. That wasn't what most people pictured or wanted when they hired a private detective. So Matt, who is an actor . . ."

"You're not actually a detective?" Rod asked as he looked at Matt, who shifted uncomfortably.

"Not in the traditional sense," Matt said defensively.

"But I'm learning on the job and I'm getting better every day."

Rod took all this in, not sure how to react.

"I'm sorry, Rod. We should have been up front from the beginning," Poppy said.

"Yes, you *should* have," Rod said sharply.

He was angry.

And it made Poppy feel terrible.

He had trusted them, trusted her, and she had betrayed that trust.

"What ticks me off the most, Poppy, is that after all these years, considering our history, you would consider me some kind of misogynist."

"You're right. We hadn't seen each other in a long time and I was surprised when you wanted to hire us to find Lara. I was worried you wouldn't take me seriously. . . ."

"You were wrong. I've come a long way since the nineteen eighties. I've raised a daughter. Maybe I haven't come around as quickly as a lot of more enlightened men, but I'm getting there, and I would have applauded you doing what you've done."

Poppy nodded, eyes downcast. "I wouldn't blame you if you found someone else to work on this case. . . ."

"And let you think you were right? Forget it," Rod scoffed. "I want you to find my daughter. *You*, Poppy, I've hired *you*. So don't disappoint me."

"Yes, Rod," she said softly before turning to Matt. "Go wait in the car. I'll be right there."

Matt, who was relieved to have been let off the hook for messing up, scrambled back around the house, leaving Poppy and Rod alone.

Rod walked toward Poppy.

She wasn't sure if she was in for more scolding or not but she managed to hold her ground as he approached. He took her by the shoulders. "Actually, I think it's incredibly hot that you're no longer the secretary and now you're the real-life Jack Colt."

She smiled. "Thank you, Rod. And thank you for believing I can do this."

He leaned in to resume kissing her.

She raised a finger to his lips to stop him. "And now that you know the truth, thank you for allowing our relationship to go back to being professional, at least until I get the job done."

She could not have any more moments of weakness.

Rod looked at her and instinctively knew that she was resolved in her determination and that that was the best he was going to get for now.

"Go find her, Poppy," he said impatiently.

Poppy nodded and then hurried around the side of the house to catch up with Matt.

# Chapter 20

Poppy couldn't believe her ears.

Matt was an impressive crooner with a powerful charismatic voice, both charming and seductive at the same time as he belted out Frank Sinatra's "New York, New York," a karaoke staple that Matt had chosen on the car ride over as his audition song for Carl Menkin.

Poppy could do nothing but sit back and enjoy the show, occasionally glancing over at Carl, who sat behind his desk, his meaty hands clasped together, his round, pudgy face betraying very little reaction to Matt's singing. She thought she had seen the corners of his mouth curl up into a smile at one point, but when he caught her watching him, he quickly frowned again, not willing to show his cards just yet.

Matt hit his final note, holding it longer than Poppy thought possible. And then he was done. He bowed his head and gave them both a bashful smile. Poppy couldn't contain herself. She leapt to her feet and started to wildly clap her hands. Matt waved her off. He was trying to play the dutiful son, embarrassed by his mother's over-the-top response to her "son's" performance, but she could tell he was reveling in the accolades.

After hugging Matt and kissing him lovingly on the cheek, Poppy whirled around to Carl Menkin, a hulk of a man bursting out of a pink dress shirt two sizes too small for him, who leaned forward, his hands still folded on top of his desk.

"Well, what did you think?" Poppy asked.

The silence was interminable.

Carl seemed to enjoy drawing out the suspense.

Finally, he cracked the slightest smile and nodded. "The kid's good."

"*Seriously?*" Matt gasped.

"There's something there. Kind of a Justin Timberlake vibe. Of course, you're a lot older than Justin was when he first got started. You have a lot of catching up to do."

"So you'll represent him?" Poppy asked.

"I'll think about it," Carl said, not quite ready to commit.

"But you think he has talent," Poppy said curtly, not satisfied with him dragging his feet.

"Oh, for sure. But I have to consider the whole package. He's good looking and has a certain sex appeal. The girls will love him, and some of the boys, too. I can see him onstage, strutting around, but I'm not sure I can picture his face on the cover of *Rolling Stone*. I mean, is he *too* much of a pretty boy?"

"I can be tough. I'll grunge it up, get some tattoos," Matt said.

"And like I said, you're old. What are you, twenty-four, twenty-five . . . ?"

"Twenty-four," Matt lied.

He was actually twenty-eight.

Or maybe he had just had a birthday and was twenty-nine.

Either way, Poppy knew he was not going to cop to his real age.

"I like to take on kids who haven't been fully formed yet, who I can mold and shape. At twenty-four, you pretty much get what you get," Carl said.

"My son is a fast learner, and open to whatever suggestions you may have to make him a famous singer. We've both been waiting for this opportunity his whole life. Please, Mr. Menkin, give him a chance. I know he will not disappoint you," Poppy pleaded, adopting her stage-mother role wholeheartedly. She had seen *Gypsy*, all versions in fact, and knew just how to play it.

Carl Menkin was still wavering.

"I'm not too old," Matt argued. "In fact, I know you just started representing a friend of mine who is already twenty-two years old."

Carl's ears perked up. "Who is that?"

"Lara Harper," Matt said, locking eyes with Carl.

Carl raised an eyebrow. "You know Lara?"

"Yes. We ran into each other at a few parties around town and got acquainted. I heard you recently signed her. That's why I zeroed in on you to try to get this audition," Matt said.

"I see," Carl said. "But she came to me with a modicum of fame already. She was on *American Idol*."

"I promise you, if you represent me, I will get my face on *Idol*, *The Voice*, whatever gets me a social media following I can build on. I'm ready to do this. I just need someone besides my mother to believe in me."

"Like I said, I'll think about it," Carl said. "I appreciate you coming in, Matt. You too, Mrs. Cameron."

Matt smiled and shook Carl Menkin's hand, slightly deflated.

Poppy could see he was no longer playing a part.

He genuinely wanted Carl to sign him.

She had not expected this when they had first showed up at his office in a complex on Sunset Boulevard.

Matt headed for the door but stopped. He turned around. "Lara gave me her number and told me to get in touch with her but I lost it. Can you—?"

Carl quickly cut him off. "I wish I could help you, but I have a strict rule never to give out contact information for any of my clients. If you want to speak to her, you have to go through me."

"A mutual friend of ours is having a party in Malibu this weekend and he was hoping to invite her. I told him I was coming here and so he asked me to—"

Carl cut him off again. "Tell your friend that Lara sends her regrets. She is not going to be in town this weekend. She is at an undisclosed location recording her first album."

Poppy knew from the credit card receipts that Lara Harper had to still be somewhere in the Coachella Valley.

How many recording studios could there be in the desert?

She felt like they were slowly getting closer to finding her.

"Thank you so much, Mr. Menkin. I look forward to hearing from you," Matt said.

"You probably will," Carl said with a smug smile.

As Poppy turned to follow Matt out of Menkin's office, she noticed a photo of Tony Molina hanging on the wall.

"I love Tony Molina," Poppy said casually. "What a voice."

"He happens to be a longtime client of mine," Carl boasted. "It's because of him alone that I own my ranch in Santa Barbara."

"Well, you obviously know talent," Poppy said with a sly smile. "So I'm sure we will be hearing from you because the last thing you would want to do is jeopardize your winning streak by letting someone else sign my boy, Matt."

"Spoken like a true stage mother. Good-bye, Mrs. Cameron," Carl said as she left the office.

# Chapter 21

When they got into the elevator and rode down to the parking garage of the office complex, Matt could no longer contain himself. He turned to Poppy excitedly. "Do you honestly think he's going to sign me?"

Poppy's eyes widened. "What?"

"I know, I know. This was supposed to be an undercover assignment, just a means to get some kind of lead to Lara's whereabouts, but you heard him—he really liked my singing. I honestly think he might take me on and guide my career. . . ."

Poppy could not blame Matt for being so hyperfocused on this incredible opportunity. After all, he had already been an aspiring actor before their paths first crossed and they had entered into this private eye con job together, along with Iris and Violet. She suddenly worried that she, too, had been hyperfocused on getting her business off the ground, and she had needed him to help her do that, and so she had willfully ignored what he really wanted and what was best for him.

As they got into Matt's Prius and drove out of the parking garage underneath the office building, heading east on Sunset back toward Palm Springs, Poppy listened as Matt prattled on about how he had always been told he had a good singing voice, but he had never really had the confidence to pursue any kind of music career. Acting was another matter altogether. He had shined in one high school production after another and studied acting in college. He had always felt at home on the stage or in front of a camera, but the idea of becoming a professional singer, well, that had never really occurred to him before today.

Poppy remained silent, listening to him. When he finally ran out of things to say, almost forty minutes after they had been on the 10 Freeway heading east, she finally spoke. "Matt, I think you should consider moving back to LA."

This took him by surprise. "What do you mean?"

"You are a wonderful actor. I knew it from the moment I saw you in that play in Palm Springs last year, the murder mystery, when I came up with the idea of you becoming Matt Flowers. And you've played the part superbly. Look at Rod. He's been a successful actor since the nineteen seventies and he totally bought you in the role. He truly believed you were a real-life private investigator. You're a natural. You have huge potential."

He was genuinely touched. "Thank you, Poppy."

"And now we find out you're multitalented. You can sing, too, good enough for someone like Carl Menkin to sit up and take notice. You need to be in Los Angeles."

There was a long pause as Matt considered this. He kept his hands gripped on the wheel of his Prius and stared at the busy highway that lay ahead of them. He didn't quickly reassure her that he wanted to continue playing the part of a private eye, a role he had relished playing for over a year now. Finally, he glanced over at Poppy. "If I did move, what would happen to the Desert Flowers Detective Agency?"

"You can't worry about that. None of us—me, Iris, or Violet—would ever want to hold you back from something better. Besides, the three of us are very resourceful. We'll somehow manage to get by without you."

"I know, but—"

"You were only supposed to be a temporary fix anyway. Just to help us get the business off the ground when it became clear people were reticent to hire three old broads to solve their cases. We needed you, but now we're established and maybe the clients will be a little more understanding and open-minded. It could be time for us to take the training wheels off anyway."

She was trying her best to sell this to Matt, but she wasn't sure it was working on herself. She was deeply concerned about what would happen if Matt left at this critical time, just when the agency was starting to gain some traction. But she was not going to show him that she was worried. This wasn't about her or the agency. This was about Matt and his promising future.

She could tell Matt was wavering because he hardly ever shut up and right now he wasn't talking at all.

He just stared straight ahead.

"Matt?"

"Let me think about it."

They drove in silence for most of the way back to

Palm Springs, making small talk a few times, but spending the majority of the drive wallowing in their own thoughts. Poppy couldn't even consider her poor daughter, Heather, and how it would affect her.

When they finally arrived back at Iris's house, they found Iris and Violet waiting for them in the garage office.

Poppy looked around. "Where's Wyatt?"

"He's at school," Violet said.

"I forget he's still in the seventh grade and not twenty-five years old. He acts so much older sometimes," Poppy said. "Did he get my text?"

"Yes, he called right before you got here," Violet said. "During recess he had some time to do a little research. He contacted all of the professional recording studios in the area, which frankly aren't that many because most are in LA, and none of them had even heard of Lara Harper."

"Maybe she left the desert and is making the album somewhere else," Matt said.

"Or perhaps she is here but using an assumed name," Poppy suggested.

"Why would she do that? She is a fame whore. She wants everybody to know who she is," Iris huffed.

"It looks like we are back to square one, I'm afraid. *Again*," Violet sighed.

Poppy's phone buzzed. She glanced at the screen. It was a text from Rod.

**Just arrived in PS. The drive was lonely without you. When can I see you?**

"Anything important?" Matt asked.

Poppy smiled and quickly pocketed her phone, ignoring Rod's text. "It's nothing. Now let's sit down and strategize about what to do next."

But Poppy wasn't sure what they should do next. The fact was, their client, Rod, seemed to be slowly losing interest in finding his daughter and was more focused on chasing after Poppy. It was making her uncomfortable, and yet, that kiss they had shared back at his mansion had been downright swoonworthy even though it had undoubtedly crossed a line. As hard as she might try not to succumb to his charms, it was becoming nearly impossible for her to resist him. If Matt hadn't interrupted them, there was no telling where they would have ended up.

And that was cause for deep concern.

# Chapter 22

Poppy had just drifted off to sleep when she heard a loud banging on the door to her apartment. At first she thought it was a dream. She rolled over on her side, clutching her pillow as she buried her face in it. A few seconds passed and suddenly there was more banging. Poppy shot up in bed. This was definitely not a dream. She checked the digital clock on her nightstand. It was almost 1:00 a.m.. She crawled out of bed and grabbed her blue terrycloth robe, which was draped over a chair, and put it on over her white sleeveless nightgown. She slipped on her cozy fur-lined slippers and quietly headed out of the bedroom and crossed to the front door. She paused, leaning in and pressing an ear to the door, trying to hear who or what was on the other side. There were three more loud bangs, startling her enough that she let out a short scream.

"Who's there?" Poppy demanded to know.

"It's me. . . ."

It was a man's voice, but his words were slurred, like he was intoxicated, and she had trouble recognizing who it belonged to.

"Me *who*?" Poppy snapped, worried she might have to call the police.

"Rod . . ."

Poppy felt an overwhelming sense of relief. At least her midnight marauder wasn't a complete stranger. But at the same time, she wondered what on earth Rod was doing here at such a late hour.

Poppy unlocked the door and opened it to find Rod swaying from side to side, with glassy eyes and a red nose, totally obliterated.

"Can I come in?" he managed to get out, although it was mostly garbled.

"Rod, *what* are you doing here?"

"I need to talk to you. . . ." He was trying to focus on her, but she surmised he was probably seeing two of her at the moment.

"Please, it's really important!" he shouted.

Poppy feared he might wake the neighbors with his yelling so she grabbed him by the shirtsleeve and pulled him inside the apartment. She quickly shut the door and locked it again. "I certainly hope you didn't drive here."

"No, I walked. . . . You're really close to the bar. . . . I put your address in my phone and a really nice woman directed me here. . . ."

"That would be Siri," Poppy said, although he had no idea what she was talking about.

Poppy led Rod to the couch. "Sit down here, Rod. I'm going to put on a pot of coffee for you."

He didn't want to sit down so Poppy gave him a slight

shove. He lost his balance and toppled over, landing on the couch sitting upright. He stared straight ahead trying to focus his vision.

Poppy scurried to the kitchen to make the coffee, and by the time she returned to the living room with a cup, she suddenly stopped in her tracks at the sight of Rod, who was now on one knee, staring up at her with his bloodshot eyes and a goofy, expectant smile on his face.

"Will you marry me?" he asked. "I haven't had the chance to buy a ring yet, but I'll do that tomorrow, I promise. . . ."

"Rod, you're being silly," Poppy admonished.

"I'm one hundred percent serious, Poppy," Rod drawled as he put one hand down on the floor to maintain his balance. "I love you. . . ."

"Stop it right now," Poppy said. "You're going to be awfully embarrassed when you sober up in the morning."

"No . . . I want to marry you," Rod sputtered, like an obstinate little boy who wasn't getting his way.

Poppy crossed to him and set the cup of joe down on the coffee table, took him by the arm, lifted him up to his feet, and set him back down on the couch. She then handed him the cup. "Here. Drink this."

Rod refused to take a sip at first, pouting that his proposal hadn't quite gone the way he had hoped it would.

"It's because of what happened back when we were doing *Jack Colt*, isn't it?"

"I don't know what you're talking about, Rod," Poppy said.

"Yes you do," he slurred. "We slept together that one time in my trailer at the end of the second season, and then I didn't call you and it got awkward on the set after that. . . . Don't you remember?"

"Yes, Rod, I remember."

Rod finally took a gulp of his coffee. It was still too hot and he opened his mouth and let out a yelp. "I burned my tongue."

"Sorry about that," Poppy said. "I should have warned you."

But she was secretly glad she hadn't. That's what she liked to call karma.

"I . . . I should've called you," Rod stammered.

"You were a big star. You had women falling all over themselves trying to get your attention."

"That didn't make what I did right," Rod said. "I broke your heart. I'm so sorry. . . ."

He became wistful and sad and Poppy thought he might cry. The alcohol was obviously making his emotions run high.

"Don't beat yourself up, Rod. You weren't ready for anything serious at that time in your life. I totally understood that eventually. And then after the show got cancelled, I met Chester and it all worked out the way it was supposed to anyway."

"But that's the thing—you and I *were* meant to end up together. I see that now. . . ."

"Oh, Rod . . ."

"The moment I saw you again, after all these years, I knew right away. . . ."

Poppy sighed and then said softly, "We all just try to live our lives. We make choices, some good, some bad. That's just the way it is."

"Okay then, I've made a choice. I want to marry you," he said.

"You're drunk. I am sure you will feel differently when you wake up tomorrow."

"No I won't. . . . I love you, Poppy. I think I've always loved you. . . . Have I told you that?"

"Yes, Rod, several times now," Poppy sighed. "But my life is very complicated right now, Rod. I cannot marry you, or anyone else, for that matter. I've started this business, and I have my daughter Heather's situation to deal with. It's not a good time to make any major life decisions, least of all getting married again."

"I'll give you time to think about it. . . ." He was not about to give up. He had it in his mind that he wanted to marry her and he was not about to be deterred. "Is there someone else?"

He tried to get up from the couch, but because he was so inebriated he couldn't stand, so he fell back against the cushions and pretended he hadn't even tried.

Poppy hesitated, wondering if she should mention Sam Emerson. Rod would certainly remember him. The ex–police detective had worked on the show for all three seasons as a consultant and scriptwriter. She decided in that moment not to bring him up to Rod. It wouldn't be helpful to tell him in his current state that she and Sam had reunited about a year ago and were casually dating.

"Poppy . . . ?"

"Yes, Rod?"

"Poppy . . . ?"

"I'm listening."

"Will you . . ."

"What?"

"Will you marry me?"

Poppy smirked. She found it amusing that Rod had completely forgotten he had proposed to her not five minutes earlier. Luckily she didn't have to put him through two rejections in one night because before she had time to answer his burning question for the second time she heard him snoring loudly. He was still sitting upright on the couch, his head tilted to the right, his tongue hanging out of the side of his mouth. His chest heaved up and down as he wheezed and snorted.

Poppy leaned over him and gently put a hand behind his head and lowered him down so it rested on a pillow propped up against the arm of the couch. She then grabbed hold of his feet and heaved them up to the other end so he was lying horizontally. She removed his shoes, threw a blanket over him, kissed him lightly on the forehead, and then headed toward her bedroom, praying that when Rod woke up in the morning he would have no recollection of proposing marriage.

Twice.

# Chapter 23

Poppy was roused out of a deep sleep by what she thought was more knocking at the door. She opened one eye and stared at the digital clock. It was already after 9:00 a.m. Rod's late night appearance had interrupted her sleep pattern so she had been deprived of her usual eight hours. She closed her eye and rolled over on her side, not quite ready to get out of bed and check on Rod, when she heard it again.

She was not mistaken. Someone else was outside the door to her apartment knocking. She couldn't believe it. Poppy once again crawled out of bed, threw on her robe and slippers, and walked out into the living room, where Rod was curled up on the couch, still sound asleep with the blanket over him. He was no longer snoring and was very still, but Poppy knew when he eventually did finally stir awake, he would be nursing a massive hangover.

Before she reached the door handle, someone rapped three more times on the door. Before unlocking it, Poppy asked gruffly, "Who is it?"

"Sam."

Poppy's heart skipped a beat.

Sam Emerson.

What was *he* doing here?

Poppy twisted her head around to look at Rod, sprawled out on the couch.

How was she going to explain *that*?

She would just have to be honest.

After all, nothing untoward had happened.

Except for the fact that Rod Harper had proposed to her.

*Twice*, she reminded herself again.

Poppy took a deep breath and opened the door a crack.

Sam stood outside, looking refreshed and sexy as all get-out in his manly plaid shirt, rugged jeans, scuffed cowboy boots, and weathered brown leather bomber jacket. His mustache was full and gray, and just the sight of him caused Poppy to swoon a little bit. He had a big, warm smile on his face that wavered slightly at the sight of her still in her nightgown.

"Poppy, did I wake you? You're such an early riser I was sure you'd already be up and about," Sam said apologetically.

"No, Sam, it's fine. I was unexpectedly up late last night so I just decided to sleep in a little later than normal. What are you doing here in Palm Springs?"

Sam lived in a cabin up in Big Bear and ventured down from the mountain only when absolutely necessary.

"I had some business to take care of in Palm Springs today, so I thought I'd stop by to see if I could take you to breakfast," Sam said, still sporting that sexy, inviting smile.

"Right *now*?"

Sam glanced at his watch. "Last time I checked it was still too early for lunch."

"I'm not sure I can today, Sam. . . ."

She casually averted her eyes back to check on Rod and was surprised to see he was no longer on the couch. She frantically looked around for him but he was nowhere to be seen. Then the toilet in the bathroom flushed. She whipped her head back toward Sam, praying he hadn't heard it.

"Is this a bad time?" Sam asked, slightly concerned.

"No . . . I mean, yes . . . I don't think I can join you for breakfast today, Sam. I'm sorry. Can I have a rain check?"

"Of course. Is everything all right? You look a little nervous."

"Nervous? Me? No, I'm not nervous. What would I have to be nervous about?"

Sam studied her suspiciously. "You tell me."

Then, with the world's worst timing, she heard Rod come out of the bathroom and practically yell at the top of his lungs, "Hey, where do you keep the toothpaste?!"

There was no way Sam hadn't heard *that*.

In fact, he was now craning his neck to peer through the crack in the door to see who had said it. Poppy bowed her head. There was no hiding the fact any longer that Rod Harper was in her apartment. With a heavy sigh, she opened the door all the way and turned around to see Rod, his shirt open, standing in the middle of her living room.

She looked back at Sam, whose eyes widened with recognition. "*Rod?*"

Rod had to squint in order to focus on the tall, handsome stud standing in Poppy's doorway, but it took only a few seconds for him to figure out who it was. "*Sam?* Sam Emerson? My God, I haven't seen you in over thirty years!"

Rod bounded over, almost pushing Poppy out of the way, to shake Sam's hand. Sam was still taken aback by Rod's presence in Poppy's apartment, but he made a valiant effort to hide it. The two men pumped hands and Rod even went in for a half hug.

Rod, who remarkably showed no apparent signs of a hangover after his bender last night, clapped a hand on Sam's shoulder. "How've you been, buddy?"

"Pretty much the same. Living up in Big Bear now," Sam said, with one eye on Poppy.

"So you're no longer consulting on cop shows?" Rod asked.

"Hell no. I got tired of the Hollywood scene when Bush Junior was still in office," he said. "I'll be happy if I never have to drive west of Riverside again."

"Smart man," Rod said, grinning. There was a slight pause as it finally dawned on Rod. "What are you doing here? I didn't know you and Poppy were still in touch."

Poppy could feel her pulse racing. She had no idea how to handle the situation except to just stand by silently and let it unfold naturally.

"We see each other now and then," Sam said, trying his best to be diplomatic. "I came by to see if she was hungry for some breakfast."

"Well, I'm starving," Rod said before turning to Poppy. "What do you have in your kitchen? If you've got eggs, I could whip us up some omelettes."

"I . . . I'm not . . . sure," Poppy stammered.

Sam slipped his hands in the back pockets of his jeans and arched an eyebrow, still confused by Rod's unexpected presence.

Rod quickly disappeared into the kitchen in a flash to inspect Poppy's refrigerator.

Poppy rushed forward closer to Sam. "Sam, I know what you must be thinking. . . ."

Sam chuckled. "You have no idea what's going through my mind right now."

She spoke fast. "Rod came over last night and he had been drinking and—"

Rod was suddenly back. "You've got all the ingredients I need. And I spotted some frozen hash browns in the freezer to boot. Come on in, Sam. Stay for breakfast. We can catch up on what's been going on with each other the last thirty years."

"I'd settle for just last night," Sam cracked.

Rod didn't hear him or chose to ignore the comment. He was already heading back to the kitchen to start making breakfast.

"He just showed up at my door. He was very drunk. I didn't know what to do," Poppy said. "Please don't be mad. . . ."

"I have no right to be mad, Poppy. We've never had any kind of discussion about what it is we have going on between us. From my perspective, at this point until further notice it's very low key and casual, right?"

"Yes, I suppose so, but—"

"So you can do whatever you want."

"I understand, but I don't want you to think—"

"It's all good."

Rod interrupted them, calling from the kitchen. "Hey, I'm getting lonely in here. Come have some coffee with me."

They marched into the kitchen to find Rod wearing one of Poppy's aprons and cracking open eggs into a glass bowl.

The two men spent the next twenty minutes reminiscing about their time together on *Jack Colt, PI*; how Rod was still a working actor today and what shows he had guest starred on recently; how the business had so fundamentally changed and was more challenging than ever. Sam wasn't as chatty as Rod but did talk about how leaving the business saved him from a heart attack and how he had always been a cowboy at heart, which was why living in Big Bear now was the right fit. Mercifully, neither of the men discussed their history with Poppy back in the 1980s as they took their trip down memory lane.

Rod poured on the charm and Poppy was in awe at his uncanny ability to shake off the effects of all that alcohol from the night before. She knew Rod had been downing cocktails at the bar working up the nerve to come over to her apartment and ask her to marry him. She just prayed he wouldn't bring that up again over omelettes with Sam.

"You married these days, Sam?" Rod asked, winging the frying pan upward to flip the omelette up into the air over the stove.

"Naw, I'm kind of a loner," Sam said, stealing a quick glance at Poppy.

"I've been single a while, too," Rod noted. "But I'm hoping that might change one of these days."

He winked at Poppy.

And of course Sam saw him do it.

Poppy wanted the floor to open up and swallow her at this point.

Luckily the topic of conversation eventually steered toward sports for a while as Rod finished making the omelettes and hash browns and sliced up some tomatoes and they all sat down at the kitchen table to eat.

Poppy ate her food at record speed, hoping to end this little buddy reunion as soon as possible, but neither Rod nor Sam seemed to be in any kind of hurry.

In fact, after they were done eating and Sam helped Poppy clear the plates since Rod had done the cooking, the two men exchanged numbers with promises to keep in contact. That was the last thing Poppy expected or wanted to happen.

Sam finally said, "I'd better get going. I have an appointment at the bank in fifteen minutes."

"You heading toward Palm Canyon?" Rod asked.

"Yup," Sam said.

"Would you mind giving me a lift to my car? I left it parked out on the street in front of a bar last night," Rod said, rubbing his eyes. "What a night."

Sam looked at Poppy with a knowing smile.

"He was in no condition to drive home and needed a place to crash for the night so he walked all the way here. . . . I wasn't expecting him," Poppy said, feeling the need to explain again.

"But she couldn't have been more welcoming . . . the perfect hostess," Rod needlessly added, winking at her again.

She just wanted him to stop talking.

Poppy could tell Sam wanted to say something and it was killing him not to, but he was being a gentleman and kept his mouth shut.

As Poppy ushered the two men out the door, Rod turned to her and said, "Thank you for everything, Poppy. I'll call you later."

He went in for a kiss, but she deftly avoided it and patted him on the back and practically pushed him out the door.

Sam, on the other hand, didn't even make any kind of attempt at physical contact with Poppy. He just nodded, smiled, and thanked her for breakfast. She knew she would have a lot of cleanup to do later, and she wasn't thinking about the dirty dishes in her kitchen sink.

Rod threw an arm around Sam's neck as they headed for Sam's car and said, "It's so good seeing you again, buddy."

"Same here," Sam said.

Poppy shut the door, spun around, and leaned up against it, relieved they were both gone, and at a total loss as to how she was going to handle any of this.

# Chapter 24

Poppy had not expected Iris and Violet to be waiting for her, arms folded, stern looks on their faces when she breezed into the garage office. She stopped dead in her tracks. "What? Did I do something wrong?"

Violet, who rarely got upset and always put a positive spin on things, instantly melted at the sight of Poppy's worried look. "No, of course not, dear, no one can blame you really. . . ."

"*I* can," Iris insisted. "We are trying to run a business and make money and you are preoccupied. . . ."

Poppy suddenly felt nauseous. She knew what this must be about. "I'm trying to remain professional, but it's Rod. He's the one who thinks he is in love with me. I swear I am not encouraging him in the least!"

Iris turned to Violet. "What is she talking about?"

Violet shrugged. "I have no idea."

"I may have crossed the line allowing him to stay over last night at my apartment," Poppy sputtered.

"Wait. *Who* stayed at your place last night?" Iris demanded to know.

"Rod," Poppy said before quickly adding, "He showed up drunk and clearly couldn't drive himself home. What was I supposed to do?"

"Our client, our *only* client, spent the night with you?" Iris asked, incredulous.

"On the couch! He passed out! Nothing sordid took place!" Poppy cried.

Iris and Violet exchanged curious looks, not sure how this conversation had taken such a wild and unexpected turn.

Violet stepped forward. "Can we back up just a bit, dear? Did you say Rod Harper thinks he is in *love* with you?"

Poppy nodded. "Yes, and frankly it's making me very uncomfortable. He will not leave it alone, but luckily he passed out after he proposed to me. . . ."

Iris and Violet exchanged stunned looks.

"Rod Harper *proposed* to you?" Violet gasped.

"What did you say?" Iris asked.

"Of course I said no. At least I think I did. It was all a blur. I was very nervous," Poppy howled.

"I thought you were dating Sam," Violet said.

"I am! And he showed up at my door this morning when Rod was still there!" Poppy wailed.

"What happened?" Violet gasped again.

"Rod made us all breakfast!" Poppy said, not quite believing it herself.

There was a long pause as Iris and Violet stared at her blankly.

Poppy suddenly realized that the two women had a *lot*

of questions for supposedly already knowing what was going on. "I cannot imagine what went through Sam's head when he saw Rod in my apartment this morning. Did Matt say something to you? He was probably suspicious when he saw Rod fawning over me at his house in LA."

"Matt didn't say anything to us," Violet said.

"Then how do you know about Rod?" Poppy asked.

"We did *not* know about Rod," Iris huffed.

"Then why were you upset with me when I came in?"

Iris and Violet moved apart to reveal Wyatt sitting at his desk, his chair turned around so he was facing her. He had a silly grin on his face and said in a singsong voice, "Poppy has a boyfriend!"

"Why didn't you tell me Wyatt was here? He shouldn't be hearing about things like this!" Poppy scolded.

"You did not give us a chance!" Iris snapped, indignant.

"If this has nothing to do with Rod, then what is this all about?" Poppy asked.

"Show her, Wyatt," Violet said gently.

Wyatt excitedly picked up a box from the floor and excitedly thrust it out toward Poppy, who had absolutely no clue what it was except that it seemed to have a picture of a lot of metal parts on it.

"I'm totally lost here. What is it?" Poppy asked.

"It's a robot arm–building kit!" Wyatt exclaimed. "It has six axes of movement and up to two hundred and seventy degrees of rotation from all the different parts! Once I assemble it, it will be able to vacuum and pick up objects!"

"Impressive," Poppy said, still thoroughly confused about what any of this had to do with her.

"It's actually quite educational," Violet said with a bright smile. "It will help him learn about the power of hydraulic systems."

"I see," Poppy said, turning to Wyatt. "Is it your birthday? Did I forget?"

Wyatt shook his head. "My birthday's not until November."

Poppy turned to Violet. "Did you give it to him?"

"No," Violet said, shaking her head. "*You* did."

"*Me?* No, I most certainly did not," Poppy said. "I'm sure I would remember giving him a robot arm!"

Iris, tired of beating around the bush, stepped forward. "But you did. He bought it with the hundred dollars you gave him to find out information about Alden Kenny."

"*Oh . . . ,*" Poppy mumbled, the subject of their displeasure finally coming into focus. "I meant to tell you both about that."

"Well, clearly you did not," Iris huffed. "We are supposed to be finding Rod Harper's AWOL daughter and you are completely distracted with that young man from your jury whom you found facedown in his swimming pool!"

"Someone drowned him. It's only natural that I'm curious to find out who did it!" Poppy said, lamely trying to defend herself, but she knew in her gut that Iris was right.

"That's perfectly reasonable," Violet said, rushing over and squeezing her arm. "Nobody can blame you for wanting to know!"

"Stop saying that, Violet! *I* am blaming her! She should not be bribing your grandson to do a background check when she should be focused on a case that is actually making us *money!*"

"To be fair, she did spend the whole night with our client!" Violet said.

"Please don't say it like that, Violet," Poppy said.

"I'm just trying to help you, dear," Violet said quietly.

"I know and I appreciate it. But you make it sound like Rod and I have a thing and we don't. He is just a client and I am determined to keep it that way," Poppy cried.

"What about *after* the case is closed?" Iris asked, folding her arms again and glaring at Poppy.

"Well, then we will see where we are at that point," Poppy stammered, now totally discombobulated.

"Poor Sam . . . ," Violet whispered, shaking her head.

"Nothing has changed with Sam!" Poppy cried.

"For the record, I did come up with some stuff," Wyatt sighed, tired of hearing about Poppy's romantic travails.

"Like what?" Poppy asked.

Wyatt picked up a folder from his desk and handed it to Poppy. "Alden Kenny was the co-owner of a carpet-cleaning business in Rancho Mirage. Now that he's dead, his partner gets full control of the company."

"That's not necessarily a strong motive for murder," Poppy said, flipping through the pages of Wyatt's research.

"But since he was Alden's business partner, he probably knows a lot about him. He might be able to point us in the direction of someone who *did* have a strong motive," Wyatt suggested.

Poppy nodded. She really liked this kid.

Her phone buzzed.

She pulled it from her pocket and grimaced.

"Who is it?" Iris asked.

Poppy hesitated, not wanting to share the identity of the caller.

Wyatt put his robot arm–building kit down on the floor and chuckled. "It's her *boyfriend*!"

"He is *not* my boyfriend!" Poppy snapped before catching herself. "Look at me. I'm arguing with a twelve-year-old boy about my love life. When did it come to this?"

"Please don't keep the client waiting," Iris said.

Poppy threw Iris an irritated look and then answered the call. "Hello, Rod."

"Hey, babe," Rod said.

She wanted to ask him not to call her "babe," but she decided to let it slide this one time. "What can I do for you?"

"I just received a call from Lara," he said.

Poppy gasped. "*What?*"

"Yes, she's fine. Apparently she went off to Nepal to find herself. That's why she fell off the radar. She said she was in a bad place and needed to figure some things out, but now she is back and is willing to see me. . . ."

"*Nepal?* But that doesn't make any sense," Poppy said tentatively.

"Actually it does," Rod said. "Her mother used to take off all the time and disappear for weeks, sometimes months, at a time. She could be a little too independent, which is one of the myriad reasons we're not married anymore. I suppose Lara takes after her in a lot of ways. . . ."

"No, Rod, what I mean is, we have credit card receipts showing Lara has been in the Coachella Valley recently, and I talked to her new agent in Hollywood, who claimed she was recording an album. For whatever reason, she's lying to you."

"I'm sure she has her reasons and hopefully she will tell me when she sees me," Rod said.

Poppy could tell from his tone that he didn't really believe what he was saying. "Rod, I think there is something else still going on here—"

"Maybe, but she's back in touch with me, and that's all I ever wanted," Rod said. "The end goal has always been to repair my relationship with her and now I have hope it might happen."

Poppy wanted to tell him that she strongly suspected Lara had called him only because she wanted something, probably money, to keep bankrolling her, maybe this new album. He had threatened to cut her off previously, and now here was her chance to become Daddy's Little Girl again to make sure the coffers remained full. It was a cynical theory, but one that made sense.

"I will mail a check to your office. Tell Matt and the ladies I appreciate all they have done," Rod said.

"But we didn't solve anything," Poppy muttered.

"Yes, but it was worth every penny because it brought you back into my life. Now that I am no longer a client and you no longer have to keep a professional distance, I think a romantic dinner is in order."

"Rod . . ."

"I have to go. My agent is on the other line. I'll call you tonight."

He hung up.

"Well?" Iris asked.

"Lara called Rod. They're back in touch. Our services are no longer required," Poppy said.

"That's it? The case is over?" Iris said.

"It would seem so," Poppy said. "I think there are more unanswered questions about what is going on with her, and I suspect that she might be playing him for some reason, but for our part, we are apparently done."

"Well, now that he is no longer a client, you no longer have to see him," Iris said, staring at Poppy. "Right?"

"Right," Poppy answered half-heartedly.

"But you will anyway," Iris added.

"He wants to have dinner," Poppy moaned.

"Poor Sam," Violet murmured.

"Stop saying that!" Poppy cried.

# Chapter 25

What Jay Takamura lacked in stature, he certainly made up for in exuberant personality. The energetic twenty-something Japanese American with his toothy smile and sparkling eyes was a born salesman who wasted no time in talking Iris into adding on the Scotchguard and deodorizer services to her simple initial order of cleaning two area rugs and the carpet in the walk-in closet in her bedroom.

"You won't regret it! The deodorizer is especially strong against typical pet odors," Jay pitched excitedly.

"I don't have any pets!" Iris bellowed.

"Well, you never know when a friend might drop by with her dog or cat in tow," Jay reasoned.

"I don't have any friends!" Iris insisted.

Poppy couldn't help but snicker as she sat in the

kitchen, sipping coffee, pretending to be Iris's sister who was visiting her from Duluth. She took an immediate liking to Jay when he had first shown up at the door bearing his elaborate powerful carpet cleaner machine.

Poppy had initially suggested they make an appointment to visit Jay Takamura, Alden Kenny's partner in his Fresh Scrub Carpet Cleaners business, at his office, but Iris had been complaining about her dirty, ragged carpets for weeks and decided Takamura might talk more openly if he believed they were actually paying customers instead of private investigators pumping him for information.

What neither of them expected was for the diminutive Jay Takamura, who barely cracked five and a half feet, but was packed with charisma, to be such a charmer and a big fan of older women. Within just a few moments from the time Iris had first opened the door to greet him, he had complimented her hair, her outfit, her decorating taste, and her sense of humor although Iris had yet to crack a joke. Jay took his sweet time assembling his equipment as he flirted shamelessly with the impenetrable Iris Becker.

"Stop smiling at me like that. You're making me nervous," Jay said playfully.

Iris stared at him, stone-faced. "I am *not* smiling."

"Sure you are. I can see the corners of your mouth curling up. It's very distracting," Jay said with a wink.

Poppy could see the scene unfolding from her vantage point in the kitchen and had to cover her mouth to stop from bursting out laughing.

"You are being *ridiculous*!" Iris barked.

"What can I say? You bring out the worst in me!" Jay

said as he finished putting together his carpet-cleaning machine.

"Do you think you can get those stains out of that area rug by the fireplace?" Iris asked, trying desperately to change the subject.

Jay stood up and walked over and stood close to Iris. He was a few inches shorter than her, barely up to her collarbone. But his size hardly deterred him from his mission to melt her heart. "I promise I won't leave this house, Iris, until that carpet is as good as new. If you're not satisfied, I won't charge you a penny."

"Well, that seems fair," Iris said, still a bit discombobulated. "I'll let you get to work then. I will be in the kitchen with . . . my *sister* . . . who is visiting me from Duluth."

"Yes, you mentioned that already," Jay said.

Poppy nearly spit out her coffee and howled. She had to clap a hand over her mouth again. It was Iris's idea to give Poppy a cover story of being her sister and now she was overdoing it by reminding herself of it over and over again so she wouldn't forget.

Jay wasn't finished flirting. "But I don't mind. You can say it as many times as you want because I could listen to that rough, demanding voice of yours all day. Bossy women are always such a turn-on for me."

The kid's aggressiveness rendered Iris speechless. At least for a few seconds. And then she shouted, "Stop doing that!"

"Doing what?" Jay asked innocently.

"Talking that way!" Iris bellowed.

"Yes, ma'am!" Jay said, snapping to attention like a

uniformed soldier responding to the firm order of a commanding officer. "Whatever you say, ma'am!"

"And don't call me ma'am!" Iris growled.

"How about 'sexy mama'?" Jay said with a wink.

"You are not acting professional at all!" Iris yelled. "I should tell you to leave my house right now!"

Jay winked at her again. "Like I said, you bring out the bad boy in me."

"Just clean the rug!" Iris snapped.

Iris raced into the kitchen as the carpet-cleaning machine roared to life and Jay began running it over the area rug.

Poppy was doubled over giggling, unable to contain herself.

Iris sat down at the table and shot her a look. "I figured you would be in here enjoying this!"

"You didn't even mention Alden Kenny," Poppy reminded her once she managed to stop laughing.

"Of course I didn't! He did not give me a chance! He kept making those lewd and inappropriate comments! Shamelessly flirting with a woman my age! Nobody should have to put up with that! I should mention his behavior in my Yelp review."

"Given some of the women you golf with, I'm sure if you did that his business would skyrocket!" Poppy said with a sly smile.

Iris shrugged. "You are not wrong about that!"

"Why are you in here with me? You should be out there talking to him and finding out more about Alden Kenny!"

"Why can't *you* do it?" Iris huffed.

"He likes you! Which means he will probably tell you

more than he would ever tell me. So get back in there Mata Hari and do your job!"

"Don't be so bossy!" Iris snapped.

"Okay, but you need to be because apparently that's what he likes."

Iris gave Poppy a withering look and then got up and marched back into the living room just as Jay shut off his machine.

"How about that?" Poppy heard Jay say to Iris.

"You were right. It looks brand new. You did a nice job," Iris reluctantly admitted.

"I couldn't bear disappointing you," Jay said. "I'm very good at what I do."

"Don't get cocky," Iris warned. "Now follow me up to the bedroom and I will show you the carpet in the closet I want cleaned."

"The bedroom . . . music to my ears," Jay said.

"The last one from your company who was here was much better at people skills! He did not come on as strong as you!" Iris yelled.

"You've used us before? Because when you made the appointment I didn't see you in our billing records."

"I paid cash," Iris insisted.

"But that wouldn't matter because we keep all receipts. . . ."

"Are you calling me a *liar*?"

"No, ma'am. It's just that—"

"His name was Alan or Alvin, something like that."

"Alden," Jay said quietly.

"He came here and cleaned the carpets, kept to himself, and I didn't have to put up with any silly shenanigans!"

Poppy, listening from the kitchen, quickly could tell Jay's demeanor had suddenly changed. There was silence in the living room.

"Are you all right?" Iris asked, softening her tone.

"Yes . . . I'm sorry," Jay said, sniffing.

Poppy got up and hurried into the living room to find Jay, his head down, wiping his eyes with the sleeve of his shirt.

"Really . . . I'm sorry," Jay said.

"It is fine! Stop apologizing!" Iris demanded. "Are you *crying*?"

"No . . . ," Jay said, his voice cracking.

He was clearly crying.

"I didn't mean to upset you. It's just that you are not my type. I like men who are a bit older . . . ones who are too old to be my grandson!"

"It's not that," Jay tried to explain.

"Would you like to sit down?" Poppy asked. "Can I get you something to drink?"

Jay shook his head. "No, I have another job to get to after this. I can't be taking any breaks. I'm a one-man operation now. My partner . . . Alden . . . he recently passed away."

"Passed away" was underselling the point just a bit. The poor young man had been murdered. But Poppy kept up the impression that she was completely in the dark about the circumstances. "I'm so sorry to hear that."

"He was like a brother to me," Jay managed to get out between sniffles. "I'm so ashamed. . . . I shouldn't be acting like this. . . . It's so unprofessional. . . ."

"*Now* you want to act professional?" Iris asked sharply.

"Iris, cut him a break. He has clearly suffered a loss and is very upset," Poppy said, crossing to Jay to put an arm around him. She was far better at showing empathy than Iris, who didn't have time for such theatrics. "Are you sure I can't get you anything?"

"Yes, I'm sure, thank you," Jay said, finally getting hold of himself. "We had this business together for only six months but we were friends way before that. . . . We met when he moved out here from Texas a few years ago. . . ."

Poppy didn't want to reveal that she knew Alden, so she casually commented, "He must have died very young. . . ."

Jay nodded. "I shouldn't be talking about this."

Poppy signaled Iris, who was standing across the room, to come over and offer her condolences. Iris vigorously shook her head at first, refusing, but Poppy glared at her, insistent. Finally, Iris sighed and shuffled over and sat down on the couch and, through gritted teeth, put an arm around Jay and said, "I am sorry for your loss."

Jay wasted no time in hugging her and burying his head in her chest.

Iris's eyes popped open but Poppy motioned for her to continue holding him.

Iris was hating every minute of this but did what she was told.

"There . . . there," Iris said mechanically.

With his face in her breasts, Jay said in a muffled voice, "He had been through a lot, and had some trouble with the law. . . . He wasn't in a very good place . . . but I helped him out by bringing him into this carpet-cleaning business idea I had. . . ."

"That was very generous of you," Poppy said gently.

They could barely make out his words because he was face-planted in Iris's cleavage. "He'd fudge the books sometimes and try to cut corners that weren't exactly legal to help the bottom line, but I told him I didn't want to run the business like that, and so he stopped. . . . After that he tried to stay on the straight and narrow. . . . Despite his demons, he was a really good guy."

"I'm sure he was," Poppy said. "Was he sick?"

"No, the cops say he was murdered," Jay said, in no rush to remove himself from Iris's embrace.

"*Murdered?* How awful!" Poppy yelped, feigning surprise.

Jay nodded his head. "We were roommates, too. We shared a house. I was out working when some friend of his . . . some woman I didn't know . . . found him floating in the pool."

*Some* woman?

Poppy was relieved Jay had not done his homework to find out exactly who it was who had discovered the body because then she would have had to explain why she was pretending to be Iris's sister.

"The cops said there were signs of a struggle, like someone drowned him," Jay said softly.

"Who would do such a thing?" Iris asked impatiently.

Jay shrugged. "I wish I knew. . . . I tried so hard to keep him out of trouble. But I couldn't be with him all the time. He may have had a whole other life outside of work I didn't know about. . . . I just know he was a damn good carpet cleaner."

Iris patted him on the head and mouthed to Poppy, *Are we done?*

Poppy nodded.

That was all Iris needed. She immediately pushed the kid away from her, startling him. "What a tragedy. Well, I have always found it is best to buck up, stay strong and move on! That has always worked for me!"

She jumped up from the couch and marched back into the kitchen, relieved to be finished with her role of chief consoler.

Jay, somewhat dumbstruck, looked at Poppy for an explanation as to what had just happened.

Poppy smiled and shrugged. "She's German."

# Chapter 26

Poppy sat in the back of the parole hearing room next to Matt, who fidgeted and squirmed and was more nervous than she was. When they had first arrived, Poppy had quickly steered them toward the back of the room for the hearing because she in no way wanted to distract Heather, who was in front of the board making her case to be released early from her sentence for good behavior.

Heather had discouraged her mother and boyfriend from driving all the way here for the hearing because she didn't want to have to see their crestfallen faces if she was denied, especially since this was her first time in front of the parole board. But Poppy and Matt had both insisted on attending because they had a good feeling about the outcome and did not want to miss out on celebrating if Heather was fortunate enough to be granted an early release.

The hearing had already been in session for almost forty minutes as the three-person panel of commissioners peppered Heather with questions about her crime, her time inside the prison, and her plans for the future in the event that she was ultimately granted parole.

One of the commissioners, an older African American woman, rather stout, with a sweet, sympathetic personality and who was a psychiatrist, seemed to be more on her side than the other two on the board. "Heather, it says here in your report that you have been a model prisoner, you've undergone therapy to deal with the events that brought you here, and you have used your own social work degree to counsel other inmates. Is all of this true?"

"Yes," Heather answered.

"Well, I commend you on your efforts to make the most of your time here," she said with a kind smile.

The commissioner who sat in the middle, a rather gruff, sour white man who looked as if he would rather be anywhere else, chewed gum and flipped through the file in front of him, distracted and uninterested in the proceedings. "It says here you have only been here thirteen months. What makes you think that's enough time served for your crime?"

Heather looked at the man and cleared her throat before speaking. "I don't think it's enough time at all."

Poppy's heart sank.

Matt physically clenched up next to her.

What on earth was she doing?

Heather sat still at the small table that had been set up in front of the parole board, not moving a muscle except to speak. "I don't think five years, or ten years, or even twenty years will be enough. . . ."

Poppy stared down at the floor, twisting the strap of

her purse, devastated that Heather was torpedoing her chances of an early release.

"I think about what I did every day, and whether or not I am an inmate here or a free woman on the outside, I will always think about it. I will think about it until my dying day. That I can promise you. It's not my decision where I will be when I think about it. In my cell or at home with my mother. The fact is, I will never forget. And my only recourse is to work hard to make amends, and be the best person I can possibly be, and a contributing member of society."

"What are your plans if you are granted release?" the third commissioner asked, an Asian woman whose face was totally unreadable. She was the wild card, the undecided vote who would likely determine Heather's fate.

"I want to go back to school and study criminology, and maybe, if I'm lucky and I get enough loans, pursue a law degree."

Her advocate on the board smiled and said, "You want to work hard and get on the right side of the law, I see."

Heather didn't answer her.

The man in the middle stared at her, unimpressed.

The third commissioner, Miss Hard to Read, sat back in her chair. "You mentioned your mother. Is she here?"

Poppy sprang to her feet, startling everyone in the room. "Yes, I'm here! Poppy Harmon, nice to meet you all!"

The man in the middle sat up straight, as if he recognized her, but didn't say a word.

"Are you willing to house Heather at least temporarily until she can afford to rent her own place?"

"Of course, yes, I wouldn't have it any other way!" Poppy blurted out.

The woman turned back to Heather. "Would that be suitable for you, Heather?"

Heather nodded. "Yes, my mother and I get along quite well."

That remark might have been a stretch.

They had suffered through difficult times, to be sure. But they loved each other and in times of need were certainly there for each other, and Poppy was absolutely determined to be there for her daughter.

"That's good to hear. Thank you, Ms. Harmon," the third commissioner said with a slight nod.

"Thank *you*! I'm just so proud of Heather and all she has accomplished during these difficult circumstances, and I want you all to know that she is a good person who found herself in a very unfortunate unavoidable situation—"

Heather whipped around to signal her mother that she was overdoing it.

Luckily before she could embarrass herself any further, Matt reached out and squeezed Poppy's hand, then pulled her back down next to him.

"Thank you," Poppy choked out before covering her mouth to stop herself from speaking anymore.

The parole board adjourned to meet in private, but not before instructing Heather's lawyer to have Heather and her loved ones stick around for a few minutes while they discussed her case.

Poppy wasn't sure if that was a good sign or not, but she decided to remain optimistic. Usually it took up to six months for a parole board to make a decision one way or the other.

Out in the hallway, they were allowed to spend time with Heather, who was very quiet and guarded, as if she was trying not to get her hopes up too much.

Matt sat down on the bench next to her and put a comforting arm around her. "You did great. How can they not
let you out?"

"I have friends inside who went up in front of the parole
board and were certain they were going to get released
only to be denied. You just never know," Heather said
softly.

"Well, I have a good feeling!" Poppy declared, looking to Heather's lawyer, Harvey Kaplan, to back her up,
but the young, disheveled attorney just shrugged.

"Who knows?" Kaplan mumbled.

Matt kissed Heather on the cheek. "Well, I want you to
know that when you do get out I am going to be there for
you. We can pick up right where we left off, like nothing
ever happened. How does that sound?"

Heather looked at him and smiled. "You're a good
man, Matt, and that's very sweet of you to say, but I'm
going to need some time. . . ."

"Time for what?" Matt asked, confused.

"Time to put my life back together. It's been over a
year. A lot has changed. . . ."

"My feelings for you haven't!" Matt declared. "Have
*yours*?"

"No . . . ," Heather said. "They haven't."

Poppy frowned. She didn't think Heather sounded all
that convincing.

Neither did Matt, who seemed to deflate in front of
them.

She had been so worried over the possibility that Matt
might leave Heather she had never seriously considered
Heather pushing him away.

Heather took his arm. "What I said in there, about
going back to school and perhaps working toward a law

degree, that's the one concrete decision I've managed to make . . . and so I'm going to go for it. Anything beyond that, I have to take one day at a time. I'm not sure I'm ready to start, let alone resume, any kind of romantic relationship."

Matt nodded, glancing at Poppy, who was trying to stay strong and not break down and cry out of pity for Matt. He turned his gaze back to Heather and whispered, "I understand . . . honestly I do."

Poppy believed him. Although he was an actor, a good actor, and he might have just been delivering a solid, convincing performance.

A few moments later, they were called back into the room before the parole board, which announced in a unanimous decision that they were going to recommend Heather for parole.

# Chapter 27

Poppy's apartment had belonged to Heather before her incarceration, so when she brought her back to it after her release, Poppy suddenly felt displaced. In preparation for Heather's return, Poppy had moved out of the master bedroom, where she had been sleeping the last thirteen months, and set up her belongings in the smaller guest room so Heather could have her old room back. She wasn't quite sure how all of this was going to work, but she figured they would make it up as they went along. Poppy's late husband, Chester, had left her in a lot of debt, some of which she was still paying off, and she had lost her home to boot because of his gambling and financial mismanagement, so it had made sense for Poppy to take over Heather's lease on her much cheaper apartment while she was serving her sentence.

Poppy had spent much of the day restoring the two-bedroom apartment to exactly how Heather had left it so she would feel as if she was coming home to her own place and not her mother's. Poppy had hoped they could spend Heather's first night together cooking and drinking wine and making a plan for Heather to get her life back on track again, but it wasn't meant to be. Heather was lethargic and tired and excused herself to go take a nap. That had been five hours ago. It was now past eleven at night, and Poppy had made herself a sandwich and sat down at her computer to keep herself busy. She realized Heather probably was not going to wake up until the morning, so Poppy used the time to do a little research on Tony Molina's wife, Tofu.

A Google search brought up pages and pages of press interviews and fan Web sites and endless beauty shots and glamorous red carpet photos from the past thirty years, most of them dating back to before she had married Tony. Poppy assumed that Tony probably was not too keen on his wife working much after they got married. Those Italian superstars could be pretty chauvinistic, possessive, and controlling, which was why Frank Sinatra had divorced Mia Farrow in the 1960s after she refused to quit the Roman Polanski classic *Rosemary's Baby* to spend more time at home with Frank. Sinatra was Tony Molina's hero so it was more than likely that he modeled his behavior after him.

As Poppy scrolled through the countless articles on Tofu, she happened upon a short *People* magazine profile from around the time she released her biggest hit song, the one that had been used as the theme song for a James Bond movie. She was skimming the article when something popped out at her. The reporter had asked her if she always knew she wanted to be a star and Tofu answered,

"From the time I was a little girl, growing up in Abiline, Texas, I knew I was destined for greater things, and so the day I turned eighteen, I was on a bus out west with sixty dollars in my pocket and the phone number of a distant cousin who was a set decorator for soap operas. He was willing to take me in for a few months until I got on my feet."

Abilene, Texas.

The same town where Alden Kenny grew up.

And Tofu had somehow known that.

In Poppy's mind, that was just too much of a coincidence.

There had to be almost a thirty-year age difference between Tofu and Alden.

But it was at least something to finally go on.

Poppy went to bed in the guest room, but the mattress was lumpy and unfamiliar and she didn't get a wink of sleep. Finally, she rose at five in the morning, showered, dressed, made some coffee, and watched the news. She waited for Heather to finally rise from the dead, but when she still hadn't stirred by eight-thirty, Poppy scribbled a note to call her and she left for the Desert Flowers garage office at Iris's house. She had no intention of waking Heather up. The poor thing probably hadn't had a decent night's rest in over a year. She deserved to sleep in for as long as she desired.

Violet was already at the office when Poppy arrived, sweeping and dusting and polishing. Violet was a bit of a neat freak, which was just fine with Poppy, who despised all housework.

"Is Iris still in the house?" Poppy asked.

"No, she had an early golf game this morning at the club," Violet said.

Poppy frowned. She was anxious to sit down with everyone and rally them to help her look into the Alden Kenny case now that Rod no longer needed or wanted their services. When Poppy brought Violet up to speed on the Abilene connection between Alden and Tofu, Violet excitedly scurried over to the desktop computer.

"Wyatt had me buy this new computer program for the office that he said would help us with our cases!" Violet gushed. "It sounds so high tech! It's some kind of a facial recognition program!"

"How much did that set us back?" Poppy asked, not sure she wanted to know.

"Three hundred dollars," Violet said. Sensing Poppy bristling, she quickly added, "Not to worry. It was my treat!"

Violet put on her reading glasses, fired up the computer, and clicked on the program, which was in the center of the desktop display. "Wyatt's been teaching me how to use it. I'm not very good at it yet, but I'm getting there."

It took forty minutes for Violet to figure out how to upload a photo, but eventually she managed to attach a recent picture of Tofu. Then it took another hour and fifteen minutes for her to figure out how to actually run the program. But after a lot of false starts and enough time for Poppy to go out for some Danish at Starbucks and return before Violet got it working, they finally hit pay dirt. The Abilene High School had put digital versions of all its yearbooks dating back to the early 1970s online, so running the current photo of Tofu against all the photos on the Abilene High Web site finally resulted in a match.

"Oh goodness, Poppy, I think I did it!" Violet cried.

Poppy tossed her Danish down on the little kitchenette

counter and rushed over to Violet and hovered over her. Next to the recent picture of Tofu was a black-and-white photo of a pretty young girl with her hair in a barrette and a full smile with a mouthful of crooked teeth. She wasn't nearly as attractive as her adult self.

"Her name is Maria Martinez and she graduated Abilene High in nineteen seventy-nine."

"She must have gotten braces in college!" Poppy declared.

"Alden Kenny graduated in twenty twelve," Violet noted, bringing up his photo. "He looks exactly the same way as he did in the photo that was in the newspaper."

"I wonder if he knew that Tony Molina's wife went to the same high school as he did," Poppy said. "That is a really big coincidence, right?"

Violet nodded. "But it could just be a *coincidence*."

Poppy wasn't buying it.

She felt there had to be more to it, especially since Tofu automatically knew Alden was from Abilene when it had never been mentioned in the press. Where had she gotten that information? Or was she aware of it because she already knew Alden Kenny before her husband's trial?

The opportunity to find the answer literally burst through the door at that very moment.

Iris was back from her golf game. She was in a buoyant mood and practically bouncing off the walls from the moment she entered the office. Iris was never one to wear her emotions on her sleeve, so Poppy assumed she had just come from an extraordinarily successful golf game.

"A hole in one!" Iris boasted. "I could not believe it myself! You should have seen the looks on the other ladies' faces!"

"Congratulations, Iris! I'm so happy for you! Violet

and I have had a successful morning, too. Violet bought this facial recognition program and—"

"May I please relish in my victory for just a few more moments, if you don't mind?" Iris scoffed.

"I'm sorry, it's just that Violet and I are working on a case—"

"What case? We were just fired from our one and only case!" Iris wailed.

"I'm talking about Alden Kenny," Poppy tried to explain. "And for the record, we were *not* fired!"

"Who is the client? You? Are you paying us? And how much did this facial recognition contraption cost us?" Iris asked.

"Five hundred dollars," Violet said.

Poppy twisted her head around and stared at Violet. "You said *three* hundred!"

"I know, I shaved off a couple hundred because I didn't want you getting mad that I spent that much until you saw how helpful it could be," Violet said sheepishly. "But now you see how valuable it is. We found Tofu!"

Poppy had to agree. "It's really a wonderful program. We were able to match a photo of Tofu taken recently with one—"

"I don't care!" Iris said. "I was out on the golf course—"

"Hitting a hole in one, we know," Poppy muttered.

"It was a masterful stroke, once in a lifetime, but do you think I was out there just having fun? No, while you two were here playing computer games, I was out there getting us invited to Dena Cantwell's cocktail party tomorrow."

"I'm not sure I'm up for socializing right now, Iris," Poppy said.

"Who said anything about socializing? Do you know

who Dena Cantwell is?" Iris asked pointedly, folding her arms, annoyed.

"I've heard of her!" Violet said, shooting her hand in the air. "She's very rich and she gives millions of dollars to the arts and is the center of the Palm Springs social scene."

"She is also friends with Tony Molina and his wife, Tenderloin or Turmeric or whatever her name is," Iris said.

"Tofu," Violet said with a helpful smile.

Iris threw her hands up, losing patience. "Whatever! Who cares! Whenever Tony is in town, he always makes a point of attending Dena's cocktail parties. And so after I whipped Dena's butt on the golf course this morning, and she saw firsthand what a superior golfer I am, especially after scoring a hole in one, if I forgot to mention that, and after shaming her in front of all her friends by mentioning how she has never invited me to one of her fancy parties—"

"She invited you," Poppy said, nodding.

"Yes, under duress. Her rich, snooty friends practically demanded it after I scored that hole in one! I'm a legend at that club now! I told her I would be happy to attend, and I would be bringing a few friends along with me. She didn't dare say no. So now you can pump Tony and his wife all you want about this Alden Kenny kid."

"Iris, I don't know what to say," Poppy said, moving forward to hug her.

Iris backed away. "I am *not* big into hugs, Poppy."

"Right. I forgot," Poppy said, backing off.

"But I *am* open to your praise," Iris said.

"And you are the best investigator at Desert Flowers. Going out there and snagging us party invitations to help us get answers to the Alden Kenny murder," Poppy said.

"Actually I wasn't thinking about that at the time. I just wanted to be invited to one of Dena Cantwell's parties, but I guess it all worked out for the best. What about you, Violet? What nice things do you have to say about me?"

"Gosh, I've never really done well under pressure," Violet said.

"I scored a hole in one, Violet. Does that help you?" Iris huffed.

Violet nodded and quickly piped in, "You are the best golfer in the world, Iris! You could win the Dinah Shore tournament if you wanted to next year!"

"Thank you. I appreciate your kind words," Iris said.

Poppy was more than happy to indulge her.

Because she was about to be in the same room as Tony Molina and his wife, Tofu, again, as well as many of their friends, who knew a lot more about them.

And she was certain chances were good that somebody at that cocktail party would have direct knowledge as to why Alden Kenny ended up floating facedown dead in his swimming pool.

# Chapter 28

Dena Cantwell's cocktail party was held at her palatial home located in the Thunderbird Country Club in Rancho Mirage, the same exclusive gated community where former President Gerald Ford and his wife, Betty, once resided. According to Iris, Dena made her money from her family's worldwide liquor distribution business as well as her late husband's real estate investments. Iris, who was from far more modest means, still captured the attention of the partygoers as word of her astounding hole in one the day before spread far and wide. Iris, of course, basked in all the glory, as she recounted the fateful moment when she realized her golf ball that was racing across the green after her perfect swing was destined to drop in that tiny hole and make history.

Poppy, who huddled with Violet and Matt in a corner, kept scanning the crowd for Tony and Tofu Molina, but they still had not arrived. Poppy was starting to fear they might be no-shows, but finally, just as she was about to give up hope, the front door swung open, and Tony, looking rested and happy, breezed in with his wife, Tofu, on his arm. Tony glad-handed a few buddies by the bar as Tofu floated over to Dena to alert her that they had finally arrived, giving the hostess an air kiss on both cheeks.

Poppy dispatched Matt to mingle with the other guests, and Violet headed toward the bar while Poppy casually made her way toward Tony. If she had any apprehension that he might not remember her from the trial and the restaurant, that worry was quickly dispelled when his eyes fell upon her and he immediately lit up with a bright smile.

"Well, if it isn't the lovely Poppy Harmon," Tony said, excusing himself from his rat pack at the bar. "Why do we keep running into each other like this? Is someone trying to tell us something?"

Poppy smiled demurely. "We do seem to run in the same circles."

"How do you know Dena?"

"I don't. I came with a friend."

Tony waved Dena over to them. She was an elegant show horse, preening and proud and immaculately put together. She eyed Poppy warily and said as she extended a bony arm, "Hello, I'm Dena."

"This is Poppy Harmon," Tony said, speaking for her. "She was a juror at my trial."

"Oh!" Dena exclaimed. "Well, we are very grateful you didn't send our poor Tony to the big house. He would have struggled mightily without his afternoon golf game and nineteenth-hole dry martini."

Poppy refrained from mentioning that if it had been up to her she would have sent him straight to the big house for a long time.

So did Tony.

"It's lovely to meet you, Dena," Poppy said, shaking her hand.

Dena studied her intently, trying to figure out just what she was doing here. "I'm so happy you could come."

Poppy decided to help her out. "I am a friend of Iris Becker's. Part of her plus-three."

Dena lit up and smiled. "Iris is the big hero at the club! She's certainly got a lot of tongues wagging around here." She turned to Tony. "The hole in one I was telling you about."

Tony nodded. "Our resident Tiger Woods."

"If Tiger were an outspoken, imposing German woman in her sixties," Poppy added.

Dena and Tony both laughed.

"Well, make yourself at home, Poppy, and help yourself to a drink at the bar. Tony, there is someone I want you to meet," Dena said, steering Tony away.

Poppy turned to see Tofu at the bar, sucking down a cosmo, glaring at her. She wondered if Tofu had signaled Dena to get her husband away from Poppy. But then, Tofu turned her attention toward the handsome young bartender, who mixed her another drink as she flirted with him, giggling and playfully touching his arm.

Poppy walked over to Matt, who was charming a gaggle of older women near some expensive-looking Art Deco pieces, and whispered in his ear, "She's by the bar."

Matt nodded and whispered back, "I'm going in." Then he turned and flashed that megawatt smile that he had been blessed with at his bevy of admirers, who had been hanging on his every word. "Excuse me, ladies."

They practically sighed with disappointment as he scooted off to find Tofu. Poppy wandered over to Violet, who was standing alone in a corner, nursing a glass of white wine. "Why are you hiding all the way over here?"

"This is not exactly my crowd," Violet said. "Too rich for my blood. I wouldn't know what to say to these people."

"How about 'Hi, my name is Violet,'" Poppy suggested.

"I'm much more comfortable over here away from everybody, you know, keeping an eye on things. Let me tell you, that Tofu gal is quite the operator. In the time it's taken me to drink half a glass of Pinot Grigio, she's tried picking up three different men."

Poppy glanced over at the bar, where Tofu had just abandoned her efforts to snag the bartender and was now laser focused on Matt, who was no doubt reeling her in with his unbridled charm. Poppy scanned the crowd for Tony, to make sure he was preoccupied and not about to have a jealous fit if he saw the handsome young actor captivating his wife, but luckily he was still chatting with Dena and a couple of her super-rich friends.

"Tofu obviously has an attraction to much younger men," Violet said, trying not to ooze judgment but ultimately failing. "Just what do you hope to accomplish here, Poppy? Besides helping boost Iris's ego, not that she needs it!"

Iris was still reliving her defining moment on the golf course, surrounded by a half-dozen fans in the center of the room, without a thought or care about why they had crashed Dena Cantwell's cocktail party in the first place.

"This is Tofu's primary social circle. These people probably know her better than anyone. I'm betting someone here can tell us something about her predilection for young men, and if one of those men happened to be Alden Kenny."

"That sounds like a real long shot to me," Violet said, looking around at the intimidating crowd, not eager to go talk to any of them.

"It only takes one, Violet," Poppy said. "Matt's working on Tofu so why don't you strike up a conversation with one of the guests."

"I wouldn't know who to start with," Violet protested.

Poppy looked around and settled on an elderly woman with a hunched back and granny glasses, her white hair in a bun, sipping a glass of white wine. "Start with her. She likes white wine, too. That's your icebreaker. I'm going to talk to a few of the men smoking cigars outside by the pool."

Violet sized the old woman up, decided she could handle her, and shuffled off toward her. Poppy glided out to the pool and spent the next twenty minutes chatting up a few of the men, who were more interested in talking investments and sports than about Tony Molina's one-hit-wonder wife. Frustrated and bored, Poppy wandered back inside to see Tofu literally hanging off Matt as he entertained her with yet another story. Tony was still downing martinis with a couple of his buddies and was mercifully oblivious. Iris was nowhere to be seen although Poppy suspected she was now outside on the front lawn re-creating her now famous swing that led to that hole in one. And Violet was still immersed in conversation with the old woman who was fond of white wine. Finally, the two women hugged, and Violet excitedly bounded over to Poppy.

"You were right! She was a fountain of information!" Violet cried.

Poppy was taken aback.

She hadn't seriously expected Violet to get anywhere with the old woman. She just wanted to give her something to do so she wouldn't feel bad about being a wallflower at the party. "What did she say?"

"Lydia—that's the woman over there, she is such a dear—well, she told me that Tofu has had an unhealthy attraction toward much younger men for years, boys even young enough to be her grandson!"

"How did Lydia know about that?"

"Pretty much everyone knows. It's an open secret around here. Tofu is not exactly discreet, according to Lydia," Violet said, waving at her new friend, who adjusted her granny glasses and grinned and waved back as she stood in line for another white wine at the bar.

"What about Tony? Does he know?" Poppy asked.

"He tolerates it because, according to Lydia, it makes his life easier. He can have his own dalliances without having to worry about Tofu complaining and causing a ruckus. She would be the world's biggest hypocrite if she did, so the unspoken arrangement basically works."

"The key to a happy open marriage," Poppy remarked. "More power to them, I guess."

"They never had a problem until last year. Lydia, who is about to be a great-grandmother, isn't that wonderful news; her granddaughter in Phoenix is about to give birth to twins, a boy and a girl—"

"Violet, that's lovely, but can we stay on point?"

"Of course, it's just that she is the sweetest thing and we exchanged numbers and I am so happy you made me go over there because I hardly expected to make a new friend today—"

"Violet . . ."

"Right, sorry. Anyway, last year Tofu went home to Texas for her mother's funeral, and apparently while she was there she had a brief fling with a local boy, the son of the preacher who delivered the sermon at the memorial service."

"Alden Kenny?"

Violet shook her head. "Lydia never heard his name, but it was quite the scandal. Tony was touring Canada at the time and couldn't be there, which allowed Tofu to get up to her old tricks! Well, after she returned to Palm Springs, she thought that was the end of it. But it wasn't. The boy she left behind was head over heels in love with her and couldn't let her go, and so he followed her out here from Texas like a puppy dog, with love in his eyes."

"And by this time Tony was home from his tour?"

"That's right! He caught the kid leaving flowers for Tofu outside the gate of their estate and all hell broke loose! Lydia said Tony threatened to kill him if he didn't leave his wife alone! And so the kid, fearing for his life, apparently did what he was told because that's the last they heard of him. Lydia assumed he went back to Texas."

"But he didn't. He stuck around. And I'm betting his name was Alden Kenny, who went in on a carpet-cleaning business with a friend in order to make a living. I'm certain if we do a little digging about his past in Abilene, we'll find out he was the son of a preacher man."

"Isn't that the title of a song?"

"Yes, Violet."

"I did good, didn't I?" Violet asked, an expectant look on her face.

"Violet, you are a rock star," Poppy said, proudly patting her on the back.

Poppy homed in on Tofu, who was leading Matt by the hand over to the couch, where they sat down to continue their flirtatious conversation.

How on earth did Alden Kenny wind up as a juror for Tony Molina's assault trial?

And how did his history with the defendant's wife not come out during the jury selection process?

It left Poppy to wonder, was it sheer coincidence or had Alden Kenny, as she had long suspected, been a plant?

And did that have anything to do with why he was murdered?

# Chapter 29

The following morning, Iris was not at all pleased when Poppy strong-armed her into calling Jay Takamura, Alden Kenny's friend and business partner, and asking him out to dinner. It had been quite clear when Iris had first hired the sprightly eager young entrepreneur to clean her carpets that he carried a not-so-secret torch for her. And so it made perfect sense for the detectives at Desert Flowers to use that to their advantage. Given Iris's rather remote and brusque personality, Jay at first thought it must be some kind of prank when he answered his cell and it was the elusive Iris Becker.

"Iris, is this really you?" Jay asked hesitantly.

"Of course it is me. Who else would it be?" Iris barked as she sat on the couch in the garage office of the agency, surrounded by Poppy, Violet, and Matt.

"I just didn't think you were interested in me," Jay said.

"Have you never heard of playing hard to get?" Iris asked pointedly.

"Well, yes, but if that was what you were doing when I was over at your house the other day, then you were playing really, really hard."

"I play to win. Do you want to have dinner with me or not?" Iris sighed, getting annoyed at the entire conversation.

"Yes, I'd like that very much," Jay said, starting to get excited that this was real and actually happening.

Violet poked her in the arm and signaled to her to be nicer.

Iris hated being nice, but she reluctantly went along with the helpful advice. "You are a very nice man, and as far as I can tell you have very good taste if you want to spend more time with me, so we might as well have a meal together and see how it goes."

It wasn't exactly whispering sweet nothings in his ear, but it would have to do.

The important thing was that Jay was buying it.

"How about tonight?" Jay suggested.

"Let me check my schedule," Iris huffed, putting down the phone, counting to ten, and then picking it up and pressing it to her ear again. "That will be fine."

"Shall I pick you up at your place? I still have your address in my phone from when I came over to clean your rugs."

"No! I will come to you!" Iris said quickly.

Jay told her seven o'clock and then hung up before Iris could change her mind. The plan had worked. Iris would go over to Jay's house, the same house he had shared with Alden, and they would leave for dinner. Iris would make a note of the security code of the house and text it to Poppy, who would be waiting around the corner with Violet and Matt to use the code to gain entry and search for any clues that might lead to why someone would want to kill Alden Kenny.

Iris had argued vigorously against this cockamamie plan, but once Matt buttered her up by explaining how Jay simply could not resist her classic beauty and sparkling personality, and was clearly blinded by her celebrity as a now legendary golfer in the Coachella Valley, Iris finally relented. She explained her reasoning for finally going along with the hair-brained scheme: "I might as well use this power for good."

When Iris showed up at Jay's house, he suggested they have a cocktail by the pool since their dinner reservation wasn't until eight, but Iris refused, explaining she didn't want to sit near a pool where a corpse had been floating around like an inflatable pink flamingo. Jay said he understood and quickly ushered her out the door, suggesting they have a cocktail at the restaurant's bar instead. Just as Poppy had instructed, Iris managed to memorize the security code and text it to Poppy as they left, and within minutes, Poppy, Matt, and Violet were inside the house with flashlights searching desk drawers and closets.

After forty-five minutes, they still had turned up nothing. Poppy was starting to believe their efforts had been a waste when suddenly Violet discovered a manila folder of Alden Kenny's personal papers lying among some other items—a stack of old Prince CDs, a beer bong, and some vintage Playboy magazines—in a cardboard box underneath his bed. As Violet pulled some old store and restaurant receipts from a trash can to go through, Poppy spread the personal papers out on the floor. She and Matt spent the next half hour sifting through them all. They quickly found a few items of interest. According to his recent bank statements Alden's account had been overdrawn. There was also a threatening note from the IRS and two jury summons. Poppy checked the dates on each summons and gasped.

"What? What did you find?" Violet asked, poring through her own stack of receipts and wadded up balls of paper in the trash can.

"These two separate jury summonses," Poppy said. "They're from the same year. There is one from February, where he showed up and was not put on a trial, and then this second one, which was right about the time of the Tony Molina trial."

"So?" Matt asked, not understanding the significance.

"No one is called twice in one year to serve jury duty. Once you have fulfilled your obligation, even if you are not selected to serve on a jury, they don't call you again for at least a year. He was summoned four months later."

"Maybe it was a clerical error," Violet said, shrugging.

"Maybe, but maybe it wasn't," Poppy said, suddenly suspicious. "And if it was a clerical error, why didn't he bring the first summons with him to the courthouse to get out of jury service? Unless he *wanted* to be called!"

Matt suddenly jumped to his feet. "What was that?"

"What?" Violet asked.

"I heard something," he said before bounding out of Alden's bedroom and into the living room.

A few seconds later he raced back in. "They're home!"

"*Already?*" Poppy cried, checking her watch. "They've only been gone a little over an hour."

"They just pulled into the driveway!" Matt urgently whispered.

Poppy scrambled to her feet as Violet frantically tossed all the papers back into the box and shoved it underneath the bed where she had found it.

"We can sneak out the back by the pool," Poppy said in a hushed tone.

The three of them hurried out of the bedroom into the hallway and were halfway toward the sliding glass door that led outside to the backyard when the front door swung open and Jay, accompanied by Iris, walked inside.

"I swear I set the security code when we left," Jay said, confused.

"You were nervous and trying to impress me so perhaps you just got flummoxed and forgot," Iris suggested helpfully.

Poppy, Matt, and Violet were trapped in the hallway. If they made a dash for the sliding glass door now, Jay would surely spot them from the living room. Poppy waved for Matt and Violet to follow her and they quickly doubled back, scurrying into a small bathroom off the hallway.

"How about a nightcap?" Jay asked Iris.

"No, as I told you in the car, I just need to use the ladies' room and then I will be on my way," Iris said.

"Down the hall to the right," Jay said. "I'm going to make myself a scotch. Give me a holler if you change your mind."

Poppy could hear Iris approaching. The three of them had piled into the bathtub and whipped the curtain closed to hide. Iris walked in and shut the door behind her. She was checking herself out in the mirror when Poppy slowly drew the light blue curtain back and whispered, "Iris . . ."

Iris let out a whoop and jumped back, her eyes nearly popping out of her head at the sight of Poppy, Matt, and Violet crowded in the bathtub behind a shower curtain.

They heard Jay pounding down the hall. "Is everything okay in there?"

"Yes. Why?" Iris barked.

"I thought I heard you scream," Jay said from behind the door.

"I don't scream," Iris growled. "I'll take a bourbon straight up."

"Coming right up," Jay said, sounding delighted that she had decided to stay a while longer.

When she was certain he was gone, Iris turned back to her Desert Flowers partners. "What are you still doing here?"

"We didn't expect you back so soon. You were barely gone an hour," Poppy whispered.

"We had a cocktail, an appetizer, and an entree. You can only drag that out for so long," Iris sniffed.

"You couldn't have stayed for dessert?" Matt asked.

"You know I have been trying to cut down on my carbs," Iris said huffily.

"How are we going to get out of here?" Violet asked in a hushed tone.

Matt jumped out of the bathtub. He took Poppy's hand to help her out and then did the same for Violet.

Poppy whipped around to Iris. "You're going to have to distract him so we can slip out!"

"How am I supposed to do that?" Iris asked.

Matt grinned. "Oh, I'm sure you will think of something."

Iris wasn't sure what he meant at first, but as it slowly began to sink in, she snorted and hissed, "Not on your life. He is half my age."

"He's a third of your age if you want to quibble about it," Violet said a bit too loudly.

"Nobody asked you, Violet," Iris almost yelled.

"Shhhh! Quiet, everybody," Poppy insisted. "He's going to hear us."

Matt tried keeping his voice really low. "I'm not suggesting you go to bed with him, just be nice and flirty and keep him busy enough so he doesn't see us leaving."

After a few more minutes back and forth, Iris finally agreed to do what she could, but she stopped short of leaving the bathroom.

"What is it now, Iris?" Poppy asked.

"The reason I came in here is I have to go," Iris said, embarrassed.

"Go where?" Matt asked.

The women turned and stared at him and then he quickly got caught up. "*Oh . . .*"

"Everybody turn around," Poppy said, herding Violet and Matt back into the tub and closing the curtain as Iris lifted her skirt.

"I have never been more humiliated in all my life!" Iris wailed.

After washing her hands and applying some hand and face lotion from her purse as well as a spritz of perfume, Iris marched back out like a soldier heading into battle.

Poppy, Matt, and Violet waited a few minutes, and then Matt opened the door a crack and strained to hear their conversation. He waved Poppy and Violet to follow and they all crept down the hall until they could hear Jay talking.

"I'm so happy you decided to stay," he said.

Poppy peered around the corner from the hallway to see Jay and Iris sitting next to each other on the couch. Jay had an arm draped over the back, his hand almost touching Iris's hair. She was trying hard to smile but she was clearly hating every moment of this.

Poppy, Matt, and Violet silently made a move for the sliding glass door. Matt took a deep breath and tried opening it. It made enough of a noise for Jay to notice.

"Did you hear—?"

Before he could turn his head, Iris grabbed him by the back of the neck and yanked him forward, jamming her mouth over his. Surprised at first, Jay jerked away from her, but once it dawned on him what was actually happening, he excitedly wrapped his arms around Iris and hugged her tightly as they fell back on the couch, Iris on top, kissing passionately.

Poppy had to suppress a giggle as they all quietly padded out of the house, and then Matt gently closed the glass door behind them. The three investigators disappeared into the darkness, leaving Iris with her fresh-faced, enthusiastic admirer.

# Chapter 30

It didn't take long for Glenda Felson to buckle under pressure.

Especially when questioned by the imposing, intimidating, stone-faced Detective Lamar Jordan, who hovered over her in her cramped office adjacent to the jury assembly room at the Larson Justice Center in Indio.

Poppy stood just outside the office, not wanting to crowd the elderly woman, who was short, stout, with an obvious wig and a bit too much makeup. She sat at her desk, which was cluttered with knickknacks and Post-it Notes scribbled with daily affirmations, and stared up at the handsome but stern face of Detective Jordan.

"Bless your heart, coming all the way from Palm Springs to chat with me," Glenda cooed. "Especially this time of day with all the traffic. I feel so important."

"Well, this is a very serious matter, ma'am," Detective Jordan said.

Poppy knew in her gut that she had done the right thing calling in Detective Jordan. After all, she had no client to satisfy in this matter. She was operating on pure curiosity and determination to find out what had happened to Alden Kenny. And now, with the mounting evidence that Alden had been romantically involved with Tofu, that he had been mysteriously called twice in one year for jury duty and had miraculously landed on the jury for the Tony Molina trial, where he had stubbornly refused to acknowledge the plain hard incriminating facts, unlike his eleven other peers, there was something rotten in Indio.

Instead of dispatching her troops to get the truth from the woman responsible for the two jury summonses sent to Alden Kenny, Poppy felt Glenda might cave more quickly if confronted with an actual police detective who had the authority to place her under arrest for any crimes she was covering up.

Detective Jordan had been surprised when Poppy contacted him and brought him up to speed on what she had discovered. Instead of scolding her for poking her nose into affairs that clearly did not concern her, he very politely thanked her and assured her he would follow up on the information later that afternoon. Poppy, of course, couldn't help herself and drove straight to the courthouse, which was a half-hour drive from Palm Springs, and was parking her car in the lot adjacent to the criminal courts building when Detective Jordan arrived in his Nissan Sentra and pulled into the space next to her.

He raised an eyebrow and shook his head as Poppy offered him a friendly wave while getting out of her car. He scowled at her and she knew he probably would not be as polite as he had been when she initially called him at the police precinct with her information.

Detective Jordan jumped out of his Sentra and approached Poppy with a sigh. "I don't suppose you're here because you're fighting a parking ticket?"

"No, if you don't mind, I'd like to see what this woman in jury service has to say," Poppy said, following close on his heels as he marched toward the security line outside the building.

"What if I *do* mind?" Jordan asked brusquely.

"I would feel bad because the last thing I want to do is irritate you, but since the courthouse is a public space, and legally I am allowed to be there—"

"Just let me do the talking, okay?" Jordan said, giving up arguing with her.

After passing through security, Poppy followed Detective Jordan up to the second floor, where they found Glenda Felson shuffling through papers in her office. Before she could make time for them, she had to call a pool of jurors for a trial selection process. Once that was finished, and she excused herself to go get a candy bar from the vending machine because she was feeling tired and was in desperate need of a sugar rush to get her to five o'clock and quitting time, she was finally ready to entertain questions from Detective Jordan in her office.

After a quick exchange of pleasantries, Jordan, who was already losing patience, got right down to business as Poppy listened intently a few feet away outside in the hallway.

"Mrs. Felson, do you know Alden Kenny?"

She blinked a couple of times as she seemed to roil the name over in her mind. "It sounds vaguely familiar. But as you probably know, I see a lot of different names every day. Some are so difficult to pronounce. Take this one, for example." She picked up a jury card. "T-o-n-e. You might pronounce it like the music term. Tone. Or Tony. But no, she is Norwegian and very snootily corrected me, and said it is pronounced '*Tuna*'!"

"That's nice, but I want to talk to you about Alden Kenny," Jordan said.

Glenda shrugged. "No, I don't think I know him."

"That's strange because you called him twice for jury duty in one year," Jordan said, taking a step closer, showing her the two summonses, crowding her to the point where it got uncomfortable for her.

She took a bite of her candy bar, presumably to buy herself some time and get her story straight. "You cannot be called for jury duty twice in one year."

"I know, that's why I'm here," Jordan said.

Poppy watched Glenda slowly start to crumble although she was still valiantly attempting to act completely innocent. "I'm sure it was just a technical glitch with the computer, nothing I did wrong." As she spoke, she looked more and more guilty and she clutched what was left of her candy bar as if it were a lifeline.

"I don't believe you," Detective Jordan said, folding his arms, staring down at her accusingly.

The chocolate began melting and she quickly licked her fingers. "Well, I'm sorry about that but it's the truth!"

"Did someone *pay* you to call Alden Kenny for jury duty and make sure he was in the pool for the Tony Molina trial?"

"Nobody paid me! I never took a dime! They said—"
She caught herself and stopped talking. She popped the
rest of the gooey candy bar into her mouth as if a face full
of chocolate would be reason enough not to confess.

Detective Jordan was not done putting the squeeze on
her. "Stop lying, Glenda. You're in enough trouble as it
is. Work with me now, and I'll try to go easier on you
later. Now who is *they*?"

Glenda's sweet, breezy personality was melting fast.
She was now a bundle of nerves and her whole body was
spasming with fear. "I don't remember their names. It
was a man and a woman. . . ."

"*Who?!*" Jordan shouted.

Glenda hesitated. "I don't remember!"

Poppy guessed the couple who had paid a visit to
Glenda might be Tony Molina's married bodyguards, the
ones she had met at Chef Cicci's restaurant after the trial.
Detective Jordan just had to get Glenda to admit it.

"And they asked you to send out a summons to Alden
Kenny?"

Glenda stared at the floor, her eyes filling with tears.

"Glenda, look at me!" Jordan barked.

She did what she was told.

"Did they pay you to call Alden Kenny for jury service?" he asked.

She shook her head. "No, I already told you, I didn't
take their money."

"Then why did you do it?" Jordan asked, confused.

"Because I love Tony. He's so handsome and sweet
and he's got the voice of an angel. . . ."

Poppy thought it was awfully lucky that Tony Molina
had found an unabashed fan in the jury service office.
Without the exchange of money, it was a cleaner bribe.

Jordan looked at her, incredulous. "And so you just agreed to do it? Because you're a *fan*?"

"He was being railroaded! The district attorney was just trying to score political points by going after someone famous!" Glenda cried.

"I bet Tony promised to meet you and personally thank you after all the hoopla died down," Poppy said to herself, then realized she had spoken loud enough for Jordan and Glenda to hear because they were both looking at her. "Excuse me," she muttered.

Glenda didn't deny it.

"Could you identify the couple who approached you?" Detective Jordan asked.

Glenda, who knew she had revealed far too much already, suddenly became defiant. "No! It was in the parking lot after work, and it was dark out, and I didn't have my glasses on, so I'm afraid I couldn't possibly tell you what they looked like. . . . But I do know they most certainly did *not* work for Tony Molina, of that I am quite sure. No, they had no connection to Tony at all. I have no idea who wanted Alden Kenny on that jury. I'm sorry I can't be of more help," Glenda insisted.

The phone on her desk rang and she picked it up. "Yes? Okay, right away." She hung up and started frantically shuffling through her jury cards. "I'm sorry, but I have to get back to work. Judge Hayes in courtroom four is ready to bring in some prospective jurors."

Detective Jordan pulled out some handcuffs. "I'm sorry to tell you this, Glenda, but I'm placing you under arrest."

"Whatever for?" Glenda asked, wide eyed.

Jordan couldn't believe he had to tell her at this point. "Jury tampering."

He snapped the cuffs on Glenda's wrist and escorted her out of her office into the hallway, where Poppy stood watching.

A younger woman, maybe in her midforties, suddenly appeared, her eyes big, her mouth open in shock. "Glenda, what's happening?"

"Nothing, dear," Glenda said, refusing to accept the fact that she was being arrested. "I have a little personal issue I need to deal with. Can you cover for me for a few minutes?"

The woman nodded and watched in horror as Detective Jordan led Glenda away. Poppy turned to the woman. "Just so you know, this might take more than a few minutes. Glenda is probably going to need to take some vacation time."

Poppy then hurried off after Detective Jordan.

# Chapter 31

"Are you sure you don't want me to go to a movie tonight with Iris and Violet?" Poppy asked as Heather checked on her bubbling tray of turkey lasagna that was heating in the oven.

"Of course not," Heather said, sliding the rack back inside the oven and shutting the door. "This is just as much your home as it is mine. You don't need to go anywhere. Would you please open the wine and let it breathe?"

"Certainly," Poppy said, picking up the wine bottle opener and screwing it down into the cork. "I just thought maybe you and Matt would like to enjoy some alone time without me hovering around all night."

"Please, hover. I want you to hover," Heather said with a wry smile. "Matt is desperate to have a serious talk about our relationship and I'm just not ready to do that. I need you here as a buffer."

"You can't put it off forever," Poppy said as gently as she could. She popped the cork out of the bottle of Merlot and set it down on the counter next to three wine glasses that had been set out.

"I know, but I just got out. I haven't even met with my parole officer yet or gotten a job or applied to any schools. It's very overwhelming. I need time to get my act together and sort things out before I can address any kind of future with Matt."

"I completely understand," Poppy said. "I'm happy to gorge on your homemade turkey lasagna then."

"Thank you, Mother," Heather said before reaching out and taking her mother's hand. "Thank you for being here for me . . . for everything."

"You have no reason to thank me. It's a mother's job to take care of her children."

"Children, yes. But I'm past thirty. It's rather embarrassing for me to be living with my mother at this point."

"There is *nothing* to be embarrassed about. Everyone goes through a rough patch. Look at what happened to me after Chester died and I found out I had nothing. It takes time to get back on your feet."

Heather let go of Poppy's hand. "I'm going to work hard to make you proud of me."

"I'm already proud of you," Poppy said.

The doorbell rang and Heather crossed over to answer it. Matt, looking dashing in an open yellow shirt and blue blazer and bearing a bouquet of fresh flowers, leaned in for a kiss. Poppy saw Heather stiffen for a moment and hoped that Matt hadn't noticed it when he landed a peck on her cheek. He then handed her the flowers.

"They're lovely, Matt. Thank you," Heather said. "Please, come in."

Matt bounded into the apartment, waving at Poppy. "Hey, boss! I heard you were at the courthouse today when the cops arrested that woman for jury tampering."

"Our instinct was right. It was not a clerical error. Tony Molina wanted to make sure Alden Kenny got selected for that jury, and the young man did his job. He made sure the judge was forced to declare a mistrial. Of course, with Glenda Felson refusing to identify Tony's bodyguards as the two who approached her, the police can't prove anything yet."

"I'm going to put these in water," Heather said, thoroughly uninterested as she crossed back to the kitchen carrying the flowers.

Poppy started pouring wine into the glasses while Heather filled an empty green vase with water from the sink.

"I was listening to the news on the way over here. Molina has gone on the offensive," Matt said. "He swears that he has no idea who Glenda Felson is and that he is one hundred percent innocent and will sue anyone who suggests otherwise. Can you believe that?"

Poppy shook her head. "He sounds desperate and scared."

"He should be. The prosecutor is on the warpath and has promised to retry the assault case against him, and not only that, she plans to pile on a bunch of new charges, including the jury tampering," Matt said, crossing around the island to Heather's side. "Can I help?"

His sudden presence next to her startled Heather, who gasped, and then turned and smiled at him. "No, I have everything under control. You talk to Mother."

Poppy finished pouring the wine and handed them each a glass and then picked up hers and raised it. "I would like to propose a toast. . . ."

Heather and Matt also raised their glasses.

"To my daughter, Heather, who we are so happy to finally have home again," Poppy said, choking back tears.

"Here's to that," Matt said happily as he took a gulp of wine.

Heather smiled shyly, not one to enjoy being the center of attention, and took a small sip before setting the glass back down and tending to her lasagna, which she pulled out of the oven using a pair of mitts. She set it down on a rack on the counter to cool and then opened the refrigerator and took out a wooden bowl with greens in it.

"Why don't you two take a seat at the table and I'll serve the salad," Heather said.

Poppy and Matt did as instructed while Heather picked up some tongs and began tossing the greens in the wooden bowl after adding some homemade dressing.

"So Tony Molina gets his goons to convince Glenda at the courthouse to call Alden Kenny for jury duty, but why *him*? Why pick the guy who was having an affair with your wife?" Matt wondered, then gulped down some more wine.

"That's the big question, but once Glenda Felson figures out the DA has an airtight case against her, she will hopefully finally cooperate and identify the couple who came to see her and ask her to help Tony," Poppy said.

Matt leaned forward. "Do you think Tony had Alden Kenny killed in order to make sure he never talked about what he had done, you know, as a way to tie up a loose end?"

Poppy nodded confidently. "That sounds exactly like what a typical mafia don would do, and if Tony Molina reminds me of anything, it's a mafia don. I'm sure Detective Jordan will have this whole thing wrapped up in no time."

Heather appeared with salad plates and set them down

in front of Poppy and Matt. Poppy suddenly felt bad about
talking business.

"No more shop talk. Let's enjoy this lovely meal Heather has prepared for us," Poppy said.

"I'll drink to that," Matt said, swallowing the rest of his
wine.

As they made their way through the salad course,
Poppy tried steering the conversation back to Heather
and her plans, but Heather answered in one-word sen-
tences or with a simple shrug.

Matt put a hand on top of Heather's as she set her salad
fork down. "Whatever you decide to do with your life,
I'm sure you'll be a huge success."

Heather withdrew her hand from underneath his just as
Poppy had done with Rod recently. Matt looked down at
the table, crestfallen. Poppy felt terrible for him. He had
stayed so loyal to Heather throughout the duration of her
incarceration, but she clearly was struggling with her
feelings for him. But she also understood this was a very
difficult and vulnerable time for her daughter and she was
determined to support whatever path she took.

Matt tried lightening the mood by moaning rapturously
after taking his first bite of Heather's turkey lasagna. Heather seemed to appreciate the reaction. Poppy followed suit,
and Heather started to feel more comfortable and started to
open up and share stories about just how awful the food was
in prison, describing one particularly stomach-churning
mystery meat served in a bland, tasteless stew twice a
week. They were on safer ground now, not talking about
Heather's feelings for Matt, or vice versa. The evening
took a turn for the better and became almost celebratory
over the fact that Heather's worst days were behind her

and she had much to look forward to, and Poppy felt dinner was going to end on a high note.

But then, out of the blue, Matt's phone buzzed. He couldn't resist pulling it out of the back pocket of his pants and glancing at the screen. His face suddenly went pale.

Poppy held her wine glass close to her mouth but stopped before taking a sip. She knew something was wrong. "Matt, what is it?"

He looked up from his phone. "It's a breaking news alert."

"What? What's happened?" Poppy asked.

Matt set his phone down on the table and looked at both of them, stunned. "Tony Molina's wife, Tofu, was just found in their home here in Palm Springs . . . shot to death."

Poppy dropped her glass and it shattered on the floor as splashes of red wine stained her dress.

# Chapter 32

His hands were shaky as he read from a statement. He looked tired, worn, haggard, as if he hadn't slept in days. Tears streamed down his cheeks. He was dressed in a jacket and tie and stumbled a bit as the reporters surrounding him with their microphones jostled him to get a little bit closer.

"Tofu was my life, my everything. I cannot imagine going on without her. This is an incomprehensible loss to me, to my family, and in the days and weeks ahead, as the reality of this unthinkable tragedy sinks in . . ." Tony Molina wiped his tear-stained right cheek with his hand. "I'm sorry. . . ." He cleared his throat and tried to continue, but he couldn't. He crumpled up the paper and stuffed it in his coat pocket and then pushed his way out of the throng of reporters and through the yellow police tape and back inside his house.

A handsome Asian reporter stepped in front of the camera. "There you have it. Tony Molina, clearly a broken man, unable to speak to reporters after a housekeeper found his wife's body, shot to death. Although the police are not talking, and there has been no press conference as of yet, our source who is close to the investigation is reporting today that Mr. Molina was not at home at the time of the shooting. According to our source, Mr. Molina was playing golf with some longtime friends at the time of his wife's murder, and thus is not being considered as a suspect. This is Ralph Kim reporting live from Rancho Mirage. Back to you, Tanya!"

A raven-haired beauty in a bright pink blouse beamed into the camera as if she had just been watching a heart-warming piece about a dog rescue adoption center. "Thank you, Ralph. A local Cathedral City man hiking the Gene Autry Trail learned the hard way that snakes are not friendly household pets. . . ."

Violet scooped up the remote and shut off the TV. "And the Oscar for Best Actor goes to . . ."

Poppy stared glumly into space, still in shock over the unsettling news. "So you think he was lying?"

"I hate judging anyone before all the facts are in, but I'm struggling to buy that loving husband act!" Violet said.

Iris, who was sitting on the couch with Poppy, shrugged. "He struck me as sincere, Violet."

"This is such a switch. You're always telling me how I am the most naive and trusting person you know!" Violet said, shaking her head. "How you are more worldly and skeptical, and naturally trained by experience to detect a man's real character, but just because you are a fan of

Tony Molina's music, you're willing to believe anything he has to say!"

"Don't be ridiculous, Violet! The man has an alibi!" Iris argued.

"He knew he was going to need an alibi to cover his tracks! The police always start by looking closely at the spouse!" Violet said. "He could have hired an assassin to do the dirty work for him!"

"A professional assassin? In Rancho Mirage?" Poppy asked with a raised eyebrow. "You really need to stop reading so many John le Carré novels, Violet."

"I agree!" Iris piped in.

Violet threw her arms up in the air. "You call me Rebecca of Sunnybrook Farm, say I always see the best in people, and turn a blind eye to the realities of the world! Well, this one time, Iris, I'm looking at that man on TV and I'm telling you, he is *guilty*!"

Poppy stood up. "After sitting through two days of testimony at his trial, I have no illusions about Tony Molina. I don't think he is a good person, I think he pals around with a lot of shady people, and I think he is capable of a lot of criminal activity, including assaulting Chef Cicci and tampering with a jury, but seeing him on TV talking about his wife, I just don't think he was faking it."

"If it wasn't her husband, then who on earth *did* kill her?" Violet asked.

Poppy began pacing back and forth around the office. "It might have been a robbery gone bad. Maybe thieves somehow broke in and didn't know she was home at the time and panicked—"

"It's a gated community. How did they get onto the property?" Violet asked.

Poppy stopped and thought about it. "Perhaps they were

disguised as air-conditioner repairmen, or gardeners, or plumbers. Home owners in gated communities give out gate codes all the time to service people."

"Or maybe Tony Molina gave them the code so they could get in there and kill his wife!" Violet said matter-of-factly.

"All I'm saying, Violet, is my gut is telling me Tony didn't kill his wife based on what we just watched on television. However, I do not have the same feeling about Alden Kenny, who we now know was having an affair with his wife."

Violet marched over to Poppy, waving her hands. "Poppy, the truth is right in front of you. Tony found out about the affair and had them *both* taken out! Everyone knows he has mafia connections!"

Iris pouted, not wanting to believe the worst about her beloved Tony Molina.

"Yes, Violet, I suppose that's possible! But your new friend Lydia told you Tony already knew about the affair long before Alden was killed! There is a lot more to the story, in my opinion," Poppy said. "And I look forward to finding out what the whole story is!"

"You mean when the *police* find out!" Violet said.

Poppy offered a halfhearted nod.

"Because that's their job. We, on the other hand, should focus on finding new clients with actual cases and the means to pay us! Don't you agree, Iris?" Violet turned to Iris, fully expecting her to support her since she had been the one pounding that point home for days. But Iris stayed mum, wavering.

Violet's eyes widened. "*Iris?*"

"My Tony is innocent. I would not mind helping prove it," Iris mumbled.

"You used to be on *my* side!" Violet protested.

"That was when we were just looking for some spoiled rich girl, but this is *the* Tony Molina we are talking about. A superstar! *My* superstar!" Iris said.

"Well, I guess that's it then. I'm officially outvoted," Violet said with a sigh. "We're now investigating *two* murder cases and not getting paid for either one of them!"

# Chapter 33

Poppy, who held her mug of peppermint latte to her lips ready to take a sip, had to set it back down on the table to take in what she had just heard. "I'm sorry?"

"I'm thinking of moving to Palm Springs permanently," Rod said, an expectant smile on his face.

"Why?" she found herself saying although she wasn't sure she really wanted to hear the answer.

Rod shrugged as he stirred some cream into his cup of coffee. "I don't know. It just feels right. Now that Lara's back from Nepal, I'm hoping we can forge some kind of new relationship without butting heads all the time. She seemed more relaxed and mature when we spoke on the phone. She's been talking about visiting me out in the desert. I'm hoping she might stay a while."

Poppy debated whether she should bring up the credit card receipts again to Rod. The case was over. He was satisfied with just having his daughter back in his life. But she just couldn't help herself. Her curiosity got the best of her. "Rod, did you ever ask Lara about the charges on the credit card?"

Rod nodded. "Yes. She said she had lost the card before she left the country and never cancelled it. She suspects it was a guy she met in a bar in LA who was a little sketchy and had been eyeing her purse that night. Lara didn't think much of it until she finally noticed the card was gone. But by then she was in Nepal and living in a commune and focused on her meditation and spiritual seeking and she just forgot about it and never cancelled it."

Poppy tried hard not to raise an eyebrow but couldn't help it.

Rod instantly noticed. "You don't believe her?"

Poppy leaned forward and spoke gently. "It's just that Matt and I went to a guitar shop where the card was used and we showed the clerk a picture of Lara and he thought it might be her."

"Was he one hundred percent *certain*?" Rod challenged.

"No, but it could have been her."

"Maybe this guy, the one who lifted Lara's card, has a very specific type, and his latest girlfriend just *looked* like her. And she could have been the one forging Lara's name. That's possible, right?"

"Yes, I suppose so."

They sat silently in the coffee shop located on a side street off Palm Canyon for a few moments before Rod spoke again. "Lara isn't the only reason I've been thinking about living out here in the desert full-time. . . ."

Poppy had feared she might be a factor in this hasty

decision and she definitely knew she was not ready for that. She took a breath and whispered, "Rod . . ."

"Hello," a man said, interrupting her.

Poppy looked up to see Sam Emerson standing next to their table with a relaxed smile.

"Sam, good to see you," Rod said, jumping up to his feet and pumping Sam's hand. "Pull up a chair and join us."

Sam turned and grabbed a wooden chair and slid it over to their table. Poppy was too taken aback to say much of anything as Sam sat down with them.

"Sam had to come down from the mountain for more business so I invited him to join us for coffee," Rod said casually.

Poppy was stunned but took a stab at covering, probably to no avail. "Oh . . . I didn't know you two were talking so regularly. . . ."

Rod nodded. "We might be working together."

Once again, Poppy, who had just raised her mug to her lips, had to set it back down on the table. "*What?*"

"It's all very preliminary, nothing concrete, but I've been offered a pilot, another procedural. They want me to play a police commissioner, and I thought, wouldn't it be nice to get Sam on as consultant? It would be like getting the old band back together for one more tour."

Poppy looked to Sam, mouth agape. "I thought you loved your life up in Big Bear and didn't miss the TV grind."

Sam couldn't help but laugh at her confounded expression. "Everyone says that until they're offered real TV money. I'd be a fool not to seriously consider it."

Poppy was hardly in a position to argue his point. After all, if a studio came calling for her to play a juicy role again, which was highly unlikely, she wasn't sure she could so easily say no. And Sam was very good at consulting, always sweating the smallest of details, making sure to get everything right and factual. He would be the perfect choice to help out on a new cop show given his breadth of experience and vast knowledge of law enforcement.

She turned back to Rod. "I don't understand. If you're doing a pilot in LA, then why are you talking about moving out here on a permanent basis?"

"It's not going to be shot in LA. It's filming in New York."

Poppy sat back in her chair. "New York?"

"But it's just a pilot and we all know the odds of getting an actual series pickup. We'll probably be back east for a total of two, three weeks max," Rod said.

"I see," Poppy said, finally managing to take a sip of her peppermint latte.

"And who knows?" Rod said, folding his arms and staring at Poppy. "If the series does go, then we could all end up living back in New York. Wouldn't that be fun?"

"*Me?* What on earth would I do in New York?" Poppy asked, dumbfounded.

"I don't know," Rod said playfully. "There's still a decent-size part in the pilot that hasn't been cast yet, my character's wife, Karen. . . ."

"I don't act anymore, Rod," Poppy said emphatically.

Rod didn't seem to care. "Like Sam said, we always say we're out of the business until the business comes calling again."

It was like he was reading her mind just a few seconds earlier.

But Poppy wasn't going to give him the satisfaction. "I have my business here. . . ."

Rod nodded, not believing for a second that she wouldn't seize such an opportunity if given half a chance.

That bothered Poppy because she was happy here, working with her two best friends, and even Matt, running a business she had built up from scratch.

"And if they did end up casting someone else, you could just come and be with me," Rod said, letting it hang there. It was as if he was somehow reminding Sam that Poppy belonged to him and not the cool, detached cowboy with the romantic hillside cabin up in the mountains.

Poppy was having none of it and blustered, "That's ridiculous, Rod. I have no intention of moving to New York to . . . *hang out* with you. I'm sixty-two, not some nineteen-year-old groupie."

"We can discuss it later," he said with a wink.

He was right about that. Poppy had every intention of talking to him later. She had to nip this in the bud. Yes, she still found him attractive, and she did allow for the possibility that at some point she would be willing to consider a relationship, but right now it was entirely too premature.

As for Sam, as usual, he gave nothing away. He just sat in between them, almost enjoying Poppy acting so flustered and indignant, like she was putting on a show just for him. He was quiet, laid back, and infuriatingly poker faced.

Rod finally took the hint and changed the subject. He began peppering Sam with questions about his current business investments.

Poppy sat quietly, trying to calm down until the hotness in her face subsided. As she was about ready to rejoin the conversation, her cell phone buzzed. It wasn't a call but rather a news notification. She gasped as she read it.

"Something wrong?" Sam asked, concerned.

Poppy looked up, dismayed. "There's been an arrest in the murder of Tony Molina's wife, Tofu."

Rod leaned forward. "Who?"

"Her stepson . . . Dominick, Tony's boy from his first marriage," Poppy said glumly.

# Chapter 34

As they left the coffee shop, Poppy walked ahead of the two men and Rod slid in behind her and placed a hand on the small of her back. Poppy wondered if he was just being a gentleman or if this was yet another overt gesture to signal to Sam again that she somehow belonged to him. If it was the latter, then Poppy considered the play completely inappropriate. She turned away, forcing him to pull his hand away.

Outside on the sidewalk, she finally had the opportunity to turn around and face the two men. Rod's cell phone was ringing and he already had it clamped to his ear.

"Hi, Lanny," Rod said, a finger pressed into his other ear to quiet the usual street noises. "Yes, I can talk. . . ."

Poppy and Sam faced each other with patient smiles on their faces.

Rod lowered the phone just a bit and said apologetically, "It's my agent. I'm going to have to take this."

"Of course," Poppy said.

Rod hustled away from them, down the street toward the corner for a little privacy. She turned back to Sam. "So are you really considering going to New York?"

Sam shrugged. "I'm thinking about it. Like Rod said, it's just a pilot. A few weeks tops."

"But what if it does go to series? Are you prepared to leave your life in Big Bear for nine months out of the year?"

Another shrug from Sam. "Maybe. I spend a lot of time these days alone in the wild, with just the thoughts in my head, very few responsibilities. It might be healthy for me to come down the mountain and rejoin society for a while, work hard, take a break from my completely unencumbered life."

"Well, living in New York would certainly be a dramatic change from the squirrels and raccoons and mountain lions you usually interact with."

Sam nodded with a wry smile. "There are plenty of wild animals in the Big Apple, just most of them are on two feet."

Poppy laughed. "I suppose that's true."

"You look awfully pretty today, I must say," Sam said, eyeing her from head to toe.

She shifted uncomfortably but was flattered by the remark. "Thank you. . . ." She then mustered the courage and continued, "Sam, I don't want you to get the wrong impression. . . ."

"About what?" he asked with a curious look.

"Rod and me. We're not a couple . . . not right now. . . ."

Sam looked down at his boots. "But you're thinking about it?"

"We reconnected because he brought us a case, and I have tried to keep our relationship strictly professional, at least . . ."

"Until the case is closed?"

"It *is* closed."

"I see."

Poppy didn't think she was doing a very good job at all of explaining her position. "Rod has been a little overzealous in showing me where he stands, but I have yet to decide anything. In fact, I think he may have the wrong idea about my true feelings for him because I haven't been up front with him about my own feelings for—"

Sam smiled, anxious to hear more.

"Sorry about that," Rod said, stuffing his phone into the pocket of his pants as he walked back over to them. "Money issues. The network's lowballing so don't pack for NYC just yet, Sam."

"It's all good," Sam said. "Whatever happens, happens."

Poppy wanted to kick herself. She finally had had the opportunity to tell Sam how she felt about him, and she had blown it. She had hemmed and hawed and waited too long, and now the moment was gone. It was not that she feared Sam didn't already know she had an affection for him, that the more time she spent with him had just deepened her feelings and desire for something more, but she had yet to formally communicate any of that to him. And now Rod was in the picture, a big ball of unbridled energy, the direct opposite of Sam's laid-back, man-of-few-words style, and that, she had to admit, was attractive as well. It took her late husband, Chester, two years of dating before he had finally told Poppy he loved her. Rod had declared his love in less than a week after their initial reunion. Sam had never even come close, in her mind, to revealing how he truly felt about her, which made her think that maybe she was the one with the wrong impression.

"I'd better get going to my meeting," Sam said. "You both have a great day."

"I'll keep you posted on the pilot, Sam!" Rod called after him as Sam turned and walked away.

"Good-bye, Sam," Poppy said, almost too quietly for him to hear.

But he glanced back and gave her a wink before he rounded the corner and disappeared.

"Can I give you a lift somewhere?" Rod asked.

"No, my car's just around the corner. I need to get to the office."

She was still reeling from the news about Tony Molina's son, Dominick.

"Okay, I'll be in touch," he said, reaching in for a kiss.

She didn't pull away like she wanted to, but she did turn her head to the right so his lips landed on her left cheek.

He backed away, slightly hurt. "Is everything all right, Poppy?"

"Yes, but, Rod, we need to talk. . . ."

"If I'm going too fast, I can dial it back. I'm just the kind of guy who can't help but go full gusto when he knows what he wants."

"Yes, I've known that about you for a long time and it can be heady and intoxicating, but I'm not that way, I can't rush into things—"

He felt a vibration in his pocket, grabbed his phone, and glanced at the screen. "It's my agent again. I'm sorry, Poppy, we're in negotiations and it's a very critical time."

"I used to be in the business—I completely understand. Go, take it," Poppy said, waving him away.

"You're a doll," he said. "I'll call you tonight."

He bounded away.

She hadn't lied to him. She found his enthusiasm and passion for her exciting, if not a bit overwhelming. Especially compared to Sam, who held his cards so frustratingly close to his vest, and was a much harder read.

Poppy had absolutely no idea what she was going to do.

# Chapter 35

When Poppy returned home to the apartment, she found Heather sitting on the couch with Matt. They appeared to be in the middle of a deep conversation and she hated to interrupt them.

Matt noticed her first and shot up to his feet abruptly. "Did you hear the news?"

Poppy nodded. "Yes. It's such a shock. It's hard to fathom that boy killed his own stepmother. . . ."

Matt scrunched up his face, confused. "What are you talking about?"

"Tofu's murder . . . They've arrested Dominick Molina, Tony's son," Poppy said, now wondering about Matt's news.

"I hadn't heard that. I'm talking about Heather," Matt

said, reaching down and taking her hand as she stood up. "She got a job!"

"Oh, darling, that's wonderful!" Poppy cried.

Heather tried to shrug it off. "It's nothing, really. Just a hostess job at a Mexican restaurant in town, but I figure I can start saving my money to go back to school."

"Well, you can be sure I will help, too," Poppy promised.

But inside she was saddened by the fact that she wasn't in a better financial position to cover all of the expenses for her struggling daughter. She once had been. Until she woke up one day to discover that her late husband, Chester, had lost all of their savings. But that was in the past, and she had chosen to just look ahead.

Matt put an arm around Heather. "I'm so proud of you!"

"Please, both of you, stop fawning over me. It's just a part-time job handing out menus and booking reservations," Heather demurred.

"It's a start," Poppy declared. "Think of it as the first step toward becoming a lawyer."

"I know that's what I told the parole board, but that's really just a dream," Heather said quietly.

"It's not a dream, it's a goal. All you have to do is work hard to make it happen," Poppy said. "I know how determined you are. You got that from me."

"Your mother went from penniless widow to licensed private investigator in no time," Matt said, beaming proudly.

"And I pooh-poohed her all the way. I wasn't supportive at all," Heather groaned.

"Stop kicking yourself," Poppy said. "You came around."

"I can be so negative," Heather whispered.

"You get that from your father. But that's easy to change. Be positive. You got a job. That's something to be proud of. This is a good day," Poppy said, walking over and hugging her daughter. "Matt, would you like to stay for dinner and help us celebrate?"

"Sorry, I can't. I have an appointment at a recording studio," Matt said, unable to tamp down the excitement in his voice.

"Recording studio? Does this have something to do with Lara Harper, because the case is closed," Poppy said.

"I know, but Carl Menkin wants me to record a couple of songs that he can distribute to a few companies to see if he can drum up any interest," Matt said, winking at Heather.

"Matt, that's . . . that's so great," Poppy managed to get out. She was sincerely happy for him, but she couldn't help but feel slightly sad that she might be losing him at the agency sooner than she had expected.

"The next Tony Molina," Heather said, smiling.

"Let's hope not," Poppy sighed.

"I've got to get going," Matt said, then kissed Heather lightly on the lips and hugged Poppy before he dashed out the door.

Poppy turned back to Heather. "How about we go out for dinner?"

Heather put her hands in the front pockets of her jeans and shook her head. "I'd rather stay in, if you don't mind. It's been an exhausting day." She crossed to the kitchen. "I made a casserole for us before my job interview today. I just have to heat it up."

"That sounds lovely," Poppy said, studying her morose daughter. She didn't want to pry, but now that she was a professional detective, she couldn't stop herself. "How are you and Matt doing?"

"Fine. He keeps telling me he wants to be with me for the long run," Heather said, turning on the oven and then crossing to the refrigerator to retrieve the foil-wrapped casserole dish.

"He's very sweet," Poppy said. "It took me a while to realize it, but he is."

"I know. . . ." Heather's voice trailed off.

"But . . ."

"No buts. I believe he's very sincere. It's just that I can see his career taking off, acting and singing, and who knows what else? He's very talented. I'm just not sure, given what I've been through, given the road ahead of me, that I am equipped to handle . . ."

"The harsh glare of the spotlight?"

"Something like that, yes."

"You just need to take it day by day."

"Cross that bridge when I get to it, and all those tired clichés."

"In my experience, clichés for the most part have turned out to be universal truths."

"Then I'll take your advice," Heather said, sliding the casserole onto the rack and closing the oven door.

Poppy helped her set the table. She tried telling her daughter again how proud she was of her, but Heather refused to accept the compliment, preferring to focus on her mother's personal life, which Poppy wanted to completely shut down. She had no intention of boring her daughter with the details of a burgeoning love triangle. Talk about a cliché! They had a pleasant dinner together, and Heather retired to her bedroom early, leaving Poppy to turn on the local news and gasp at the latest reports about the death of Tony Molina's wife, Tofu. The police were now confirming that Dominick Molina, after a brief interrogation, had *confessed* to the murder of his stepmother.

# Chapter 36

When Rod opened the front door of his expansive mid-century Palm Springs home to find Poppy standing there with Matt, his face registered surprise, but he quickly covered it with a welcoming smile.

"Poppy, I'm glad you came. And, Matt, good to see you," he said, waving them both inside.

When Rod had called Poppy earlier that morning on her cell and asked her to drop by for coffee, she initially resisted, but he was so insistent, so persuasive, promising her it was important, she finally reluctantly agreed. Luckily at the time she had been at the office with Matt and had enlisted him to accompany her so she would feel more comfortable. Matt was happy to oblige playing chaperone, but he told Poppy that his official opinion was that she and Rod made an "adorable" couple.

Poppy and Matt had barely stepped into Rod's foyer when Poppy spotted a tiny, wispy young woman, blond with angular features, hovering in the living room. She instantly recognized her from all the photographs she had been recently poring over.

"Lara . . ."

"Hello, Ms. Harmon," she said, shuffling over to give Poppy a strained hug. "You look as pretty as you did in all those old reruns of my dad's TV show."

"And you're all grown up," Poppy said, studying the young woman she had been so eagerly searching for the past couple of weeks. Poppy put her hands together and bowed. "I suppose I should greet you with Namaste. . . ."

Lara stared at her, puzzled.

"That's the official greeting in Nepal," Poppy said evenly.

"Oh . . . right . . . yes . . ." Lara said with a forced giggle before following suit and putting her hands together and bowing. "Namaste."

"How long were you there?" Poppy asked.

Lara ignored the question as she focused on Matt. "Who's this?"

"Oh, forgive my manners. This is Matt Flowers. We work together," Poppy said.

Lara blew past Poppy and held out her hand to Matt. "It's lovely to meet you. I'm Lara."

"Yes," Matt said, flashing his sexy smile. "I feel as if I already know you. I've been searching for you high and low for a while now."

"Well, lucky for us both you've finally found me," Lara said flirtatiously.

Rod stepped forward, attempting to put a stop to his

daughter's efforts to hit on Matt. "I thought you would like to see for yourselves that Lara is safe and sound."

"Yes, you had your father very worried," Poppy said in an admonishing tone.

Lara sighed. "I know, I feel so bad about that. I've been acting awful lately, like a spoiled child, but while I was in Nepal, the lessons I learned at a spiritual retreat run by Buddhists really centered me, and allowed me to see what was really important through long days of meditation and reflection. . . ."

"And what was that?" Poppy had to ask.

Lara batted her eyes and stared lovingly at her father. "Family, of course."

Poppy couldn't help but think the girl was here because she needed money, but she held her tongue.

Matt decided to pose Poppy's question again. "How long did you say you were in Nepal?"

Lara appeared flustered by Matt. She giggled like a coquettish fifteen-year-old being asked out by the high school quarterback. "I don't know, a month or so." She turned to her father. "How long have I been gone, Daddy?"

"A few weeks," Rod answered. "I'm just happy you came home."

"I'm not sure I could stay too long in Nepal," Poppy said. "I love eating beef too much."

Lara stared at her, utterly confused. "What?"

"Cows," Poppy said, eyes narrowing.

Lara gave her a brief, dry laugh. "What about them?"

"They are holy and sacred to the Hindus in Nepal. You could go to prison for up to twelve years if you kill one," Poppy explained. "I'm sure you heard that while you were there."

"Well, like I said, I spent a lot of time at the retreat and didn't get out much," Lara offered, although she was starting to get nervous that she was being tested.

Poppy didn't feel the need to ask any more questions because she was certain that the girl had never been to Nepal in her life and was making it all up on the spot. A quick look at her passport would prove it, but this was no longer an investigation. They were no longer working for Rod, so at this point none of this was any of her business. She just hoped Rod wasn't buying his daughter's blatant lies.

Poppy decided to drop the line of inquiry, but Matt was not about to.

"When we were looking for you, Lara, we found a lot of instances of people who saw you out here in the desert recently. Your manager, Carl Menkin, said you were at an undisclosed location recording an album. . . ."

Lara's eyes flicked back and forth as her mind raced. Finally, she nodded and smiled, then replied, "Yes, I was out here briefly with some friends. We were partying too much and getting out of control and my credit card got stolen. I didn't even know. At the time, I was in a place where I just needed to refocus, and that's when a friend who was going to backpack in Nepal invited me to join her and—"

Rod interrupted her. "Honey, I thought you lost the credit card in LA."

Lara did not appreciate being contradicted, but she resisted the urge to lose her temper. "No, Daddy, I'm sure I said Palm Springs. I was here when that loser snatched my card in the club."

Rod went over the details in his mind again but then decided to let it go. "Maybe I got it wrong."

"Yes, you did," Lara said with a tight smile. She turned to Matt. "And now that I'm home I'm going to get to work recording some new songs."

"Good for you," Matt said, obviously not buying any of her lies, either.

"Can you stay for lunch?" Rod asked. "Rosa is making her world-famous enchiladas."

"Oh, yes, please," Lara cooed, flouncing over to Matt and taking his hands in hers. "I would love the chance to get to know each other better."

"I'm afraid we can't," Poppy said quickly. "We're meeting my daughter, Heather, for lunch."

They were not having lunch with Heather because she was starting her new hostess job today, but Matt picked up the cue and went right along with Poppy's story. "That's right. We'd better get going. It's never smart to keep your girlfriend waiting."

Lara's face fell. "*Girlfriend?*"

"Yes," Poppy was happy to confirm. "They've been together a while now."

Lara dropped Matt's hands and pouted. "How nice."

"Thank you for the invitation, Rod, perhaps another time," Poppy said.

"Of course," Rod said, disappointed. "Maybe we can do dinner later this week. I'd love for you to spend more time with me and Lara."

That would never happen.

Although Poppy admittedly found Rod still attractive and nice to be around, his daughter was downright toxic. She would be happy if she never laid eyes on that impulsive, selfish young woman ever again. And it hardly took a supersleuth to deduce that she was a serial liar to start with, and who knew what else.

Poppy rightfully feared that poor Rod, who was desperate to repair the damage done to his relationship with his daughter, would stay blind to the truth until it was too late. He was opening himself up to a whole world of hurt, and Poppy hated the idea of having to watch him go through that.

# Chapter 37

Stoney Peterman's smile froze quicker than a curious kid's tongue on a metal pole in the dead of winter. Poppy and Matt stood in the doorway to his low-rent office located in a run-down mini-mall where most of the retail and office space had weathered "lease available" signs taped to the smudged glass windows. Peterman, a sleazy lawyer you might see on a billboard on the rough side of town, operated out of a tiny space on the end next to a closed barbershop. When Poppy and Matt first appeared at his door, his face lit up like a Christmas tree, his expectations raised that they were potential clients, recent car accident victims with nagging neck trouble, for instance. But Stoney's hopes were quickly dashed when Matt flashed his fake tin FBI badge he had bought on Amazon for ten bucks and announced, "I'm Agent Cameron and this is Agent Harmon. We're with the Federal Bureau of Investigation."

Poppy bit the side of her lip to keep from laughing at Matt's testosterone-laden performance, adopting an intimidating posture and lowering the register of his voice. He had been so excited when Poppy had first suggested they pose as FBI agents in order to question Stoney Peterman.

Stoney managed to keep the frozen smile from melting into a panicked frown as he stood up from his desk to greet them. "FBI? To what do I owe this pleasure?" His voice cracked slightly, but he fought to remain calm and breezy.

"We have a few questions about Alden Kenny," Matt said, narrowing his eyes, barreling inside the office as Stoney instinctively took a step back.

Poppy followed close on Matt's heels. She allowed him to take the lead because so far he was nailing it all on his own. She knew if they had just sauntered into Stoney's hovel of a headquarters introducing themselves as a pair of local private detectives with no real client, just a natural curiosity to find out who drowned Alden Kenny, he would have laughed them right out of his office. But a scuzzy attorney, keeping a low profile in the slums of Cathedral City, with his fingers in all kinds of pies, most of which were undoubtedly dirty and illegal, Stoney Peterman could not readily dismiss two professional FBI agents who had supposedly been dispatched to see him with some very serious inquiries.

The road to Stoney Peterman had been surprisingly easy to travel. Earlier that day, Wyatt had swung by to visit with his grandmother after school and was promptly put to work investigating Alden Kenny's finances. It took the whiz kid about an hour to hack into Kenny's bank accounts, or "access" as Poppy preferred to say, so it didn't sound illegal. After perusing the recent activity history, Wyatt quickly zeroed in on a mysterious cash transfer of fifty thousand dollars that had been deposited into one of the dead juror's accounts. According to the date of the transfer, it had been made on the same day that Alden Kenny was killed. Even more suspicious, the exact amount was withdrawn two days later, after Poppy had discovered Kenny floating facedown in his swimming pool. That could only mean that someone else took the cash out of the account. Poppy had her suspicions as to who would be most likely to have had access to Alden Kenny's money, the most obvious choice being his pal and business partner in the carpet-cleaning business, Jay Takamura. But her more pressing question at the moment was, *Where* did the money come from?

According to the deposit information that Wyatt had in front of him on the computer screen with just a few keystrokes, the transfer was made by a corporation known as Decision Consultants. After Wyatt did a little more digging, he discovered Decision Consultants was merely a shell company for a seedy lawyer named Stoney Peterman, who boasted on his low-trafficked Web site that one of his star clients was Tony Molina. That struck Poppy as more than just an odd coincidence. When Violet called the high-priced law firm that officially represented Tony Molina in Beverly Hills to confirm that Peterman was also looking after Tony's varied interests, the receptionist haughtily and steadfastly denied Mr. Molina had anything to do with such a shyster lawyer as Peterman. This left Poppy to assume that Peterman was the attorney Tony used to handle some of his shadier pursuits, most likely on the down low, like soliciting bribes or buying the silence of women he may have had dalliances with outside of his marriage, and, of course, paying a jury plant to vote not guilty at his assault trial.

And so a plan to visit Mr. Peterman was hatched, and now here they were, in the guise of a couple of feds, hoping to find the hard evidence that would finally connect Molina to Alden Kenny's murder. Poppy was convinced that when Kenny called and insisted she come see him, he was about to come clean. And she believed that Tony somehow had gotten to him first.

"I'm sorry, I don't know an Alden Kenny," Stoney sputtered, lying through his teeth.

"So you deny paying him a sum total of fifty thousand dollars from your company Decision Consultants?" Matt pressed, taking another step forward.

"Remember," Poppy said, folding her arms, "lying to the FBI is a felony offense."

"I . . . I . . . didn't know that," Stoney stammered, flustered. He was so nervous that sweat beads were already forming on his ample brow.

"Well, now you do, so let me try again," Matt said in a low growl. "Did you or did you not pay Alden Kenny fifty thousand dollars?"

Stoney's eyes shifted back and forth as his mind raced. He looked as if he was trying to formulate a story in his mind, one that sounded somewhat plausible and honest.

Poppy could almost see the wheels turning inside his head as he tried to come up with an answer. Finally, he nodded and answered, "Yes . . . yes I did."

"What was it for? And think before you answer because we're not stupid. It wouldn't cost fifty K to hire him to clean your carpets," Matt said before glancing down at the dirty, scuffed floor. "Especially since you don't have any."

Stoney shook his head. "I did it for Tofu. . . ."

Matt raised an eyebrow. "Tofu? Why?"

"She was having an affair with him and he got to be kind of a stalker and wouldn't leave her alone and she was terrified that Tony was going to find out about it so she came to me and asked me to fix the situation, to just get him off her back and keep quiet about their affair. I told the kid I would wire fifty grand into his bank account if he agreed to just go away and forget all about Tofu and he did. . . ."

Poppy wasn't buying it. Her instinct was telling her the money had nothing to do with Kenny's affair with Tofu, who was conveniently dead and unable to corroborate whether Stoney Peterman was telling the truth or not. Especially since Poppy had heard Tony had already been well aware of the affair. "So Tony knew nothing about the payment?"

"Hell no! He would've killed us both. . . . I mean . . . I'm not implying he had anything to do with Tofu's murder—the stepson did it, it's all over the news. Tony had nothing to do with any of that horrific business."

Poppy was convinced Tony had Alden Kenny planted on that jury and paid him handsomely for his trouble. Glenda Felson had already confessed to making sure Kenny was selected. But why *him*? Why the young man who was cheating with Tony's wife? Of all the people he could have bribed, why Alden Kenny? Tony Molina was still adamantly denying being involved and had been calling poor Glenda a starstruck liar in front of the press. And for Glenda's part, she was still refusing to identify Tony's bodyguards as the couple who had first approached her. And with Stoney Peterman claiming that the money he paid Kenny had nothing to do with jury tampering, that it was just to make Kenny go away and to keep his mouth shut about his affair with Tofu so Tony never found out, then there was still no hard evidence that could be used to indict Tony for any crime. They needed more, and Poppy knew they were not going to get it from Stoney Peterman, who was specifically paid to keep all of Tony's dirty secrets buried.

There was still the possibility that she was wrong. Maybe Tony had no idea that the kid he had paid to be a jury holdout was planning to spill all to Poppy about how he got paid to get Tony off the hook from going to jail for assault. If that was true, then Tony would have had no motive to kill him or have him killed. In fact, the only person she could think of who would have a reason to get rid of Alden Kenny was his best friend and business partner, Jay Takamura.

He had fifty thousand reasons.

# Chapter 38

Poppy watched proudly as Violet, who had gussied up in a chiffon pleated floral print dress she dubbed "a conversation starter," sashayed across the floor of the Spa Resort Casino, passing the bells and whistles and colorful lights of the slot machines, and made her way to one of the blackjack tables. Violet was eager to prove herself to be an effective undercover operative, especially when it required an older woman's touch. She had felt in recent months that she had been underutilized so she was thrilled when Poppy suggested she get off the bench and be put in the game.

It was no secret after Iris had hired Jay Takamura to clean her carpets that he had a taste for the ladies, especially those who were postmenopausal, and since Iris had already been deployed twice to pump him for information, it struck Poppy as too much of a coincidence if Iris suddenly showed up again at Jay's regular haunt, the famous Palm Springs casino where he gambled nearly on a nightly basis. Matt had spent the past two nights following him around, and like clockwork, Jay ended both evenings right here, slumped over his favorite blackjack table, downing one whiskey straight up after another, sometimes beating the house, but more often than not bleeding out his cash.

In order not to be seen by Jay, who had already met them, Poppy and Iris sequestered themselves inside the Oasis Buffet, where they could sit at a table, both of them fitted with earpieces so they could listen to Violet, who was wired with a tiny microphone pinned to her bra underneath that conversation starter of a dress, as she interacted with Jay.

Iris was already piling food from the buffet onto her second plate as Poppy sipped her cup of coffee at the table and spoke softly to Violet. "Have you spotted him yet?"

"Yes," Violet reported. "He's at his regular table and there is an empty chair next to him. I'm going in."

Poppy could hear some rustling and then Violet greeting the dealer. Violet wisely chose to ignore Jay, whom they suspected would notice her soon enough. The dealer began doling out cards to the players at the table and Poppy suddenly heard Violet gasp. "What is it, Violet? What's wrong?"

She realized Violet couldn't answer her because she was sitting at a table with several other players as well as the dealer. Poppy heard a couple of the players instructing the dealer to hit them with another card, then a slurping sound, probably Jay sucking down another whiskey. And then, after a few moments of silence, as players turned over their cards, she heard Jay murmur, "Busted," indicating he had gone over twenty-one. Then she heard Violet squeal with delight, "Look, blackjack! I won! A king of hearts and an ace of spades!"

Violet didn't really have to describe her hand to everyone at the table, who could all plainly see it, but Poppy knew Violet was doing it strictly for her benefit. She could hear the dealer pushing some chips over in front of Violet. As the next game commenced, the dealer shuffled the deck and distributed more cards. Violet gasped again.

"Don't be so obvious, Violet," Poppy warned. "Put on a poker face if you've got another good hand."

There were groans from the other players as Violet dutifully reported out loud that the dealer stood at a soft hand of seventeen, a six of clubs and an ace of diamonds. Jay went bust again with cards totaling twenty-three. Violet squealed again with delight as she turned over her cards. "Two queens! That's twenty! I win again!"

"Lady Luck seems to be shining on you tonight, ma'am," a man said, presumably the dealer.

Iris returned to the table and sat down with a plate heaped with tacos, BBQ, orange chicken, rice, green beans, pizza, and pasta.

Poppy's mouth dropped open.

"Don't you dare fat shame me," Iris growled. "I did not eat lunch and I always get carried away at buffets."

Poppy mimed zipping her mouth shut, promising not to say a word.

Iris began stabbing at her green beans. "How is it going?"

"So far Violet is cleaning up, but she hasn't broken the ice with Jay yet."

Iris opened her mouth and devoured a forkful of beans

and then began adjusting the earpiece lodged behind her lobe. "I can't hear anything. Can you turn the volume up on this thing?"

"Maybe yours has a battery issue. I can hear just fine," Poppy said.

Iris was more interested in concentrating on her plate of food than the actual reason they were at the casino, and so Poppy decided to take over surveillance duties and let her be so she could enjoy her haul of food in peace.

Poppy listened to Violet play a few more rounds, losing a few, but then making up lost ground, doubling down, and continuing her winning streak. She was worried Violet's surprising luck would turn off Jay, who might sour over losing so much, but as the dealer shuffled the cards for another game, she heard him say, "I'm Jay."

"Violet."

"What a pretty name."

"Thank you."

"A pretty name for a pretty lady."

Poppy couldn't help but roll her eyes.

"Flattery will get you everywhere!" Violet giggled, no doubt batting her eyes at the same time.

"Good to know. Can I buy you a drink, Violet?"

"That would be lovely. I'll have a Rose Kennedy."

"I'm sensing a flower theme. Violet. Rose."

"Not to mention my dress!"

"You look beautiful in it."

They were interrupted by the game.

Jay finally beat the house and got back a few of his chips.

"Looks like your luck might finally be changing," Violet said.

"I wouldn't bet on that," he said. "I don't even want to

tell you how much I've lost this week. You probably wouldn't believe it."

"Try me."

There was silence. He was hesitating.

"I don't want to embarrass myself."

"Over a thousand?"

Jay snickered. "Try twenty times that."

Violet gasped again, this time much louder.

"I know, you'd think I would take the hint and stay away from this place."

"I can't imagine losing that much money!" Violet gasped. "Well, I'm sure you do very well in business if you are able to gamble away that kind of cash."

More silence.

Another game played.

Jay won again, feeling more emboldened as the dealer shoved more chips back in his direction. Jay took a break to order more cocktails from a passing waitress, and then turned his attention back to Violet.

"Carpet cleaning," he said.

"I beg your pardon?" Violet peeped.

"I own a carpet-cleaning business."

"You must have *a lot* of customers!"

Poppy anxiously adjusted her earpiece. She didn't want to miss a word. She felt in her gut that Jay was about to give them something useful.

"I do well, but not well enough to piss away twenty grand. Luckily I recently came into some money unexpectedly."

"Did someone write you into his or her will?" Violet asked, mustering up as much of an innocent tone as she possibly could.

"You might say that," Jay sneered. "It's made my losing streak here a lot less painful."

That was it.

He had to be talking about the fifty grand deposited into Alden Kenny's account, or, more likely, a joint account for the business to which Jay had access. But that was only a motive to commit murder, hardly proof that he actually carried out the dirty deed. It was also entirely plausible that Jay accidentally discovered that money after somebody else offed Alden and simply took advantage of the fact his business partner was no longer around to spend it.

In either event, he was done talking. After losing three more consecutive rounds, Jay folded and called it a night. He asked Violet for her phone number so he could call her to set up a dinner date, but she didn't hear him because the celebratory applause of the crowd surrounding her drowned out his voice as she won big again at blackjack. She excitedly shouted that her winnings were now north of seven thousand dollars. Jay apparently skulked away to the parking lot after that.

Poppy looked over at Iris, who was chewing on a barbecued pork rib. "Finish up! We need to get Violet out of here! She's losing sight of what it means to be undercover!"

Iris dropped the empty bone on her plate and licked the barbecue sauce off her fingers. "I am not done eating yet! The buffet is open for another half hour."

Poppy stood up from the table and peered out from the buffet and into the casino to see people abandoning their slot machines to gather around the blackjack table and cheer Violet on as she continued to methodically and relentlessly beat the house. "Oh, Violet . . ."

Poppy raced toward the blackjack tables, with Iris, stuffing some dinner rolls she hadn't eaten into her large purse, on her heels, to spirit Violet, who was now burning up with gambling fever, away from the casino before she wound up on the local news.

# Chapter 39

Poppy was just about home from the Spa Resort Casino when her cell phone buzzed. Matt's name came up on the dashboard screen. She pressed the speaker button on her steering wheel to answer the call. "Hi, Matt."

"Poppy, you need to help me," Matt whispered urgently.

Poppy suddenly had a sick feeling in her stomach. "Why? What's happened?"

"She's sitting at my kitchen table and she won't leave."

"Who? Heather?" Poppy asked, thoroughly confused.

"No, Lara, Rod's daughter. She showed up at my door and said she had to talk to me, and so I invited her in, and then she started to go on about how much she loves me and wants to be with me. . . ."

Poppy nearly veered off the road from the shock. "*What?*"

"I tried to tell her I already have a girlfriend, but she

refuses to listen, and just keeps talking about how fate brought us together through her Dad hiring me to find her. It's kind of creepy. You've got to help me get her out of here. I'm in the middle of cooking dinner for Heather, who is supposed to be here any minute!"

"How did she find out where you live?"

"Beats me. Maybe she followed me home that day we met her at her father's house. Who knows?"

Poppy jerked the wheel, turning right, away from her apartment building in the direction of Matt's house in North Palm Springs. "Hang on, I'll be right there."

"Hurry, please, she's totally irrational!"

Poppy hung up and immediately called Rod, who answered groggily as if he had been asleep.

"Yes?"

"Rod, it's Poppy."

His tone immediately went from grouchy to cheery. "Well, hello, beautiful."

"We have a situation."

"I hope it's the good kind."

"I'm afraid not. It's about Lara."

There was a pause, followed by a heavy sigh. "What's she done now?"

Poppy didn't go into too many details, but simply told him she needed him to go to Matt's house and rattled off his address. Rod agreed to get dressed and head right over. By the time he had hung up, Poppy was already pulling up in front of Matt's house. The whole place was lit up and she could see Matt pacing nervously in front of the large windows in the living room. She could not see Lara.

Poppy hopped out of her car and clattered up the cement

walkway that led to the light green one-level mid-century home Matt had rented when he made the decision to stick it out full-time in Palm Springs.

The door flew open before Poppy even had time to ring the bell. Matt looked worn and tired and his whole body was tense. "Thank God you're here. Come in."

Poppy followed Matt inside, where she instantly spotted Lara, looking fresh faced and upbeat, in a revealing halter top and skintight jeans, sitting calmly at the dining table, sipping what looked like an iced tea. In the kitchen behind her on the stove top were pots bubbling with marinara sauce and boiling some kind of pasta, and there was the intoxicating smell of garlic bread in the oven. A bottle of red wine had been popped open and two glasses were set out.

Matt nervously checked his phone for the time and threw Poppy a pleading look to get Lara out of his house ASAP.

Poppy approached Lara, smiling, trying to be motherly. "Lara, dear, what are you doing here?"

"That's between me and Matt," she said matter-of-factly.

Matt sighed, irritated, and spoke directly to Lara. "I already told Poppy what you said to me. She knows everything." He began pacing again.

Lara put down her iced tea and swiveled around in the chair. "Oh, I see. You're more than willing to talk to your mother about our relationship, but not me."

"Poppy's not my mother. She's a friend," Matt said.

"Whatever. I mean, she might as well be your mother. She's old enough."

Poppy took a deep breath and said, "I believe Matt has made it quite clear that he is not available to pursue any kind of relationship with you and so I think you should respect that and leave."

"That's not the impression he gave me when we first met at my father's house. He was giving me all sorts of signals that he was available and interested," Lara insisted.

Matt was genuinely dumbfounded. "I didn't do anything of the kind!"

"I was there too, Lara, and I don't recall Matt coming on to you in any way," Poppy said gently.

"That's because you were too focused on flirting with my father to notice much of anything," Lara huffed.

Poppy was taken aback. This girl was just making up stories out of whole cloth. "However you may have interpreted things, the fact of the matter is Matt is currently involved with someone else, and I should know because she just happens to be my daughter."

"I know, you don't have to keep telling me about your precious daughter," Lara said before turning toward Matt. "Didn't she just get out of prison? Is that the kind of woman you really want to be with? Seriously?"

Poppy stepped forward, her fists clenched. "I think it would be best if you leave now, Lara."

Lara didn't make a move to stand up. It was as if she wasn't even listening. She just picked up her iced tea and took a loud sip.

Matt began to panic. "Poppy . . ."

Poppy held up her hand, assuring him she had everything under control. "Lara?"

Lara rolled her eyes and sighed. "What?"

"Are you going to finish your tea and leave?" Poppy asked quietly.

"Not until Matt admits he has feelings for me, and tells

me I'm not imagining this connection we have," Lara said, now stirring the tea with her index finger.

Matt threw his hands up in the air. "I can't do that! I would be lying!"

The doorbell rang. Matt gasped. "That's her! Poppy, what are we going to do?"

Poppy signaled him to stay calm and then crossed to the door and opened it. Rod Harper, looking confused, stood outside. "Come in, Rod."

Rod followed Poppy into the living room. He didn't see his daughter at first, seated at the dining table that had been set for two people. He was entirely focused on Poppy. "You look lovely tonight, Poppy. Have you been out?"

She had no intention of telling him that she had been at the casino overseeing an undercover operation because it was none of his business. She simply waved in the direction of Lara.

Rod glanced over to see his daughter, Lara, who had suddenly and out of the blue worked up some tears that were now streaming down her high cheekbones.

"Lara, honey, what's wrong?"

"Oh, Daddy, I've never been so humiliated!" She jumped up from the table and ran over to him. He enveloped her in a hug.

"Why, baby? What happened?"

Before Poppy had the chance to explain, Lara was already spinning out her latest web of lies. "I told you how Matt has been calling me and telling me how pretty I am and how I'm totally his type and that he would like to take me out. . . ."

"Yes," Rod said, glaring at Matt.

"Sir, I most certainly have not—"

Lara didn't let him finish. "Well, he's so handsome

and charming, and he told me he was no longer seeing Poppy's daughter, so how could I resist, right? And so when I finally relented and I came here for dinner tonight, I find out he's still seeing her!"

More tears, but these were less convincing. Because the scene she was playing was so entirely far-fetched and ridiculous, she couldn't possibly deliver an authentic performance.

Poppy could tell Rod was questioning his daughter's story, especially as he saw the disbelieving looks on both Poppy's and Matt's faces as they watched the scene. But he had wanted to reconcile with Lara for so long, had spent thousands of dollars trying to locate her, he desperately wanted to give her the benefit of the doubt.

"There are a lot of players out there, Lara. You have to be careful," Rod said, turning away from Matt, comforting her.

Poppy assumed Rod could no longer look at Matt because he knew he was choosing to believe his daughter's lies over the truth and just found it difficult to face him. Rod held his daughter and gently stroked her hair.

Matt took a step forward to defend himself, but Poppy reached out and grabbed his arm to stop him. She signaled him to remain mum.

"Why can't I find a decent boyfriend?" Lara wailed.

"You will, I promise," Rod said reassuringly. "Remember what I told you when you were a little girl—you'll come across a lot of frogs before you meet the right prince."

Poppy wanted to gag at Rod's sexist remark. As if the end goal was finding a prince. In her opinion, Rod needed to catch up on a few decades.

"Thanks for calling me, Poppy," Rod said with a tight

smile as he led Lara out. Matt dashed ahead of them to open the door, mostly to ensure they were actually going to leave, and as Rod passed him, Poppy heard him say under his breath, "Stay away from my daughter."

After they were out the door, Matt slammed it shut and turned to Poppy. "What the hell was that?"

"Be grateful he managed to get her out of here," Poppy said, relieved.

"But now her father thinks I'm a grade A sleazeball who uses women and then tosses them aside!" Matt cried.

"I'll set him straight, don't you worry," Poppy said emphatically.

"The girl does nothing but lie! One lie after another!"

"It does seem to be her favorite hobby. But at least it is over now. Hopefully, she won't be bothering you anymore."

"I still don't know how she got it into her head that I liked her! I was just being polite at her father's house the other day! I was never for one minute remotely interested in dating her or anything like that!"

"Matt, calm down. She met you and got a crush on you. It's perfectly understandable. You are super handsome with a buoyant personality. Any girl would fall for you. Look at Heather. . . ."

Matt checked his phone for the time again. "She's late."

His phone buzzed.

Matt's eyes widened, and his mouth dropped open.

"Is that Heather texting you?" Poppy asked.

Matt shook his head and looked up at Poppy, worried. "It's Lara."

"*What?* How did she get your number?"

"I gave it to Rod when he was a client. I told him to

call me day or night if he had any questions or concerns about the case. Lara must have somehow gotten it from him."

"What did she say?"

Matt stared at his phone, reading in a monotone voice, "'Stop playing hard to get. I know how you feel about me. Text me tomorrow. Good night. I love you.'"

"You need to change your number first thing tomorrow," Poppy warned.

Matt nodded. "I will."

The doorbell rang again. But instead of waiting for Matt to open the door, Heather breezed in, looking very alluring in a casual slimming fringe dress, her hair styled and her face made up. "Sorry I'm late. They asked me to work a double shift. I guess I'm doing okay in my first week."

She stopped in her tracks at the sight of Poppy. "Mom, what are you doing here?"

"Leaving. I just dropped by to discuss some business with Matt."

Heather seemed to buy it. She broke out into a smile. "Well, as long as you're here, why don't you stay and join us?"

"Yes," Matt chimed in. "Stay for dinner."

"I wouldn't hear of it. I don't want to make a habit out of being a third wheel. You two enjoy some private time," Poppy said as she headed to the door.

"You know, it's funny," Heather said, calling after her mother. "I swear I passed Rod Harper driving down the street as I was coming here. You know, I just remember him from TV but he looked exactly the same as he did on your show."

"Maybe he knows people around here," Poppy said, almost too quickly.

"Maybe," Heather said, turning to give Matt a kiss on the cheek.

There was a buzz from Matt's cell phone, which he had dumped in his back pocket. They all three stood there in silence. The phone buzzed again.

"Someone's texting you," Heather commented as she bounded toward the kitchen. "The garlic bread smells yummy!"

Matt's face drained of color. He was afraid to reach around and pull the phone out of his back pocket because he really didn't want to see who was so frantically sending him text after text at the moment because frankly he already knew.

Poppy gave him a sympathetic look before turning and walking out the door, silently hoping that Matt wouldn't have to move as well since his stalker, in addition to knowing his cell phone number, now also knew where he lived.

# Chapter 40

Matt flashed his megawatt smile and the hostess at the Sun Diner practically melted. She had to grip the rickety stand with her seating chart because her knees were about to buckle. Poppy marveled at how easily Matt could turn on his charm and win over even the most hardened, seen it all, unimpressed people, mostly women, of course. This particular woman, short, stout, with red hair and freckles, was smitten from the moment she looked up as Matt breezed through the door. Before she even had a chance to speak, he had complimented her haircut and the butterfly pin attached to her yellow blouse.

Poppy purposefully held back, not wanting to encroach on Matt's impressive skills to get her to open up and talk. But the hostess, who looked as if she was praying that the woman hovering behind Matt wasn't his much older girlfriend, asked tentatively, "Table for two?"

"We can't stay, although I hear your chicken and dumplings are out of this world," Matt said, licking his lips.

"Best in the valley," the hostess boasted.

"I'm Matt," he said with a wink, holding out his hand.

She eagerly took it, anxious to feel his touch, and couldn't help but giggle as she shook it and held on to it longer than normal. "Madge. How can I help you?"

Matt reached into his pocket and retrieved a paper slip and handed it over to Madge, who studied it. Violet had found it in the trash can at Alden Kenny's house and had added it to the other files and paperwork they had been poring over. They were now just getting around to following up on it. It was a credit card receipt from the Sun Diner, this very establishment. The meal had been charged to Alden's credit card, and the date and time were stamped on it. The same day he had been murdered, just a few hours before Poppy had stumbled across his dead body in the pool. And judging from the number of items that he had ordered, it was obvious Alden had not dined alone.

Matt circled around the hostess station and sidled up next to Madge, who eyed him hungrily and nearly quivered as their shoulders touched. He pointed to the name on the receipt. "Do you happen to know him?"

"Alden Kenny," she said, thinking hard, not wanting to disappoint this drop-dead-gorgeous man whose big hand was now resting lightly on her right shoulder. "I believe so. Young man, moved out here from Texas not too long ago."

"Yes, that's him!"

"I remember him because he was always very chatty

and had an unusual name. Alden. It stood out to me. He came in here just about every day for lunch. I think he had a window-washing business, or something like that."

"Carpet cleaning," Poppy corrected her.

Madge didn't seem to care what Poppy had to say. She kept her eyes on Matt. "He had a partner, Asian dude, who always ordered the club sandwich and a Diet Coke, every day, never anything else."

"Jay," Matt said helpfully.

Madge shrugged. "He never introduced himself so I didn't know his name. Alden was much friendlier, made a point of getting to know me and the other waitresses."

It made sense to Poppy. The waitresses at the Sun Diner were all too young for Jay Takamura to be interested in them.

Matt stepped away from her, and Madge shrunk a bit, disappointed. But it allowed him to make eye contact with her, and draw her in again. "Tell me, Madge, was Alden here with Jay on this day . . . ?"

"Oh, I wouldn't know—he was here all the time so it's hard to remember this particular day. . . ."

Matt leaned in. "It would mean a lot. . . ."

Madge was on a mission now. She could not possibly let this stunning man down. She plucked the receipt out of his hand and studied it some more. "It was a Thursday." She glanced over at the specials board. "Lemon pepper rainbow trout. Let me think. . . ."

Matt let her work through her thoughts. She suddenly looked up with a big grin on her face. "No, he wasn't with Jay. He was with some blonde. I remember now because she ordered the special."

Matt looked at the piece of paper. "Why isn't the fish special on the receipt?"

"Because she sent it back. She didn't like it. She was rude about it, too. Rosie, who waited on them, offered to bring her something else, but she said no. Alden liked his meatloaf and made a point of telling Rosie, mostly because he was embarrassed his girlfriend was being such a problem. They did order two desserts, though, two cheesecakes, and I remember seeing her scarf that down with no problem."

"So you think she was his girlfriend?" Poppy asked.

Madge looked right through Poppy, annoyed that she had to tear her eyes off Matt even for a moment to take the time to speak to her. "She was here with him maybe two or three times, tops. We just assumed they were dating. But nobody here could see them as a couple."

"Why not?" Matt asked.

Madge was relieved she could focus her attention back on Matt. "Because they didn't look like they belonged together. She was very statuesque, if that's the right word, and rather intimidating and bossy, and he was, well, he was just . . . Alden. A cute kid, kind of sweet. They made a very odd couple, if that's what they were."

"When they were here, did you hear Alden call her by name?" Matt asked.

Madge pouted, devastated that she couldn't be more helpful to Matt. "No, never, I'm so sorry."

"You've been a major help. Thank you, Madge. We have to go, but I'm coming back here for your chicken and dumplings!"

"I will serve you myself. Anything your heart desires," Madge promised.

"You're too good to me, Madge," Matt said with a wink.

"Come back anytime. You'll see how good I can be!"

Poppy nearly gagged but held her tongue, and followed Matt as he blew a kiss to his new admirer on his way out the door.

Outside the diner, Matt spun back around, startling Poppy. "So who do you think this mystery woman could be?"

"I have no idea, but according to Alden's business partner, Jay, they were close friends, so I'm sure he would know if his buddy was seeing someone."

"Where do we find him?"

Poppy checked the time on her phone. "It's too early for the casino so let's start with his carpet-cleaning business."

Matt hopped in the passenger side of Poppy's car as Poppy climbed behind the wheel. Using the Google Maps app on her phone, she drove them straight to the office location of Fresh Scrub Carpet Cleaners in Rancho Mirage. The company was located in an industrial park neighborhood in a nondescript building that housed various businesses selling kitchen supplies, picture framing and art supplies, and lamps. Fresh Scrub was on the far end and a van was parked out front. No sooner had they pulled into the drive when they saw Jay Takamura carry some equipment out the door and load it into the back of the van. Poppy pulled right up next to it. He didn't hear them because he was bopping his head to and fro to some music he was listening to through a pair of earbuds.

Matt marched foward, but Poppy hung back by the car since Jay might recognize her from when he came to steam clean Iris's carpets.

Matt yelled, "Mr. Takamura?!"

Jay didn't hear him as he wrestled with some tubes from his carpet-cleaning machine so Matt tried again. "Mr. Takamura?!"

Still no answer. Finally, Matt tapped Jay on the shoulder. He jumped and whirled around, hands raised in the air to defend himself. "What? What do you want?"

Matt always loved this part. He flashed his badge. "Matt Flowers, private investigator."

Jay studied the badge with a frown. Unlike Madge at the Sun Diner, Matt's charms were completely lost on him. "What do you want?"

"I have a few questions about your former business partner Alden Kenny," Matt said, mustering up as much authority in his voice as he could.

"Private detective? Who are you working for?" Jay asked warily.

"I'd rather not say," Matt said.

"Then I'd rather not answer your questions. I have a job and I'm running late," Jay snapped, turning his back on Matt and continuing to stuff his bulky equipment in the back of his van.

Jay was a far cry from the exuberant eager to please carpet cleaner who had shown up at Iris's house. He seemed to have a lot on his mind now. Poppy couldn't remain in the background any longer. She suddenly stepped forward, pushing Matt aside. "Please, Jay, we're just trying to find out who wanted to harm Alden. He was your best friend. Don't you want to know, too?"

Jay slowly turned back around. He stared at Poppy for a long moment. "Wait, I know you. Aren't you from Duluth?"

Matt glanced at Poppy, confused.

Poppy nodded. "Yes, at least that's what I told you. Iris's sister who was visiting from Minnesota. But my real name is Poppy Harmon and Matt and I work together at the Desert Flowers Detective Agency."

Jay's face fell. "And Iris . . . ?"

"Yes, she works with us, too," Poppy said with a nod.

"So that whole job, cleaning Iris's carpets, was just a ruse to get me to answer questions?"

"I'm sorry," Poppy said quietly. "Sometimes it's easier getting people to talk when they don't know they're speaking to an investigator." She decided not to divulge that his gambling buddy, Violet, at the Spa Resort Casino was also part of the team. Why reveal what she didn't have to?

"Then apparently I've told you all I know already," Jay huffed. "We're done here."

"That was before we found out about the fifty thousand dollars you withdrew from Alden's account," Poppy said loudly.

Jay froze, then spun back around and whispered urgently, "How did you know about that?"

"Did we not mention we are private *investigators*?" Matt said, folding his arms, happy to be back in the conversation. "That's what we do. We investigate."

"Where did it come from, Jay?" Poppy asked.

"I don't know," Jay said as he turned and slammed the back doors of the van shut and walked around to the driver's side.

Poppy and Matt exchanged a quick look, then followed after him, stopping him before he could climb in and try to speed off.

"You don't have to tell us, but I happen to be good friends with a Detective Lamar Jordan, who is also looking into Alden's murder. Maybe he's already questioned you. I'm sure he would be happy to show up at whatever house you're working at and ask you in front of your customers," Poppy said, adopting a threatening tone.

Jay sighed. "I told you, I don't know. The money just appeared in the account. I tried finding out where it came from, but the LLC was a shell company. There wasn't a lot of information. I figured it belonged to Alden given some of the stuff he used to be involved in. But he got killed before I had the chance to ask him about it. Since he was gone, and I had no way of finding out what it was for, I just withdrew it and didn't ask any questions."

Poppy and Matt stared at him, trying to gauge his honesty.

"Come on, you would've done the same thing," Jay cried. "I did nothing wrong! It was a joint account! So whatever's in there rightfully belongs to me, too!"

"Who's to say you didn't discover the money earlier? Maybe when you saw how much it was you decided to drown your partner in the pool so you could have all that cash to pay off your gambling debts!" Matt shouted accusingly.

Jay stumbled back. "How did you know—?"

"Are you deaf? *Investigators!*" Matt sneered.

"Okay, I have some gambling issues, but I did not kill Alden, okay? He was my friend, my business partner, we had a good thing going. Why would I jeopardize that? I miss him every day!" He began to tear up.

Poppy was inclined to believe him, especially since he had also appeared to be genuinely grieving for his friend when she and Iris had first met him at Iris's house.

"What about his girlfriend?" Matt suddenly asked.

Jay blinked and wiped the tears away with his shirt sleeve. "What about her?"

Poppy glanced at Matt and then back at Jay. "So you knew Alden was seeing someone?"

Jay nodded. "Yeah, not for very long. But he really liked her."

Matt took a step forward. "You got a name?"

"Tammy," Jay answered. "I don't remember her last name."

"Do you know how they met?" Matt asked.

Jay shrugged. "Nope. Just that they had to see each other on the down low because Tammy sported a fancy diamond ring on her finger, if you get my drift."

"She was married," Poppy said.

Jay nodded.

"How long was this Tammy together with Alden?" Matt asked.

Jay shrugged again. "Not long. A couple of weeks, maybe. Look, if I don't get to this job, I'm going to lose it, and there's not a lot of that fifty K left, so if you've got any more questions, you're going to have to come back later."

"No more questions," Poppy said.

Jay started to climb into the van but stopped halfway and looked back. "This Detective Jordan you mentioned, are you going to rat me out about the fifty grand because it's pretty much gone already."

"We'll have to get back to you on that," Poppy said.

Jay grimaced and then jumped into the driver's seat, strapped himself in, and peeled away, circling around at the dead end of the industrial park and out the drive toward his next job.

Matt turned to Poppy. "Do you think he's telling us the truth?"

Poppy barely heard him. She was rolling the name Tammy over and over in her mind before it suddenly dawned on her. "Tammy . . . Tammy . . ."

Matt stared at her. "What is it?"

"After Tony Molina's trial, I was having dinner with Rod Harper at Cicci's and Molina strolled in, and he was flanked by his two bodyguards. They were a married couple, which I found unusual. And I remember he called the woman Tammy and she was tall and blond."

"So Alden's girlfriend was working security for Tony Molina? That's one more awfully big coincidence," Matt remarked. "Everything always seems to point back to Tony Molina."

"Yes, and I'm convinced Tammy and her husband were the same couple who first approached Glenda Felson at the jury service office even though she has refused to identify them out of her loyalty to Tony Molina."

"So if this bodyguard was seeing Alden Kenny on the sly, why would she kill him?"

"Maybe she wasn't seeing him on the sly. Maybe it was part of her job. To get close to him and find out if he was going to remain quiet about his role in the jury tampering at Tony Molina's trial. I'm certain Alden was about to come clean to me about it. If that was the case, then perhaps Tammy found out what he was going to do, and maybe with her husband's help killed Alden to prevent him from ever talking and incriminating Tony."

Poppy's cell phone began buzzing inside her bag. She reached in and pulled it out, checking the caller ID. It was Heather. She turned to Matt. "I need to take this." She answered the call. "Hi, honey, what's up?"

"Mother, I've been arrested."

# Chapter 41

Poppy and Matt raced to the Palm Desert Police Department, where Heather had been booked for assault and was biding her time in a jail cell until her mother could post bail. Once that was completed, a rotund female officer with a severe expression and no sense of humor led Heather down the hall to the waiting area, where she was released and allowed to leave until her arraignment the following morning. Poppy hugged her daughter, who appeared disheveled, scattered, and confused. Poppy had warned Matt on their way to the station not to immediately deluge Heather with questions about what had happened. They could get all the answers later after they managed to get Heather out of police custody.

Heather turned to the female officer and in a scratchy, tired voice simply said, "Thank you."

The officer was surprised by the polite gesture and her stern expression melted just a bit, but she didn't want to appear soft so she grunted a quick reply, turned on her heel, and marched off down the hall.

Poppy and Matt wasted no time in spiriting Heather away before the cops could change their minds. Once they had bundled Heather into the backseat of Poppy's car and taken their seats in the front, Poppy turned around to look at her daughter, whose cheeks were smeared with mascara from crying.

"Honey, are you okay?" Poppy asked gently.

Heather nodded, still a bit disoriented.

Poppy reached over the seat and took her daughter's hand. "It's all right. You're with us now. Can you tell us what happened?"

Heather stared into space. "I honestly don't know. . . . I got my first paycheck at the restaurant today and I thought I would splurge and buy a new dress so I went to that shop you told me about on El Paseo. . . ."

Poppy nodded. "Lana May's Boutique?"

"Yes, they were having a sale. I was just trying a few things on and suddenly she was just there. . . ."

Matt perked up. "Who?"

"This girl . . . woman, I should say. She had to be in her early twenties. Anyway, I was standing in front of the mirror wondering if I needed to try the dress on in a smaller size since I had lost so much weight when I was in prison. . . ." Heather's voice trailed off. Just the mention of her time behind bars depressed her. But after a brief pause, she steeled herself and continued. "And I felt this tap on my shoulder. When I turned around she was standing there, and she said that she had seen the dress I was wearing earlier and it belonged to her and I should take it off that instant. At first, I thought she was joking."

"Did you know her?" Matt asked.

Heather shook her head. "No, I'd never seen her before. But she was wearing dark glasses and maybe some kind of wig. I'm not sure. She just appeared out of nowhere. I kind of laughed and turned back around to take one more look in the mirror, and the next thing I know, she's grabbing the zipper in the back of my dress and yanking it down. She was going to tear it off me!"

Poppy let go of her daughter's hand and covered her mouth. "What on earth . . . ?"

"It was awful, Mother. I let out this shocked scream and tried to push her away, but that just made her madder, and she came at me and started pounding me with her fists and pulling at my hair. She gave me a hard shove and I fell into a dress rack. The next thing I know she's on top of me and we're rolling around and I'm yelling for help and the security guard comes over and has to pull us apart! I tried to explain that she started it, and he's looking at me, and behind him I see this girl take one hand and just scratch herself with these long nails up the arm so deep she draws blood, and then she's waving it in the air and showing him and claiming I did it!"

"The girl was obviously a nutcase!" Matt cried. "How did *you* wind up arrested?"

"The boutique owner must have called the cops because two officers were on the scene within minutes, and the girl is screaming that I must be some kind of violent criminal, and they went to get a first aid kit for her arm, and that's when one of the officers took my driver's license and went out to his squad car. He must have run a check on me because when he came back he knew I was a recent parolee, and that was pretty much it. They suddenly believed her and not me and I was placed under arrest."

Poppy gasped. "Oh, Heather, no . . ."

Heather couldn't hold in her emotions any longer. She broke down and sobbed, covering her face with her hands. "What am I going to do? They're going to send me back to prison for violating my parole."

Poppy whipped back around, started the car, and peeled out onto Highway 111 heading back to Palm Springs. "You are not going back there, not if I can help it."

Matt glanced warily at Poppy, fearful she might be making a promise she could not possibly keep. But Poppy was determined. She had a strong feeling she might know what happened, but she was going to need help proving it.

She placed a call to Iris and Violet and dispatched them to Lana May's Boutique to talk to the owner. Then, after dropping Matt off and arriving back at the apartment, she put Heather to bed for a nap and started a pot of her homemade gumbo, one of Heather's favorites, for when she woke up. Poppy tried to keep busy, cleaning up, dusting, getting as many chores as she could think of out of the way, waiting for Iris or Violet to call. Just before seven, with Heather still resting, Poppy's phone finally rang. It was Violet.

Poppy quickly answered the call. "Yes, Violet?"

"Today is Heather's lucky day. There was a security camera in the store. The owner allowed Iris and me to take a look at it, and sure enough, it's very clear who started the fight, and it *wasn't* Heather! It was that awful girl."

Poppy breathed a heavy sigh of relief. "Thank God. Any idea who she is?"

"Not from the store camera. Her big sunglasses covered a lot of her face and her hair looked fake, like she was wearing a wig, and her clothes were bulky so it was hard to tell her body type, if she was on the thin side or chunky. . . ."

She could hear Iris bellowing from a distance, "She gave a fake name to the police!"

"Then I guess we will never know for sure. . . ."

"Don't despair, Poppy, because we didn't stop there. The boutique owner remembered seeing the girl flee to the parking lot in the back after the police arrested Heather, and there was a camera from the law office next door that has a view of the whole lot. Apparently they get a bunch of sordid types showing up looking to hire an attorney. Anyway, Iris got him to show her the footage, and she saw the girl get in her car and take off her wig and sunglasses and you will never guess who it was—"

"Lara Harper," Poppy said flatly.

"You guessed it!" Violet cried. "I wish we had some kind of prize we could give you!"

Poppy felt a rage building within her. She knew what Lara's game was. She had suspected it from the start. Rod's daughter was obsessed with Matt. She saw Heather as some kind of threat in her sick, twisted mind. And so she had decided to get her out of the picture by sabotaging her parole and getting her tossed back into prison so she could have Matt all to herself.

Poppy thanked Violet and hung up. The gumbo on the

stove was now bubbling, but her stew wasn't the only thing boiling. Poppy was incensed, and she was not about to let this disturbed, malevolent young woman, who was incapable of telling the truth about anything, cause any more harm.

No, Poppy was on the warpath now, like a mother bear protecting her cub.

She was not going to allow *anyone* to mess with her family.

# Chapter 42

Poppy anticipated Rod's reluctance to accept the fact that his daughter was unhinged. In fact, when she showed up unannounced at his Palm Springs house to confront him about Lara's illicit behavior, she came armed with a copy of the surveillance footage on her phone from both the boutique and the parking lot so there would be no doubt as to the identity of the person who accosted Heather while she was innocently shopping at Lana May's.

When Poppy explained to Rod what had happened at the boutique, he at first refused to believe that his daughter was capable of anything like that, stammering that it had to be some kind of misunderstanding. But before he could go on any further, Poppy simply raised her phone up in front of his face and played the video. From the moment Lara got into her car and pulled off the sunglasses and the wig in plain view of the camera, Rod gave up trying. He knew Lara had been caught red-handed.

He laughed bitterly. "So it's come to this. I'm now that nervous, seedy character who lied through his teeth in dozens of *Jack Colt* episodes, who always buckled under pressure and finally gave up the truth when Jack confronted him with the hard evidence. How pathetic."

"Don't beat yourself up, Rod. She's your daughter. It's natural for you to want to protect her."

Rod stared at the floor and mumbled, "Is Heather going to press charges?"

"No, I don't think so."

"That's very kind of her."

"Heather does not want to cause a scene. The poor girl's just trying to keep her head down and not make waves while she's on parole. But you need to have a talk with Lara. She has this idea in her head that Matt is her boyfriend and it's gotten way out of control."

"I tried discussing it with her when I picked her up at Matt's house. She wouldn't tell me much, but she did mention that she recently lost her last boyfriend and she's been feeling alone and vulnerable. When she met Matt, who, let's face it, comes across as this charismatic, powerful, confident man, well, she was naturally drawn to him."

"But Matt is with Heather! Lara needs to understand that even if she somehow got rid of her, like she tried to do today, that does not mean Matt is going to somehow magically wind up with her."

"I know. I will try to make that clear when she gets home," Rod said solemnly.

"Do you have any idea where she is now?"

Rod shook his head. "No, not a clue. I try not to pry too much because I don't want her feeling trapped here and running off again. I want us to reach a place where we can trust each other again."

Poppy wanted to suggest to Rod that he take Lara to the nearest psychiatrist for an immediate mental evaluation, but she held her tongue, concluding that her advice might not be the most helpful at the moment.

"I have a pot roast in the oven. Would you like to stay for dinner?"

Poppy chuckled. "Since when do you cook?"

"I've become quite the Gordon Ramsay. Got into it in my early sixties after my last divorce. I was tired of eating out every night. I actually find it relaxing. Come on. Stay. I think you'll find I'm not bad at it."

"I really should get home to Heather," Poppy said.

Rod appeared to be trying to read her mind. "Just dinner, I promise."

She hadn't thought the invitation was a ploy to get her to stay so he could try to woo her into the bedroom, but she was grateful that he was taking that possibility off the table.

"Lara will be home at some point, and I would also appreciate you being here to help me talk to her about what happened today. She can't lie to me if she's forced to watch the video evidence you have on your phone like I was," Rod said.

Poppy could tell he was apprehensive and scared to confront his daughter about her atrocious behavior on his own and was desperate for some backup. Poppy hesitated, not wanting any part of it, but Rod was a friend after all, someone she cared about, perhaps too much, so she nodded and finally said, "I'll stay."

Rod was elated. He clapped his hands together. "Fantastic. I'll go pour you a glass of wine." He bounded into the kitchen, leaving Poppy to look around at some of the framed pictures Rod had around the house. One of him during the *Jack Colt* days, in the Oval Office with Ronald Reagan. Another one with Elizabeth Taylor at some charity gala. She even spotted one of Rod and herself, back in the day, looking so young and fresh and happy, on the set of *Jack Colt*. She could not tell what year it was, although she guessed it was sometime during the second season from her hairstyle. There was one of Rod bouncing Lara on his knee, some years later, probably around 1998, when Lara was a toddler. She looked so innocent and carefree, exuberantly happy to be with her father. Poppy couldn't take her eyes off the picture. What had happened to that little girl to make her so erratic and disturbed now?

Rod returned with Poppy's wine and handed it to her. "I know you like a good Pinot Noir. This is Chilean. Has a nice ripeness, bold flavors, but mostly I like it because it's a twist-off top."

Poppy laughed and took a sip. "Delicious."

"I have more work to do in the kitchen. Make yourself at home," Rod said, heading off again.

Poppy heard him clanging about and wandered around, looking at more photographs, until she found herself in a long hallway that led to the bedrooms. She hadn't intended on snooping, but when she happened upon a room where Lara was obviously staying, she looked back to make sure Rod was still in the kitchen, and then slipped inside, closed the door most of the way, and turned on a light.

Lara didn't appear to have too many belongings. A few outfits in the closet. A couple of primitive sketches on a night table of possible cover art for her future album. On top of a desk in the corner was a laptop computer. Poppy walked over and sat down, then flipped the computer open. There was a box to type in a password. Poppy pondered whether or not this was a smart call, attempting to hack into someone's personal computer, but she was too worried about what Lara might be capable of not to at least try to get a better understanding of this young woman's troubled life. She wished Wyatt was with her at this moment because he would probably have no problem gaining access in a matter of seconds.

On a whim, Poppy typed in four letters. M-a-t-t. Matt. As in Matt Flowers, Lara's latest obsession. And lo and behold, it worked. Poppy was suddenly staring at Lara's desktop with several rows of folders labeled by letters. Poppy took another sip of her wine, set the glass down, and clicked on a folder marked *AI*, which turned out to be photos and song sheets from her brief time on *American Idol*. She clicked on another one labeled *F*. This one was full of photos of Lara with her ex-boyfriend, the loopy yoga instructor Falcon. They were on some kind of spiritual retreat on the Big Island of Hawaii. Poppy quickly clicked out when she happened upon a bunch of nude selfies of the once happy couple among all the lush, brightly colored Hawaiian foliage. She had seen enough of that. Her next folder was labeled *M*, and this one sent a shiver up Poppy's spine when she opened it. There were copied digital press clippings from their first big case that had put the Desert Flowers Detective Agency on the map.

Most of the photos heavily featured Matt, who was the designated face of the agency. There was also a head shot of Matt from when he first moved out to LA to pursue acting and a photocopy of a theatre program from when Matt appeared in a play in Palm Springs. Lara had done some very thorough research on Matt since she had first set her sights on him, and it didn't ease Poppy's mind at all about her mental condition.

There was another folder marked *D*, and Poppy clicked on that one next, assuming it might be yet another boyfriend since Lara clearly had a tendency to keep exhaustive records of her past relationships and current obsessions. Poppy sat back in the chair, stunned, as she took in all the photos of Lara with a more recent paramour, a strikingly good-looking, dark-haired, olive-skinned young man, who stared lovingly into Lara's eyes in most of the photographs.

He could have been of Middle Eastern descent, or Greek, judging from his complexion, but Poppy knew at first glance he was Italian.

She knew because she had seen him before.

She knew exactly who he was.

The *D* stood for Dominick.

Dominick Molina.

Tony Molina's son.

The same Dominick Molina who had been a pillar of support in the courtroom for his father and who had just been arrested for the murder of his stepmother, Tofu, and whose handsome mug was all over the news.

Suddenly a shriek startled Poppy, who spun around to see Lara Harper standing in the doorway to the bedroom, eyes blazing. "What are you doing in my room?"

Before Poppy could come up with an answer, Lara was screaming for her father. Poppy heard Rod pounding down the hall from the kitchen, drawn to the commotion.

Lara Harper wasn't the only one who had been caught red-handed today.

# Chapter 43

Rod quickly appeared at his daughter's side, his face ashen at the sight of Poppy in Lara's bedroom, sitting in front of her laptop computer.

Lara, her eyes wild with fury, pointed an accusing finger at Poppy, who calmly stood up from the small desk. "I came home and found her snooping on my computer!"

"She's right. I was," Poppy said evenly. "It wasn't difficult, either, once I guessed the password, which, not surprisingly, was just four letters. M-a-t-t. Matt."

Rod turned to Lara, who was thrown off guard for just a second. "Is that true, Lara?"

"Yes, but I know a lot of Matts; I have a gay friend named Matt. It doesn't refer to her friend Matt Flowers," Lara lied. "I'm not a *stalker*."

Poppy knew that anyone who had to claim not to be a stalker more often than not turned out to be one.

Lara charged into the room, pushed past Poppy, and slammed her computer shut. "I would appreciate it if you got out of my room now!"

Poppy stood right where she was, never flinching. "You never went to Nepal to find yourself. We were right from the beginning. You were right here in the Coachella Valley the entire time with your boyfriend . . . Dominick Molina."

Lara shot her father a worried look.

Rod was still processing what he had just heard. "Dominick . . . Tony's boy?"

Lara glared at Poppy and seethed. "Why don't you mind your own business? The last time I checked, I'm not missing anymore so you are no longer working for my father!"

Poppy ignored her and spoke directly to Rod. "I found some photos of the two of them on her computer that were taken recently during the time she *claimed* to be in Nepal."

"What's going on here, Lara?" Rod asked pointedly, stepping into the room.

"Why am I suddenly getting the third degree? She's the one who snuck into my room and was sticking her nose into my personal business!" Lara shouted angrily. "Why aren't you questioning *her*?"

"Because I'm talking to you, and I want you to tell me the truth for once. Are you involved with Dominick Molina? Is he the young man you were spotted around Palm Springs with when I was looking for you?"

"Okay, yes. I lied about Nepal. I was mad at you for trying to control my life, and I knew you didn't like Tony Molina so I made up that story about traveling overseas. I was here hanging out with Dominick. He's very sweet. If you gave him half a chance, I think you'd really like him."

"How could I give him a chance? You ran away. I had no idea where you were or who you were with," Rod said softly. "You had me so worried. . . ."

"And I'm sorry about that, Daddy, but I just needed some space, and we were fighting so much back in Beverly Hills. I wanted to put some distance between us, at least for a while, so I came out here because Dominick promised to help me with my singing career. His father has this state-of-the-art recording studio in his home and Tony was so nice. He agreed to let us use it to record my first album. Dominick wants to be a music producer. He's also a very talented songwriter. He was helping me compose some of the songs."

Poppy was having none of it. She was tired of Lara and her grating, spoiled personality. "Was this before or after he shot his stepmother?"

There was silence in the bedroom.

Rod glanced at Poppy, surprised by her directness.

Lara scowled and sighed. "I don't know anything about that."

"Really? Because right after Dominick murdered Tofu, you magically reappeared, claiming to be home from your world travels, ready to reconcile with your father and move right in here with him," Poppy said.

"Dominick didn't murder anyone! There isn't a violent bone in his body!"

"Is that so? Because it happens to be public knowledge that he has already made a full confession," Poppy snapped.

"You don't know anything!" Lara huffed, before rushing out of the room. Rod warily followed after her, with Poppy on his heels, into the living room, where they found

Lara by the front door, gripping the door handle. "Daddy, I'm serious, either she goes or I go. I don't like the way she talks to me."

"Poppy is a big part of my life now. She's not going anywhere," Rod said. "You're going to have to accept that."

Poppy wasn't sure how she should take Rod's proclamation, but she decided to ignore it, at least for the moment.

Lara shrugged. "I don't have to accept anything! I'm out of here!"

Lara spun around and was about to fly out the front door when Poppy called after her. "You were there, weren't you?"

Lara froze halfway in the threshold. She slowly turned around. It was the first time Poppy had actually seen her look scared.

The young woman's mind seemed to race for a bit and then she settled on what to say next. "No I wasn't!"

Another obvious lie.

Lara knew Poppy wasn't buying it, and neither was her father.

"Come on, Lara . . . ," Rod prodded, arms folded across his broad chest.

Lara threw her head back, exasperated. "Oh, all right! Yes, I was there! But I was in the other room! I only *heard* what happened!"

"What would drive Dominick to do such a thing?" Rod asked.

Lara shut the front door and slowly walked back into the living room. "It was an accident! It wasn't Dominick's fault! His creepy stepmother wouldn't leave him alone! She was always showing up at the studio while we were working. She'd wear these really clingy, tight, low-cut dresses, trying to get his attention all the time. I mean, ewww, gross!"

Poppy was already aware that Tofu had a penchant for younger men given her past history, but she kept mum, waiting to hear the rest of what Lara had to say.

"Dominick told me that every time I left the room she would make passes at him. It made him so uncomfortable. He didn't dare tell his father because he was afraid Tony wouldn't believe him and he might kick us out before we finished the album, so he just put up with it," Lara said. "How sleazy to be chasing after your own stepson! It was totally sick!"

"Go on," Rod said quietly.

"Well, on that day, the day he shot her, I went out to get us some sandwiches for lunch, and when I came back, she was back again and had her hands all over him, and finally he couldn't take it anymore. He pushed her away and told her to stay away from him. Well, that set her off and she got really mad and stormed off. A couple of hours later, she came back, stumbling drunk, waving a gun around, like she was going to shoot us both! I started crying and she came after me, pointing the gun, yelling that I had stolen Dominick away from her, and that's when Dominick got in between us, trying to protect me, and he grabbed the gun, trying to wrestle it away from her! I ran out of the room, screaming for help, and that's when I heard the gun go off. . . ."

Lara sniffed and blinked tears.

Rod seemed to melt. He rushed forward and embraced his daughter, holding her close and patting the back of her head, promising her it would be all right.

Poppy was utterly unimpressed with her performance.

Lara Harper was a consummate liar, and she gave Poppy no reason to believe she was telling the truth now.

"Why didn't you go to the police?" Poppy asked pointedly.

"Because Dominick wouldn't let me. He didn't want me mixed up in any of it. He told me we had to protect my career at all costs. I had already called Daddy because I missed him and wanted to reconnect, and so Dominick told me to go home and let him handle everything!" Lara sobbed, finally pulling out of her father's arms.

"But he's charged with murder!" Poppy cried. "You're a witness. You could clear everything up by telling exactly what happened, that Dominick shot Tofu in self-defense."

Lara shrugged. "I'm just doing what Dominick wants, and he wants me to stay out of it. He said if anybody can get him off, his father can."

"Oh, I have seen ample evidence of that already first-hand," Poppy said bitterly.

Rod looked completely lost as to what he should do. He glanced toward Poppy for guidance.

"You have to go to the police and tell them everything you know," Poppy declared.

"I most certainly do not," Lara sniped.

Poppy shook her head, disgusted. "So you're willing to let Dominick rot in prison? The man you're supposedly so head over heels in love with?"

Lara kept her mouth shut because she knew neither Poppy nor her father would like her answer to the question, that she didn't care what happened to Dominick because she really only cared about herself and had already set her sights on a new man.

"I'm sure Tony will somehow take care of things," Lara finally said. "Dominick will be fine."

"Keep telling yourself that," Poppy said with a sad little laugh. She reached into her bag and pulled out her cell phone.

Lara eyed her nervously. "Who are you calling?"

"Detective Lamar Jordan," Poppy said. "Just because you refuse to do the right thing doesn't mean I have to."

Lara gave her father a pleading look, silently begging for him to do something to stop her, but Rod just stood next to her, looking numb, still reeling from the fusillade of lies that kept spilling out of his only daughter's mouth.

# Chapter 44

When Poppy hung up after placing a call to Detective Jordan, Rod pulled her aside as Lara pouted on the couch. "She's very upset, Poppy. Do we have to do this now?"

"She is a key witness in a murder investigation. Either she comes with us to the police station to talk to Detective Jordan or he is going to drive over here and get her himself."

Rod looked sadly over at Lara, who was now on her phone, furiously texting.

Poppy put a hand on Rod's arm. "You have to stop coddling her."

Rod stared grimly at his daughter. "I know, you're right. I'm just so afraid of losing her again."

Poppy didn't necessarily believe that was such a bad

thing, but she refrained from comment. Rod tentatively crossed over to where Lara was sitting, her fingers tapping madly on her phone screen. "We should go, Lara."

"I don't have to do what she says. She's not my mother," Lara hissed.

"But I'm your father and I'm telling you we should go," Rod said solemnly.

Lara continued texting, not moving.

"I can do what I want. I'm twenty-two years old," Lara said, not even bothering to look up from her phone.

"Well, you're acting like a whiny ten-year-old," Poppy heard herself saying. She couldn't take it anymore. She crossed over to the couch, past Rod, and snatched the phone out of Lara's hand.

"Give that back!" Lara roared.

Poppy glanced at the screen.

She was texting Matt.

**Please, they're making me go talk to the police. I'm scared. Meet me there. I need you for moral support.**

Poppy showed Rod the text on the screen and then turned back to Lara. "I'm guessing this isn't your gay friend Matt because I recognize the number. You're texting Matt Flowers."

"So what?" Lara spit out.

"I hate to break it to you, but he may not get this message because I already advised him to change his number," Poppy said.

This got Lara's attention. "You *what*?"

"It seemed to be the only way for him to stop receiving dozens of texts from you a day," Poppy said, eyeing Rod, who seemed genuinely surprised by this revelation.

"*Dozens?*" Rod asked, eyes widened.

"Once you abandoned Dominick after things got too heated, you set your sights on Matt because you're never happy unless you are in a relationship and have someone you can manipulate, but you never bothered consulting Matt to find out if he was even the least bit interested in you. You just decided he would be the next man in your life, whether he wanted to be or not," Poppy said.

Lara jumped up from the couch and snatched her phone back from Poppy. "You know nothing about what Matt and I have together!"

"But I do, Lara. That's the sad part. I know that he has zero interest in you and that you will never be a couple, and sooner or later you are going to have to grow up and accept that and get on with your life."

Lara's face flushed with rage and her hands started shaking as she stepped menacingly toward Poppy. "I'll tell you what's sad. You, trying to keep Matt and me apart, for the sake of your loser daughter, who will never be good enough for him!"

Poppy fought the urge to raise her hand and slap Lara Harper hard across the face. She never believed violence was the answer to any problem, and she was not about to engage in it now. But it took every ounce of self-restraint not to do it. She took a deep breath, and then turned to Rod, who was still stunned at what Lara had just said to Poppy.

"Rod, I think it would be best if I left now before I say or do anything I will regret. But I implore you, take your daughter to Detective Jordan and have her tell him what she knows about the Tofu murder. It's the right thing to do."

"Poppy, I'm so sorry—"

Poppy had no interest in hearing Rod apologize for his ghastly daughter ever again, so she quickly whirled around and marched out the door before he could say another word.

# Chapter 45

Poppy wasn't sure Rod had followed her advice until the next morning when Detective Jordan called and left a message that he wanted to see her at his office. Poppy wasted no time after a quick breakfast with Heather to drive straight over to the police station. The desk sergeant asked her to wait, and after twenty minutes, she was finally escorted down a hall to a small windowless office where Detective Jordan sat behind his desk, eating an Egg McMuffin and leafing through some paperwork.

"Thanks for stopping by, Poppy," Detective Jordan said, using a napkin to wipe away some egg yolk dribbling down his chin.

"However I can help, Detective," Poppy said, feeling emboldened that the detective, who had once dismissed her as a nuisance, was now calling her in for consultation.

She sat down across from him.

"Your boyfriend was in here yesterday with his daughter. . . ."

"Excuse me, *boyfriend*?"

"The actor. Rob Harper, the one who was on that TV show I watched when I was a kid where you played his secretary . . ."

"His name is Rod Harper, and he is *not* my boyfriend," Poppy said sharply.

Detective Jordan seemed thoroughly confused. "Oh . . . he kind of gave me the impression that you two—"

"We're *not*."

Detective Jordan nodded. "Okay. Well, I listened to his daughter Lara's story, about what happened at Tony Molina's house with her boyfriend and Tofu, and although on the surface it sounds plausible, there are some details that don't exactly add up."

Poppy had expected this since Lara Harper seemed utterly incapable of telling the truth on just about any occasion.

Jordan picked up what was left of his Egg McMuffin and said, "To be frank, the young woman struck me as a little off. Possibly emotionally disturbed, if I'm being totally honest."

"You will get no argument from me, Detective."

Jordan stuffed the rest of his Egg McMuffin into his mouth and Poppy waited patiently as he loudly chewed and swallowed. Then he wiped his fingers with the napkin and dabbed at his chin again to make sure he didn't literally have any egg on his face. Only then was he ready to resume the conversation. "The Harper girl told me she was not in the room when Dominick Molina accidentally shot his stepmother."

"Yes, she told me and her father the same thing."

"She claimed that when Dominick and Tofu started struggling for possession of the gun, she ran out of the room screaming."

"Presumably to get help," Poppy said, nodding.

"Right," Jordan said, picking up a piece of bacon that had dropped out of the sandwich and onto the desk and popping it into his mouth. "The thing is, she mentioned that Tofu had been shot in the abdomen. How would she know that unless she was still in the room? When I called her on it, she said she must have read about that detail online or heard about it on TV."

"I didn't know Tofu had been shot in the abdomen," Poppy said, leaning forward, intrigued.

"Of course you didn't because that information was never released to the press. We've been keeping it under wraps while we're still investigating, so there was no way Lara Harper could know that *unless* she was still in the room when the shooting occurred."

Poppy sat back in her chair, gobsmacked. "Why would she lie about not being in the room? If she was in the room and saw what happened, that would only bolster her story that Dominick shot Tofu in self-defense. She would be an eyewitness."

"Here's the thing," Jordan said. "When I questioned Dominick Molina, he basically told the same story as Lara, except when I asked him whereabouts he accidentally shot Tofu, he hesitated, like he didn't know. When I asked if it was in the chest, he didn't figure it was a test, and just agreed and said, 'Yes, in the chest.' If he had been the one struggling with Tofu, he would've known that when the gun fired, the bullet entered her abdomen."

Poppy whispered, "It was *her*. . . . Lara was the one who shot Tofu."

"And I believe her boyfriend, Dominick, is covering for her," Jordan added. "He's taking the blame in order to protect her."

"He probably has no idea that she's already moved on and is now chasing after someone else," Poppy said disdainfully.

"When I suggested that scenario, Lara got real nervous and clammed up pretty quick. There was no way she was going to admit anything to me."

Poppy did a slow burn. She felt sorry for Rod, but she was also fiercely determined to see Lara face justice. "What are you going to do?"

"I need her to confess, but I think it's safe to say she won't confide in either you or me. I was hoping you might be able to talk to her father; maybe he can get the truth out of her. . . ."

"No, she'll never tell him anything," Poppy said, frustrated, then gasped as an idea quickly came to her. "But perhaps there is someone she may open up to given the opportunity. . . ."

# Chapter 46

"Poppy is a deeply controlling woman. She pressured me for months to stay loyal to her daughter, Heather, even though I tried to tell her a dozen times I was ready to move on, but she expected me to wait until she was released from prison, and just pick up where we left off, even though I obviously didn't love her anymore," Matt said, cold and detached.

"Why didn't you just quit and be done with both of them?" Lara asked.

"Because frankly I needed the job. I had to keep playing the role of private investigator Matt Flowers even though I hated every minute of it. I really just wanted to be back in LA working on my acting career."

"When Daddy told me you weren't really the boss, that Poppy was actually the one in charge, I felt so sorry that you were stuck working for that horrible woman! I could tell there was something weird going on when I met you."

"Honestly I just wanted to grab you and kiss you from the moment I first laid eyes on you, Lara, but I couldn't because Poppy was watching me like a hawk. I had to pretend that I wasn't interested out of fear she'd lash out and fire me."

"Well, you don't have to worry about that anymore, Matt," Lara purred. "You're finally out from under her thumb, and there is nothing she can do now to keep us apart."

"I'm going to have to find a way to pay rent," Matt said sullenly.

"You don't have to worry about that. Daddy will help me find a place in LA and take care of the rent, at least for a while, until my album comes out. . . ."

"And I start booking some roles," Matt said, his voice brimming with confidence.

Poppy, in the back of a police van parked across the street from Rod Harper's Palm Springs home, was huddled next to Detective Jordan as they listened to the conversation through Matt's phone. She put a hand to her mouth. "He sounds so convincing, it's chilling."

"You said he was a good actor," Detective Jordan said, taking a sip of his Starbucks coffee.

"I didn't know he was *that* good," Poppy said, impressed.

They heard some ice clinking, presumably one of them sucking down the rest of a drink. "Another mojito?" Lara asked.

"Are you trying to get me drunk?" Matt asked playfully.

"That's my master plan," Lara giggled.

"I'm good. If I get too sloppy, my brain will get fuzzy, and I want a crystal clear memory of everything that's going to go down this afternoon."

Poppy knew he had punctuated that statement with a charming wink. She could hear Lara breathing heavily as she excitedly anticipated a steamy seduction ahead of her.

"Come on, let's go swimming," Lara cooed.

"I didn't bring my suit," Matt said.

"It's Palm Springs, stud. Swimsuits are optional, though highly discouraged."

Poppy and Jordan could hear some rustling sounds, like Matt and Lara were shedding their clothes.

Poppy covered her eyes instinctively. "Oh, Matt . . ."

Detective Jordan chuckled. "It's not like you can see them."

"I'm suddenly getting a visual image, which is just as disturbing!" Poppy wailed.

They heard splashing sounds as the young couple jumped into the pool and then some lip smacking as they kissed hungrily. Finally, Matt spoke. "What if your father comes home?"

"He's got a meeting in LA with some studio execs about this new TV show that shoots in New York. He won't be back until late tonight," Lara promised.

More splashing.

More lip smacking.

Poppy felt physically ill picturing Matt frolicking with Rod's overindulged, damaged daughter. After what felt like an interminable amount of time, the young couple finally came up for air.

"Have you talked to Heather yet?" Lara asked.

"No, she's left me a few messages, but I'm ghosting her. Pretty soon she'll get the message and stop bothering me."

"Let's hope her awful mother follows suit, too."

Poppy frowned. This heinous, beastly young woman was working her last nerve. And she hated putting Matt in this position of pretending to be attracted to Lara Harper in order to guide her into confessing what really happened on the day Tofu was shot. He had been playing it cool and casual, but Poppy knew the opportunity had just arisen for him to make his move now that Lara had inquired about his relationship with Heather. And like the pro he was quickly becoming, Matt did not disappoint.

"What about Dominick?" he asked.

"What about him?" Lara replied, sounding almost bored.

"He's not going to be a problem for us, is he?"

"God, no . . . He's already told the police his version of what happened. He did it. He was the one who shot Tofu. If he suddenly changes his story, they'll just think he's a desperate liar trying to shift the blame away from himself."

"Why would he change his story?"

Lara giggled. "You feel so good. . . ."

"I love holding you, having you in my arms. . . ."

They could hear them kissing again.

Then, after a long pause, Matt gently said, "You didn't answer my question."

Lara was clearly struggling with herself, not sure if she should say anymore. "If Dominick says he was the one who shot Tofu, then that's what happened."

Matt gasped. "You little vixen . . . it was you, wasn't it?"

More water splashed as Lara presumably climbed out of the pool and grabbed a towel. She was much louder now because she was standing next to Matt's phone, which he apparently had put down next to a stack of towels. He must have followed her out as well because his voice was louder now, too.

"Come on, you can tell me. . . ."

"It's probably best if we drop this," Lara warned.

"You're right. Maybe I shouldn't know," Matt said.

"Why? Would it make a difference if I told you Dominick's story wasn't the *whole* truth?"

"No, of course not. Nothing you tell me would ever make a difference."

They stopped talking while Lara made them both another drink.

They clinked glasses.

"To us," Matt said softly.

Detective Jordan was starting to get impatient in the back of the van. "Come on . . . She's so close to telling him. . . ."

Poppy put a reassuring hand on his arm.

She knew just how good Matt was at getting people to talk when they shouldn't.

"Whatever secrets you have in that pretty little head of yours can stay there," Matt said. "I don't have to know. I just want to protect you from anything that might harm you."

This reasonable argument seemed to land because within seconds Lara was spilling the beans. "It was me."

"*What?*" Poppy heard Matt say, sounding as if he was surprised his charms had worked so fast.

"I shot Tofu," Lara admitted before quickly adding, "But it *was* self-defense, I promise!"

"Okay . . . ," Matt said calmly, waiting for more.

He didn't have to wait long before she was off and running.

"Dominick was telling the truth about Tofu showing up at the recording studio in Tony's house, where we were working, and making a pass at him while I was in the booth singing, and he did push her away, and she did storm off and get drunk, and then come back with a gun. . . . I saw her waving it around, yelling at Dominick, and so I came out of the booth, and Dominick held up a hand and said not to worry. She wasn't going to hurt anyone, she was just upset. He managed to calm her down until she finally put the gun down on the soundboard. Dominick said he was going to go get his father and he left the two of us there but he forgot to take the gun. Tofu was sobbing like a little baby, and I was so mad at her for scaring us like that, so I picked up the gun and I pointed it at her, just to show her what it felt like to have a real loaded gun aimed at you. I told her she was a pathetic, old has-been who was way past her prime and I found her disgusting for chasing after her own stepson, and she should probably just kill herself! That set her off and she started screaming at me. I thought she was going to attack me so I pulled the trigger. She dropped down to her knees, clutching her stomach, and blood began seeping through her silk robe, and it's kind of funny, I remember thinking, what a shame because I'm sure that robe cost a fortune."

There was a long pause.

Matt clearly had no idea how to respond to what he had just heard.

Poppy and Jordan exchanged stunned looks over the complete lack of empathy from Lara over killing a woman in cold blood.

Lara continued. "Dominick came back alone; apparently his father had left. When I told him what happened, he said he loved me with all his heart and didn't want me getting into trouble, so he decided to say it was him. He figured enough of the household staff had witnessed Tofu leering at him and would back up his claim that she had come on to him. So I slipped away before anyone called nine-one-one and came here. I told Daddy I had been soul searching in Nepal so no one would think I was anywhere near that mess at Tony Molina's house. Little did I know he had hired your detective agency to find me and you were such a smarty-pants and uncovered evidence I was hanging around here in Palm Springs the whole time!"

Lara waited for Matt to speak, but he didn't.

"So now you know everything and this can be our little secret."

Still nothing from Matt.

"Say something. You're making me nervous," Lara said with a little laugh.

"You said it was self-defense," Matt said.

"It *was*."

"You said you thought she was going to attack you. Did she or didn't she?"

"I was scared for my life! She was yelling at me! I was just protecting myself!" Lara cried, not happy that the love of her life was suddenly challenging her version of events.

"But did she make a move to grab the gun away from you, or come at you with some kind of weapon . . . ?"

"No, she was across the room," Lara said flatly.

"Then it wasn't self-defense," Matt whispered.

"It was, I swear. Isn't there some kind of stand your ground law where you can shoot somebody if you think they're a threat?"

"Not in California," Matt said.

Another long silence.

"Okay, fine. But nobody has to know. Everyone thinks Dominick did it anyway."

"That's it," Detective Jordan said, charged and ready to move. "Let's go."

He jumped up and threw open the back doors of the van and raced across the street toward Rod Harper's house. Poppy followed closely behind him. Jordan kicked open the gate leading to the backyard, and when they rounded the corner, they found Matt, with a towel wrapped around his waist, standing a few feet away from Lara, who was still totally in the buff. At the sight of the big, intimidating detective, Lara yelped and grabbed a towel and quickly held it up in front of her.

"Lara Harper, I'm placing you under arrest for the murder of Tofu . . ." Jordan stopped, not sure of a last name since Tofu was known publicly only by her first name.

"W-what the hell is going on . . . ? H-how did you . . . ?" Lara stuttered.

As the reality of what was happening finally began to sink in, especially when she saw Poppy hovering behind Detective Jordan, Lara whirled around to Matt, eyes on fire.

Matt reached down and picked up his phone off a chaise lounge. "It's all right here, Detective. Her full confession."

"Matt . . . What did you do . . . ?"

Matt scowled at Lara Harper, thoroughly put off. "You will never be even close to the kindhearted, bright, incredible woman that Poppy Harmon is."

Lara howled as the full impact of Matt's betrayal hit her, and she dropped the towel and charged at him, her fists raised in the air. "How could you? I *loved* you!"

Matt took a step back, but she never managed to reach him because Detective Jordan pounced on her and wrestled her to the grass near the pool. He got her facedown as she kicked and screamed and vowed vengeance upon Matt. Jordan finally was able to snap his handcuffs on her wrists, subduing her. Finally, she stopped fighting and lay on the ground docile, accepting that she had just sealed her own fate.

Matt dashed across the lawn toward Poppy and hugged her. "I hated saying those mean things about you. I didn't mean a word of it."

"You gave the performance of a lifetime," Poppy said, smiling. "We really need to revisit you focusing on that acting career of yours."

Matt gratefully kissed her on the cheek.

Poppy patted his face lovingly, like an adoring mother, because Lara had been right about one thing: Matt could indeed be her son.

"I'd better call Rod," Poppy said, pulling her phone out of her bag, and heading back out the gate toward the street. She knew this was going to crush him and so she wanted to prepare him before he saw it on a newsfeed or heard it from a local reporter looking for some kind of statement or reaction once the story broke.

# Chapter 47

When Poppy returned to the Desert Flowers garage office, she was in a depressed mood due to her sobering phone call with Rod, who had just left an upbeat studio meeting where the executives were wildly enthusiastic about him playing the starring role in their hot new police procedural only to be told that his daughter had just been arrested for murder back in Palm Springs.

Poppy came clean about her own role in exposing Lara, and although he said he understood, she knew from the underlying tension that he was having trouble coming to grips with it. She knew he had to be asking himself, *What if I had never reached out to the Desert Flowers Detective Agency, never hired them to find Lara? Perhaps my daughter might still be a free woman.*

Poppy assumed any father would feel guilty for setting

into motion the events that would bring about his daughter's downfall, but she hoped that with time he would be able to see that ultimately Lara was solely responsible for the death of Tofu, and she would have to pay for that crime. But that didn't make it any easier. After a cursory "thank you" Rod said he needed to get back to Palm Springs to be with Lara and abruptly hung up.

Poppy parked in front of Iris's house and walked around to the side of the garage, then entered the office to find Wyatt at his desktop computer and Iris and Violet rifling through some printed-out paperwork.

Iris glanced up, irritated. "Where have you been while we have been working hard here on a case we are not getting paid for?"

"Working on the other case we're not getting paid for," Poppy said, crossing to the minikitchen. "Do we have any chilled wine in the fridge? I need to calm my nerves."

"There is half a bottle of Chardonnay," Violet said. "We had a glass with our chicken salad sandwiches during our working lunch. Except for Wyatt, of course; he had a Sprite."

"So are you going to tell us what you were doing or not?" Iris asked gruffly.

Poppy opened the bottle of Chardonnay and poured herself a glass. She gripped the stem of the glass and tossed back a generous gulp. "Breaking Rod Harper's heart."

She then gave them a brief rundown of the events that had transpired at the Harper house not forty-five minutes earlier.

All three listened intently, with disbelieving looks on their faces.

"It's been a very difficult day," Poppy murmured.

Wyatt jumped up from the swivel chair at his desk. "Where's Matt?"

"He went to my apartment to let Heather know Lara Harper won't be bothering her anymore," Poppy said. "So where are we on the Alden Kenny situation?"

Violet glanced eagerly at Wyatt, who broke into a wide grin. He sauntered over to Poppy and began talking in a deep, professional voice, attempting to muster up the gravitas of a seasoned private investigator, lessons he had clearly learned from watching Matt play the esteemed Matt Flowers.

"We've been working on a complete dossier on Tony Molina's bodyguards, Griffin and Tammy Goodwin." Wyatt gestured toward Violet. "Show her, Grandma."

Violet popped up and handed Poppy a folder full of papers. Poppy flipped it open and began reading the information.

Wyatt was enjoying his role as lead detective to the hilt, pacing back and forth in front of her, keeping his voice deep. "As you can see from the intel I hacked from a government—"

Violet quickly cut him off. "He means from publicly available records!"

Wyatt took the cue from his grandmother and nodded in agreement. "Right. Anyway, they met while both serving in the military, worked some Black Ops missions as part of the same unit, retired early, both decorated with medals of distinction, and that's when there is a gap in available information."

Poppy flipped through more pages. "That was in twenty sixteen. They started working for Tony Molina in twenty eighteen. What were they doing during those missing two years?"

Wyatt shrugged. "Beats me. But my guess is they were doing mercenary work, hiring themselves out as private contractors on the down low to take care of problems for rich people who could afford their services."

"There would not be much information if they were doing a lot of illegal jobs," Violet added breathlessly. "Especially if they used aliases."

"But then at the end of twenty eighteen they wound up here in the Coachella Valley working security for Tony Molina," Iris said, pointing to some tax returns filed by the couple listing Tony Molina as their sole employer.

"That's when things get interesting," Wyatt said excitedly. "It turns out—"

"Griffin's been in a few illegal scrapes since moving here!" Violet piped in.

Wyatt glowered at his grandmother. "You said *I* could tell her!"

Violet put a hand to her mouth. "Oh, I am so sorry, dear. I just got caught up in the excitement of the moment!"

"I was the one who found all this information so I wanted to be the one who told Poppy!" Wyatt protested.

"I won't say another word, dear. I promise! You go right ahead, you smart boy!" Violet exclaimed.

"Someone please tell her before I die of old age!" Iris bellowed.

Wyatt waited to make sure he would not be interrupted again and then continued, as Iris rolled her eyes, annoyed. "Griffin Goodwin has been arrested twice, once for stalking and once for aggravated assault."

"So it appears he has a violent temper," Poppy said.

Wyatt nodded, drawing the moment out, enjoying being the center of attention. "That's right."

"In both cases the victims were men Goodwin suspected of having sex with his wife," Iris added.

Wyatt spun around and glared at Iris, furious.

"Iris!" Violet cried.

"What?" Iris howled.

"Don't say the *s* word in front of the child," Violet implored.

Iris wrinkled her nose, utterly confused. "What *s* word?"

Violet mouthed the word *sex*.

Wyatt sighed. "I'm twelve, Grandma! I know what sex is!"

Violet blanched at her grandson repeating the word *sex* and sighed. "Just say Griffin targeted men he thought had *relations* with his wife, and let's just leave it at that, thank you very much!"

"*Relations?* You make it sound like they were second cousins, but whatever!" Iris snorted, throwing her hands up in the air.

Poppy rolled all of this over in her mind, and then swallowed the rest of her Chardonnay and slammed the wine glass down on the counter. The pieces of the puzzle were suddenly falling into place. "That must be it! Tony Molina needed a jury plant and so his wife, Tofu, suggested Alden Kenny, whom she knew had a big crush on her, and was like a puppy dog, willing to do anything to make her happy. That would make him an easy sell. Tony probably didn't care that the kid was in love with his wife as long as it resulted in a hung jury. Griffin and Tammy recruited him; Tony paid him fifty thousand dollars, which was wired into his joint account with Jay Taka-mura; and then Griffin and Tammy got Gladys to make sure he was in the jury pool. Sometime after he got re-cruited to help out Tony by Griffin and Tammy, Alden must have entered into a secret affair with Tammy. . . ."

"Griffin probably found out sometime *after* the trial that Alden and his wife were having sex!" Iris exclaimed.

"Iris!" Violet cried again.

"*What*, Violet?" Iris squawked before realizing. "Oh, right. Sorry. Having *relations*!"

Poppy's mind raced. "Once Griffin found out about the affair, given his history, he probably flew into a jealous rage and showed up at Alden Kenny's house and drowned him in the pool just before I arrived. Griffin Goodwin is a big, strong, powerful man. He could have easily overpowered a slight kid like Alden."

"But why did Alden call *you* to come see him after the trial?" Violet asked.

"It has to be what we've suspected all along. He felt guilty for tampering with the jury and was going to come clean with the foreman. . . . *Me* . . . ," Poppy said softly.

Poppy knew in her gut that they had just solved the murder of Alden Kenny.

But she had no idea, however, that their troubles were only just beginning.

# Chapter 48

Before leaving the office, Poppy tried calling Detective Jordan to bring him up to speed on her investigative team's discovery, but she was told by a very dull and spiritless desk sergeant that Jordan was not at the station, and was not expected back anytime soon. However, he would take down a message. Poppy suspected the sergeant wasn't even going to bother to jot down what she had to say, until, that is, she got to the part where she mentioned that she believed she knew who killed Alden Kenny. That finally got the sergeant's attention, and from that moment on, he was exceedingly interested in getting all of her contact information copied down correctly.

After hanging up, Poppy was about to call Heather to let her know she was on her way home, but before she had the chance, her cell phone lit up and she glanced down at the name on the screen.

Poppy took a deep breath and turned to Iris and Violet, who had hung around for moral support after Wyatt had hopped on his bike and peddled home. "It's Rod."

"Are you going to answer it?" Violet asked.

"You absolutely should *not*, Poppy!" Iris shouted. "You need to stay out of it now and let the authorities handle whatever they are going to do with that nasty, destructive daughter of his!"

"He texted me earlier and told me he was heading to the courthouse in Indio to try to bail out Lara with whatever amount of money the judge sets at her arraignment," Poppy said, checking the wall clock. "It should be over by now."

"Don't do it!" Iris warned.

Poppy turned to Violet, who gave her a more sympathetic response, flashing her an encouraging smile.

"I can't just cut him off," Poppy decided. "It's not his fault what Lara did."

Iris snorted, signaling her disagreement. She had always been of the opinion that spoiled and unpleasant children had to learn that behavior from somewhere.

"I'm going to take this outside," Poppy said, slipping out the side door of the garage office into the walkway that led to Iris's spacious and well-kept backyard. She pressed the accept button and put the phone to her ear.

"Hello, Rod. How did it go?"

"We're home now. Judge Levy set bail at five hundred thousand dollars despite the prosecutor hammering home his point that Lara is a flight risk. I promised to keep an eye on her and make sure she doesn't go anywhere, and thankfully the judge was a fan of *Jack Colt* and mercifully granted bail."

"Well, that's a relief, I'm sure. How is she?"

"In her bedroom stewing. She's not happy about any of this. She still doesn't comprehend that she did anything wrong and maintains that she had every right to protect herself from Tofu. I've got some calls into a few high-priced lawyers who might be willing to take on her case given the headlines this is certain to generate. Ironically one represented Tony Molina at his trial."

"I'm sure it will all work out, Rod," Poppy said, and then wanted to kick herself for coming off so blasé about the situation. She cared for Rod deeply and knew this ordeal would not be easy for him, so she sincerely added, "If there is anything I can do . . ."

"Thank you for your kindness and support, Poppy, but that's not why I am calling you. . . ."

She prayed he wasn't going to ask her to come over for dinner again because she had no desire to be in the same room, let alone the same house, with his daughter ever again.

"I just went to check on Lara, and to see what she would like for dinner, and she was on her phone, talking to someone."

"Who?"

"She didn't mention a name, but they were discussing Matt."

Poppy's face fell. "*Matt?*"

"Yes, I heard Lara say that she knew for a fact that Matt has been sneaking around with this man's wife, and that he has been pressuring her to file for divorce and run off with him. Do you know anything about this?"

Poppy felt her heart hammering in her chest. "She's making the whole thing up."

"I figured as much," Rod said sourly. "But why would she do that?"

"Revenge," Poppy answered flatly. "Revenge on Matt for messing up her plan to be with him and get away with shooting Tofu."

There was a pause as Rod took all of this in before he spoke again. "After she hung up, I went into the bedroom and confronted her, and asked who it was she had called, but she refused to divulge anything. She just told me it was none of my business. I wasn't sure if I should bother Matt with this or not since it was probably not true, but I wanted to let you know in case—"

"I have to go, Rod, I'll call you later," Poppy said hurriedly, ending the call and then speed dialing Matt.

She got his voicemail.

Poppy was suddenly experiencing shortness of breath as panic quickly set in.

She had to find Matt.

There was no doubt in her mind that the man Lara had called was Griffin Goodwin. She must have been aware of Griffin's short-fused temper and raging jealousy, and given the amount of time she had spent at the Tony Molina estate, there was also the probability that she was also aware that he had drowned Alden Kenny. If she knew that Griffin was capable of violence whenever he suspected his wife, Tammy, of cheating, like he did with Kenny, why not plant the seed in his head that she had been doing the same thing with Matt? That would make Matt another cheating louse who needed to be dealt with, just like he had dealt with Alden Kenny.

Poppy tried calling Matt one more time.

Voicemail again.

Poppy leaned up against the side of the garage.

Her hands shook as she quickly made another call.

Heather mercifully answered. "Hi, Mom, what's up?"

"I'm looking for Matt. It's an emergency."

"He's not here," Heather said, suddenly worried. "Why? What's wrong?"

"There is no time to explain. Do you know where he is?"

"Yes, he texted me about a half hour ago and said he was going to take the tram up the mountain and hike the trails. Mom, what is it? You're scaring me!"

"I'll call you as soon as I can," Poppy said, ending the call and trying Detective Jordan again. She got the same disinterested desk sergeant.

"Is Detective Jordan back? It's Poppy Harmon and I need to speak to him right now. It's urgent!"

She heard the sergeant sigh. "No, ma'am. As I told you the last time you called, he's out working on a case and I have no idea when he'll be back—"

"Can't you call him on his cell phone?"

"Not unless it's an emergency," the sergeant said with another sigh. "I'd be happy to take another message—"

Poppy cut him off. "It *is* an emergency! A man's life is in peril and he may be killed if we don't help him immediately!"

"I'm going to need more information than that, ma'am," the irked sergeant barked.

Poppy ended the call.

Time was running out.

She had to somehow get to Matt before Griffin Goodwin did.

Otherwise, Matt Flowers was a dead man.

# Chapter 49

Iris squeezed her eyes shut and howled in fear as the Palm Springs Aerial Tram left the floor of the Coachella Valley and began its two-and-a-half-mile ascent past the cliffs of Chino Canyon up to the near peak of the San Jacinto Mountain. Minutes before, when Poppy, Iris, and Violet had raced toward the Valley Station in Violet's Mini Cooper in order to ride the next tram up to the top in a desperate bid to find Matt, Iris had made it quite clear she had a nauseating and debilitating fear of heights. As Violet had raced to the window to buy them tickets, Poppy had explained to Iris that she would completely understand if she waited at the bottom until they returned, hopefully with Matt safe and sound.

But at the last minute, Iris chose to board the tram, in an unexpected and last-minute heroic decision. However, once the door shut and the tram began to move, she instantly regretted it and started banging on the windows to be set free. Unfortunately, none of the staff heard her, and as the rotating tram left the station, rising higher and higher from the ground, Iris knew she was trapped. Luckily other than the three of them, there were no other passengers on board.

"Iris, calm down. I assure you that no one has ever died riding the tram," Poppy promised.

"That's not quite true. Back in nineteen eighty-four a bolt from a shock absorber crashed through that Plexiglas window and struck a woman," Violet said, oblivious. "Killed her instantly."

Poppy shot Violet a peeved look. "Okay, only one person has died since they built the tram in the early nineteen sixties! That's a darn good track record, if you ask me!"

"We are all going to die!" Iris wailed, covering her eyes.

Poppy chose to ignore her and continued trying to call Matt's cell phone. She knew there was no cell service at the top of the mountain and it was pointless, but, she couldn't just stand there and do nothing.

"Iris, you need to confront this head-on," Violet said, determined, as she marched over and put an arm around her and lifted her up to her feet. "That's how I got over my fear of heights." Violet led Iris over to the window and faced her out. "Now, open your eyes, Iris, and take in this breathtaking view."

"No!" Iris cried, refusing to look, clenching her eyes shut even tighter.

"It's beautiful! It would be a shame for you not to see it," Violet said gently.

Iris stopped struggling, working up the courage to open her eyes.

"You can do it!" Violet said with all the enthusiasm of a licensed life coach.

Finally, Iris slowly opened her eyes and stared out the window at the lush scenery and almost smiled until Violet abruptly ruined the moment by commenting, "Now look down there. We're almost eighty five hundred feet off the ground! Isn't that amazing?"

Iris screamed, shut her eyes again, and flew into Poppy's arms, rocking the tram back and forth with her sudden movement, panicking herself even more.

The tram ride to the top felt endless, but the fifteen-minute voyage finally came to an end, and as soon as the doors opened, Iris pushed past Poppy and Violet, hurled herself to the ground, and kissed the dirt, smearing her Satin Pink & Proper lipstick.

Poppy meanwhile approached a staff member and showed him a picture of Matt. The young man recalled seeing him about an hour ago get off the tram, along with a family of four and one other man, who had the same description as Griffin Goodwin. Big, brawny, and kind of mean looking. There were a bunch of trails Matt could have chosen to hike, but, to Poppy's vexation, the staff member did not happen to see which direction he went.

"We'll just have to split up! Violet, you take that trail over there, and I'll head this way!" Poppy said, before turning back to Iris, who was struggling and failing to climb to her feet. "Iris, are you coming?"

"I do not feel very well. I think I may be sick," Iris sobbed.

"Your body probably is having trouble adjusting to the elevation," Violet offered. "You have altitude sickness!"

"Stay here, Iris!" Poppy yelled. "In case we miss Matt and he comes back this way!"

Poppy and Violet set off toward the wooded trails, leaving Iris back at the tram, on her hands and knees, nauseated.

"Matt! Matt!" Poppy called out as she veered off from Violet and pounded down a marked trail. Poppy had to keep telling herself that Matt was capable, strong, lean, and fast and could probably outsmart and outrun a big, lumbering brute like Griffin Goodwin. But not knowing he was a target put Matt at an extreme disadvantage, and she prayed that they would not be too late.

She could hear Violet in the distance calling out for Matt as well.

Poppy had perhaps run about a quarter of a mile down the trail when after another attempt at screaming his name over and over, as her throat started to burn and her voice became hoarse, she stopped dead in her tracks.

She had heard something.

It sounded as if someone had called her name.

Was it Violet?

Poppy stood there, freezing cold from the forty-degree drop in temperature, and listened intently. The wind was blowing and the trees were rustling. She began to suspect it was her imagination. She took a step forward to continue her hunt when suddenly she heard it again.

"Poppy . . . ?"

It was faint, but it definitely was not Violet.

It was a man's voice.

It was Matt!

He had heard her.

"Matt! I'm here! I'm over here!" Poppy cried, running forward, following the sound of his voice.

A few minutes went by and she didn't hear him again.

She feared she had traveled in the opposite direction, away from his location, or the unthinkable had happened and he had already encountered his pursuer, Griffin Goodwin. But then, she saw him. Matt jogged around a corner, in gray running pants and a black LA Raiders hooded sweatshirt, surprised to see Poppy in his sights, standing in the middle of a hiking trail on top of a mountain. He ran toward her, smiling.

Suddenly Poppy noticed a flash of light off the trail, near a thicket of trees, which distracted her. She zeroed in on a man dressed in military camouflage clothing and tactical gear. He had a rifle aimed at the trail. The telltale flash was from a rifle scope reflecting off the sun. She was certain it was Griffin Goodwin, in sniper mode, about to take out his target.

"Matt, look out!" Poppy screamed, pointing in the direction of Griffin, who spun around toward Poppy, frustrated she had just given away his position. Griffin turned back to Matt, raised his rifle, about to take his shot. But Poppy's warning had come just in time and Matt launched himself off the trail, hit the ground, and rolled out of view. Poppy also dashed off the trail and hid behind a tree, pressing her back against the bark, and staying as quiet and still as possible.

After five minutes, she carefully peered around the tree to see if she could spot Griffin, but he was gone. She looked around for Matt but there was so sign of him, either.

Poppy dropped to her hands and knees and crawled through the brush until she reached a large rock and hid behind that. She lifted her head and scanned the area again. Still no sign of Griffin or Matt.

She then stood up and ran along the trail back toward the tram station when suddenly a shot rang out and a bullet ricocheted off a granite rock nearby.

Poppy screamed and zigzagged, trying not to run in a straight line, which she knew would make her an easier target. She stayed off the trail this time and darted behind another tree. She was out of breath and her legs were tired, but she knew she had to get back to the tram station, where someone on the staff could radio for help. She started off again, leaving the tree cover, and ran smack into a man's chest. Before she had a chance to scream, his hand was clamped over her mouth. She feared it was Griffin, but he whispered urgently in her ear, "Poppy, it's me, Matt!" He let her go and she hugged him tightly.

They were alive, but still in grave danger.

They ducked down into a crouch to stay hidden.

"What's going on? Who is that?" Matt asked.

"One of Tony Molina's bodyguards. It's a long story, but he thinks you're having an affair with his wife and he wants to kill you!"

Matt's eyes widened in shock.

This was not what he was expecting to hear.

Suddenly they heard Griffin's gruff voice. "Flowers!"

Poppy clutched Matt's arm. "Don't say anything! You'll give away our position!"

"Flowers! I think you'd better answer me!" Griffin yelled. He waited a few seconds before adding, "I've got something of yours that you might want back!"

They were now lying flat on the ground, behind some bushes, trying to keep out of sight, but Poppy couldn't resist and lifted her head just a bit to get a good view and gasped, horrified. "He has Violet!"

"What?" Matt raised his head and grimaced.

Griffin had his rifle in one hand and was clutching Violet with the other. "If you don't come out now and face me, I'm going to have to shoot this little bunny rabbit!"

"Don't do it, Matt!" Violet cried. "He'll shoot you!"

Matt made a move to stand up, but Poppy grabbed his sweatshirt. "No, Matt!"

"I can't let him hurt Violet," Matt said, and then he bravely stood up, hands in the air, and stepped out in the middle of the trail.

Poppy watched, terror stricken and trembling, as Matt slowly walked down the trail toward Griffin and Violet, about to get himself killed.

It happened in slow motion.

As Matt approached, Griffin pushed Violet aside, so hard she tripped and fell to the ground. Griffin raised his rifle, aiming it right at Matt's chest. Poppy couldn't see Matt's face but she envisioned him closing his eyes, preparing himself for the inevitable.

Poppy, in that moment, felt so helpless, so despondent.

And then, out of the shadows, appeared a wild woman, screaming like a banshee, brandishing a thick tree branch. She came up behind Griffin Goodwin in a flash, and whacked him in the back of the head with it. Griffin dropped to the ground with a thud, allowing Violet to crawl over him, grab the rifle, then haul herself to her feet and scamper away.

Matt lowered his hands as he stared at the woman in utter shock. Where had she come from? She had just swooped in at the last minute and saved the day. He squinted to get a better look at her. She was older with white hair and bright pink lipstick and she had this perpetual look of annoyance.

No, it couldn't be.

But it was.

Poppy was on her feet and walking toward Matt, who was turned enough now that she could see a smile creeping across Matt's face. "*Iris?*"

"You can thank me now!" Iris shouted.

And then she promptly turned and threw up in the bushes.

Apparently she still hadn't adjusted to the high elevation yet.

# Chapter 50

When Poppy opened the door to her apartment and found Rod Harper standing outside, she was surprised to see him looking so relaxed and refreshed. After all he had been through with his daughter recently, with her arrest and impending trial, she had expected him to appear more worn and worried. He had called earlier, asking if he could come over to talk to her, and she had agreed. It was noon, and she had a lot of errands to do, but he said it was important and couldn't wait and so she told him to drive right over. It had taken him only fifteen minutes, and now he was here, reaching out with his muscular arms and drawing Poppy in for a long hug. He raised his hand and gently placed it on the back of her head, which rested on his broad chest. Poppy felt safe in his warm embrace but was the first to pull away, and, with a bright smile, welcomed him into her home. After offering him a drink, which he declined, she led him into the living room and they both took a seat next to each other on the couch.

"Is Heather working?" Rod asked, glancing around.

"No, today is her day off. She and Matt went on a hike around Andreas Canyon on the Cahuilla Indian Reservation."

"I'm happy to hear Matt is hiking again after what happened."

"Matt has always been one of those get-right-back-up-in-the-saddle type of people," Poppy said with a laugh.

"And he and Heather are good?"

"I believe so, yes. Taking things slow, but I'm hopeful they can make things work," Poppy said confidently before adopting a more somber tone. "And Lara? How is she?"

Rod shrugged. "Okay, I guess. Still defiant, still refusing to admit to any wrongdoing. Her lawyers have been trying to cop a plea deal, but Lara's having none of it. She wants to go to trial. I've been trying to reason with her, her lawyers are adamantly advising against it, but Lara is going to do what she is going to do. I'm afraid this is all going to end with a hefty sentence."

Poppy reached out and took Rod's hand, not as some kind of romantic gesture, but as a longtime friend who wanted him to know that she would always be there for him.

There was a long pause. Rod looked deep into Poppy's eyes, and she was afraid he might try to propose marriage again, and she would have to gently shut him down, but he didn't. He just shook his head and, with a sad smile, said, "How did we both reach this point, Poppy? Both our daughters so adrift and so troubled?"

Poppy bristled, but deep down she knew Rod had meant no offense. He was just trying to find someone who understood his dire situation, his only daughter on the verge of being sent to prison for a long incarceration. However, Poppy could hardly compare the devious Lara Harper with her own daughter Heather's situation. The circumstances could not have been more vastly different, and Heather had owned up to her mistakes almost immediately and wanted to make amends and serve her time. It was her only path to living a normal, happy life. Lara was going to fight doing the right thing until the bitter end, and that's what made the two women so stark in contrast. But Rod did not need a lecture about his morally bankrupt daughter, so Poppy chose to stay mum and just be a friend during this terribly turbulent time he was going through.

"On a brighter note, that network pilot I was in negotiations for is apparently a go. They need me in New York in two weeks to start shooting."

"Oh, Rod, that's wonderful!" Poppy cheered. "Congratulations!"

"My first starring role in a network series since *Jack Colt*, if you can believe it," he said, almost not believing it himself. "I thought my days as a TV star were over, which is a big reason I made the decision to move out to the desert permanently. Now I have to close up the house or rent it. I've already found a place I like in Manhattan, right near Central Park. The network is very bullish on the show, and they are hinting about a golden time slot, Monday nights at ten."

"Rod Harper is back!" Poppy declared, squeezing Rod's hand, genuinely happy for him.

"Of course, I told them I needed to be back here if Lara's case goes to trial, and the producers have offered to work with me to make that happen."

"I'm sure Lara will appreciate it."

Rod looked down at Poppy's hand holding his and without looking back up at her said softly, "I was hoping you might consider coming with me."

Poppy slowly let go of Rod's hand and she could tell at that moment that he knew her answer. "Rod . . ."

"I know. . . ."

"It's a tempting offer. . . . You know how much I care for you. . . ."

Rod sighed, his head bowed. "But there's someone else. . . ."

Poppy nodded.

"I guess I knew all along. . . . But you know me . . . Rod Harper, always one to give it the old college try."

Poppy lovingly touched his cheek with her hand. "You're a good man, Rod."

"Will you at least come visit me in New York sometime?"

"Of course."

"Maybe consider a guest spot? The role of my wife was cut. Now I'm a widower. You can play my new love interest. If I can't have you in real life, maybe we can date on television. . . ."

"Every Monday night at ten on CBS."

They both laughed and hugged each other again.

There was another long beat before Poppy spoke. "Rod, if you need someone to come with you to the trial, if it comes to that, I want you to know I would be happy to be by your side so you don't have to go through this alone."

"I appreciate that, Poppy. Thank you."

She couldn't tell if he would actually take her up on the offer, but she was glad she had made it.

Rod finally stood up. "I should go."

He was halfway to the door before he turned back around. "By the way, Sam Emerson turned down the consulting offer. I'm not sure why. Maybe he's got something more important here in the desert. I just thought you should know." Then he gave her a knowing wink.

She beamed, happy they were parting as good friends, and then he was gone.

Poppy waited a few moments before crossing to the kitchen, grabbing a bottle of wine from the fridge, and then scribbling a note for Heather. *Gone to Big Bear. Don't wait up. Love, Mom.*

And then, after packing an overnight bag, she headed out the door.

*Private investigator Poppy Harmon likes the anonymity of working behind the scenes for the hottest names in Palm Springs. But when solving a case demands dragging her old acting career out of retirement, it's lights . . . camera . . . murder!*

Cast in her first role since the 1980s, Poppy has never been more rattled or unprepared on a film set. It's an embarrassing but necessary cover to keep an eye on client Danika Delgado, a rising starlet and social media influencer with a large following—including a dangerous stalker who won't disappear. The leading lady's fame is growing, and so are the threats against her life . . .

Unfortunately for Poppy, there's more to fear than flubbed lines. When she finds Danika smothered to death in her trailer at Joshua Tree National Park, the horrifying crime stirs up memories of a man known as the Pillow Talk Killer during her time as a young actress, bringing unsolved murders from the past back into focus . . .

A trail of clues urges Poppy, hunky sidekick Matt Flowers, and the rest of the Desert Flowers Detective Agency gang on a frantic chase after Danika's crazed #1 fan. But as co-stars and production crew members start looking equally suspicious, Poppy must expose a slew of insidious industry secrets before a murderer rolls out the red carpet for someone else . . .

**Please turn the page for an exciting sneak peek
of the next
Desert Flowers mystery
POPPY HARMON AND THE PILLOW TALK
KILLER
coming soon wherever print and e-books are sold!**

# Chapter 1

It had been over thirty years since Poppy Harmon had stepped foot on an actual Hollywood film set. Granted, this shoot was set up at a high-end resort hotel in the heart of Palm Springs and not some cavernous soundstage on the Paramount lot where her mid-1980s television series *Jack Colt, PI* had been filmed, but there was a feeling of warm familiarity, an infusion of happy memories, because back in her heyday when Poppy was an actress with a regular TV role, she had never once taken it for granted. She had always been hyperaware of just how lucky she was to have scored such a cushy, well-paying gig at the time, especially after so many years in her late teens and early twenties struggling, waiting tables, modeling skimpy swimwear at car shows, and answering phones at a call center for a household appliance company.

Poppy watched as the crew busily set up lights by the shimmering pool where the next scene was to be shot as a bright-eyed, eager, enthusiastic PA who had introduced himself as Timothy led her and Matt through the resort.

Matt was like a kid in a candy store, excitedly soaking up everything he saw: a makeup woman powdering the face of a vaguely recognizable actor; a forty-something man in a gray T-shirt and red baseball cap, slumped over in his director's chair, perusing a script; some kind of set decorator or production designer painstakingly arranging red bougainvillea in the background of the set as the cinematographer stared through the lens of his camera, working on getting his shot just right.

Poppy knew Matt was in his element. This had been his dream for most of his young life. He had wanted so desperately to become a successful actor, the next Ryan Gosling or Chris Hemsworth, or whoever was the hot superstar of the moment. But life never works out exactly as you expect, and now the talented young man found himself playing the role of Matt Flowers, the public face, the de facto head, of the Desert Flowers Detective Agency. He wasn't on billboards and buses, or in the front row of the Academy Awards, but he was successful and surprisingly good at the part he was playing.

When Poppy, along with her two best pals, Iris and Violet, had first started the Palm Springs–based investigative firm, no one would hire them. Mostly due to people's ageist preconceptions that three mature women in their sixties were utterly incapable of solving cases or handling potentially dangerous situations. Enter Matt. Young, virile, disarmingly charming. He had risen to the challenge of playing a master detective wholeheartedly, and his performance had put their fledgling business on the map.

Now they had more clients than they knew what to do with.

Including Danika Delgado, a rising young actress and social media influencer who had heard about Matt's daring exploits online and had called the Desert Flowers office, which was located in Iris's garage, to inquire about hiring them.

Actually, Danika did not call personally. One of her three personal assistants had left the message on voicemail. Poppy, Iris, and Violet were clueless as to who Danika Delgado even was, but Matt had certainly heard of her, which became quite clear when he whooped and hollered about being a big fan at the first mention of her name in their morning staff meeting. His outburst had startled Violet so much, she spilled coffee all over her new blouse she had just bought on sale at TJ Maxx.

The assistant had not explained why Danika wanted to hire local private detectives, just that she would like to meet with them ASAP. Once Poppy read Danika Delgado's net worth online, she immediately called the assistant back and happily informed her that they luckily had an opening to meet this very afternoon.

Danika was at the Sundial Luxury Resort just outside of downtown Palm Springs shooting a reboot of the early 1960s camp classic *Palm Springs Weekend*. The original had featured the sizzling hot stars of the time including Troy Donahue, Connie Stevens, Robert Conrad and Stefanie Powers. In fact, Poppy had been friends with Stefanie Powers, who was co-starring with Robert Wagner on *Hart to Hart*, about a globe-trotting wealthy married couple who solve murders, at the same time Poppy was appearing in *Jack Colt*. Now, after all these years, Netflix, or Hulu, it was one of those giant streaming services, was currently producing a remake, or reboot, Poppy could never keep the lingo straight, of *Palm Springs Weekend*, with an all-new Gen Z cast.

The production assistant, Timothy, cranked his head around to Poppy and Matt, who was so distracted by a bevy of bikini-clad extras, he tripped over a lounge chair, and asked, "Would you like to stop by craft services for some coffee, or a Danish before I take you to Danika's room?"

Matt opened his mouth to speak, but Poppy cut him off with a curt, "No, thank you, Timothy." She was too anxious to hear what kind of case Danika wanted to hire them for and didn't want to waste time while Matt dithered over whether he should have a cruller or go for a healthier option like a granola bar.

Timothy nodded and they kept moving until they reached a glass door leading inside toward the large corner suites. Timothy opened it and stepped aside to allow them both in ahead of him when the man in the T-shirt and red baseball cap, his script rolled up in his fist, bounded toward them.

"Wait!" he yelled, catching up to them, breathless. He took a moment, his eyes fixed on Poppy before continuing. "I'm sorry, I'm Trent, Trent Dodsworth-Jones," he said in a clipped decidedly British accent.

"Trent's our director," Timothy said, slightly concerned he had done something wrong, bracing himself to be dressed down in some unexpected way.

Trent ignored him and remained focused on Poppy. "Are you who I think you are?"

"That depends on who you think I am," Poppy said dryly.

"You are, aren't you? I'd recognize that smoky, sexy

voice anywhere! You're Daphne!" Trent practically exploded.

Matt smirked. He loved it whenever Poppy got recognized for her signature role on *Jack Colt*.

Poppy graciously extended her hand. "Poppy Harmon."

Trent excitedly pumped her hand. "I grew up watching you back in the eighties. I was a huge fan of *Jack Colt* when it finally made its way across the pond! My family comes from a dreary little town called Preston in Northern England. There is absolutely nothing to do there. Our only claim to fame is that we are about an hour's drive from Liverpool where the Beatles got their start. That's it. There is no other reason to ever go to Preston. We were dirt poor, but we did have a color TV which was my only lifeline to the outside world and I would watch you every week!"

Poppy had heard from friends that Preston was a lovely little city, but was not about to argue with someone who had grown up there and had probably harbored dreams of getting out to make it big in the film business.

"I am so happy to have played a small part in your adolescence," Poppy said politely.

"Yes, if anything, you helped get me through puberty!" Trent said, a lascivious smile suddenly plastered on his face.

Okay, way too much information, in Poppy's opinion.

"What brings you to our little set?" Trent inquired.

"They're here to see Danika," Timothy offered.

"Oh, are you friends?" Trent asked, curious.

"No, this is a professional call," Matt chimed in.

Poppy resisted rolling her eyes at him. She did not like to burp out information she didn't have to, but Matt was her exact opposite, exceedingly chatty and unfiltered. It could be a burden sometimes.

"I see. Are you an agent, or a manager?" Trent asked, eyeing Matt.

"Neither," Poppy snapped, staring down Matt, who finally got the message to keep his mouth shut from further comment. She turned back to Trent. "It was a pleasure meeting you, but we should go before we're late for our meeting."

"Of course," Trent said, turning to Timothy. "Tell Danika we should be ready to shoot in ten."

"Got it!" Timothy chirped.

Before Poppy had a chance to escape, Trent reached out and touched her arm. "Please, Poppy, before you go . . ."

She turned and warily eyed his hand on her, but didn't want to immediately shake it off and appear rude. "Yes?"

"Let me just say, in my humble opinion, you never got your due," he said solemnly.

Poppy was confused—what on earth he was talking about? "I beg your pardon?"

"As an actress. I know you probably got cast as Daphne because the show needed window dressing, and you certainly fit that bill . . ."

This was now getting downright creepy but Poppy held her tongue.

Trent sighed, realizing how inappropriately he was coming across and quickly added, "But you were quite good in that role. You gave Daphne depth and heart, and I always thought with the right opportunity, you would have risen to the heights of a Jessica Lange or Sissy Spacek."

"Well, I don't know what to say," Poppy murmured, flabbergasted.

"And she's *rarely* speechless!" Matt cracked.

Poppy threw him a stern look, like a mother trying to drive the car while her rambunctious preteen son caused too much of a ruckus in the back seat. She then returned her attention to Trent. "I appreciate your kind words, Mr. Jones. Good luck with the rest of your film shoot."

"A pleasure, Poppy," Trent said, beaming, before jogging back to the set.

Timothy led them down a long hallway to the largest suite in the hotel and knocked on the door. One of Danika's personal assistants, a harried-looking girl carrying two different phones, whipped it open and ushered them inside. "Hurry, we don't have much time and Danika is *dying* to talk to you!"

Timothy hung back as the girl waved Poppy and Matt inside and tried to get out, "Trent wanted to let Danika know we'll be ready to shoot again in—" but the assistant slammed the door in his face.

Poppy and Matt followed the assistant into the main room of the suite. Sitting in a chair in front of a mirror while an African American hairdresser fussed with her wavy dark curls was Danika Delgado, petite, unblemished brown skin, in a pink robe. She held her phone up in front of her face as she recorded a video for her fans. "So this is day eight of the *Palm Springs Weekend* shoot, guys, and it's going awesome! I love my co-stars! Chase Ehrens is such a sweetheart! And a first-rate kisser, too, if I'm going to talk out of school! I'll share more juicy details from the set in my next post at bedtime! Love you all! Oh, and the lipstick shade I'm wearing is called Flawless, in case you were wondering!"

The assistant turned to Poppy. "Danika has a marketing deal with Color My World products. She's one of the highest-paid social media influencers out there."

Poppy nodded as if she had a clue what this girl was prattling on about.

Danika threw her phone down on the table next to her and glanced at herself in the mirror. "Does it look kind of flat to you, Chanel?"

The hairdresser quickly began fluffing Danika's locks out. "No worries, girl, we'll get it where it needs to be."

The nervous assistant cleared her throat. "Excuse me, Danika . . . ?"

Danika was still staring at herself in the mirror, dissatisfied with her appearance. "I'm not liking this eyeliner at all. We may have to reshoot before we post anything to Instagram."

The assistant apprehensively tried again. "Danika?"

"*What?*" Danika snapped, swiveling her head around.

"The private detectives are here," the assistant whispered, practically shaking.

Danika instantly slapped on an inviting smile. "Oh, good!" She popped up from her chair. She was a short little thing, about five feet two inches. Her eyes instantly fell upon Matt and without even a pause, cooed, "You are *so* much hotter in person!"

Unlike Poppy, Matt had no qualms about soaking up compliments. "Why, thank you. As one of your one hundred and twenty-eight million Instagram followers, dare I say the same?"

"Oh, you are the charmer!" Danika said, laughing, eyeing him up and down lustfully. "When my people found you online, I said to myself, this guy's a detective? He should be an actor!"

Matt beamed brightly. "Funny you should say that—"

"Miss Delgado needs to be back on the set soon, so why don't we get down to business," Poppy quickly interjected.

Danika's eyes finally strayed away from Matt and over to Poppy. "And who are you?"

Obviously, unlike the film's director, Danika was far too young to ever know who Poppy had been in a previous life.

"I'm Poppy, Matt's . . . *assistant*."

She always had trouble actually saying it.

Especially since it was not true.

"Oh, nice to meet you, Poppy," Danika said pleasantly as she pointed out a lush comfy-looking couch nearby. "Why don't you both sit down while Chanel tries to work miracles on this rat's nest?" She sat back down in her chair as Chanel rubbed some gel on her hands and went about smoothing out Danika's chic hairstyle.

"How can we be of service?" Matt asked.

"I'm having trouble with a stalker," Danika said matter-of-factly.

"Do you know who this stalker is?" Poppy asked, reaching inside her shoulder bag and pulling out a pen and some paper to take down notes.

Danika shook her head, forcing Chanel to stop for a second. "No. I have no idea. I mean, let's face it, I have a zillion crazies following me. Everyone with my kind of online profile does. It's impossible to keep track of them. But this guy, he's different. It started out innocent at first. The usual flowers and chocolates and little personalized gifts he knew I liked just by following me on Instagram and subscribing to my YouTube channel. But lately, things have taken a dark turn. His messages are far less adoring and more worrying."

"How so?" Poppy asked.

"There's a rumor going around that I'm dating Chase Ehrens."

"Your co-star on this film," Matt offered.

"Yes, which I am most certainly not. Chase is a decent enough guy, but definitely not my type. We're just friends."

Poppy cocked an eyebrow. "I'm a bit confused. When we walked in here you were making a video with your phone and talking about him as if there might be something going on between the two of you."

"That's just for show. Keep people interested, you know? It promotes the movie and us as well. It doesn't matter if it's not true. The problem is, this wacko thinks it *is* true and it's making him mad! Like, stalker-y, I'm going to murder you, mad!"

"He's threatened you?" Matt asked.

"Yeah, about five hundred times. He knows I'm here in Palm Springs shooting this movie, and he's made no secret of the fact that he is here too and ready to come after me at a time and place of his choosing. That's a direct quote from his last post, by the way."

"Have you called the police?" Poppy asked.

Danika laughed derisively. "Duh. Of course. But what can they do? Oh, sure, they rushed down here acting all concerned and serious and made some kind of report, but that was it. Until this guy literally guts me with a carving knife, they're totally useless. The studio is paying a fortune for a kick-ass security detail while I'm here, but they're not trained detectives. I want to be proactive about this. I want a local firm, one that knows this city, that can track down this lowlife creep and put him away for good before he throws acid in my face, or worse."

Poppy swallowed hard at the prospect.

This young actress was doing a good job of keeping up her bravado, but it was clear on her beautiful, heavily made-up face that she was scared and feeling vulnerable.

"I have a lot of people looking out for me, with good intentions, but for my own peace of mind, I want someone who knows about things like this, who I can call day and night, who is not here to protect the movie or my brand, but to protect *me*! That's where you come in, Matt."

Matt sat up straight on the couch next to Poppy.

He nodded confidently. "Trust me, Danika, I'm your man."

"I had a strong feeling you would be," Danika said, smiling seductively.

Poppy wasn't so sure.

Keeping a highly public figure with over a hundred million fans safe and secure seemed like a daunting challenge, not to mention the task of locating one of those millions of fans out in the world who was unstable and possibly homicidal, ready to strike at any time. But once Danika offered to pay triple their usual going rate, Poppy was suddenly feeling slightly more emboldened.

How hard could it be?

If only she had listened to her initial instincts.

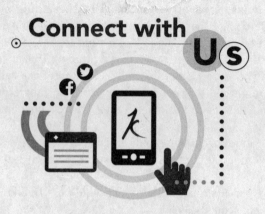